INHERIT THE STARS!

What you're holding is a book about the struggle for peace—about what it means to be human, about how an honest, thoughtful recognition of what we are as human beings can show us the way toward a real peace. Not an easily dreamt peace, no—not one where men and women lie down lobotomized in the garden of Eden with lambs and lions and somehow, in the process, lose their very humanity—but a peace achieved in the face of their humanity . . . apples, serpents, fear, rage, prejudice, and all. Intelligence is the key, of course—but so are trust, compassion, respect, and a very real recognition of the paradoxes, the conflicts within us, that make us human.

The struggle isn't easy, but then it shouldn't be. . . .

—From the Introduction

Tor books by Harry Harrison

Also by Bruce McAllister

THERE WON'T BE WAR

edited by
Harry Harrison &
Bruce McAllister

A TOM DOHERTY ASSOCIATES BOOK
NEW YORK

This is a work of fiction. All the characters and events portrayed in this book are fictitious, and any resemblance to real people or events is purely coincidental.

THERE WON'T BE WAR

Copyright © 1991 by SF Horizons

Cover art by Alan Gutierrez

A Tor Book
Published by Tom Doherty Associates, Inc.
49 West 24th Street
New York, N.Y. 10010

ISBN: 0-812-51941-8

First edition: November 1991

Printed in the United States of America

0 9 8 7 6 5 4 3 2 1

ACKNOWLEDGMENTS

"The Liberation of Earth" by William Tenn copyright © 1953 by Columbia Publications, Inc. Originally published in *Future Science Fiction*. Reprinted by permission of the author and Henry Morrison, Inc.

"The Lucky Strike" by Kim Stanley Robinson copyright © 1984 by Terry Carr. Originally published in *Universe 14*. Reprinted by permission of the author and the author's agent, Patrick Delahunt.

"We, The People" by Jack C. Haldeman II copyright © 1983 By Jack C. Haldeman II. Originally published in *Analog Magazine*. Reprinted by permission of the author.

"The Terminal Beach" by J. G. Ballard copyright © 1964 by J. G. Ballard. Originally published in *New Worlds Science Fiction*. Reprinted by permission of the author.

"General of Noah" by William Tenn copyright © 1951 by Farrell Publishing Corp. Originally published in *Suspense*. Reprinted by permission of the author.

CONTENTS

Contents

Introduction

Just before this book went to print, I turned to my oldest daughter, Annie, who was sitting beside me in the car, and asked her:

"Would you read a book about *peace*?"

She hesitated, that cautious look that eleven-year-olds often have in her eye. "I don't know . . ."

I thought I understood and I said: "Because it might not be *exciting* enough?"

"No . . . I'm wondering what it would be *about*, Daddy."

"What do you mean?"

"What would the book *really* be about?"

I lied. "About a peaceful world, I guess—people living in harmony, getting along, respecting one another."

There was a long pause. "I'd rather," she said at last, "read about how we got there. How we made a world like that. . . ."

1

Introduction

This from an eleven-year-old. Maybe there's hope after all.

"Thank you," I said. "That's exactly what my good friend Harry and I have put together—a book about the *struggle* for peace, *not* peace itself. I do hope you like it."

I'd been expecting, as Harry knows, the reaction of so many adult readers to *peace*—or for that matter, to utopias, those perfect societies we keep making in fiction that somehow never ring quite true: *"Why would I want to read about perfect harmony?"* we hear. *"There's no conflict, no drama. It's* **boring**, *isn't it?"*

No, it isn't. It's actually the most exciting idea in the world. But far too many people just don't think peace is *possible*. We don't believe that human beings—by their nature—can achieve harmony, can reach everlasting peace on a global (let alone a domestic or personal) scale. *Looking Backward*, that 19th Century utopia that invented credit cards, feels like an essay, reads like a joke—while *Brave New World*, *Nineteen Eighty-Four* and *Anthem*, all of those *anti*utopies we keep on reading decade after decade, somehow feel more real to us . . . truer.

Is it simply that we believe a vision of global peace denies what makes us human, and is therefore a lie—or is it that, in historical terms (no matter how many interludes of peace we've had over the millennia) we've always known war, and fiction must echo that "reality"? Is it that, as human beings, we're doomed never to make everlasting peace—or is it simply that we distrust ourselves, that we're cynical, the way any idealist who very much wants something and never gets it in life becomes cynical—though indeed we do have the potential to make peace?

The latter is more hopeful certainly.

Even with Gorbachev and *glasnost* and the opening of Eastern Europe, we remain distrustful. It's a lie, a temporary fantasy, a Soviet manipulation, at best an attempt that will fail. Perhaps because to assume otherwise—to have faith in our own best nature as intelligent, caring human beings—may set us up for disappointment once again in the long history of the world?

That very distrust, however—that cynicism, as we continue to dream our dreams of peace—may tell us more about what it means to be human than we realize.

It may tell us that there is indeed hope . . . because, though we stumble, though we fear and distrust and are disappointed, we keep on dreaming. The dream, though we often misuse it, pulls us on. The dream within us is as real as our failure historically to reach it, and in turn must therefore be a "reality" deep within our neural wiring that good fiction should, must, and always will address as well.

When an eleven-year-old prefers reading about *how we can get there*, there is indeed hope. She could have said: "I'd rather read about perfect harmony, Daddy—I don't *care* how we get there." And that would have been hideous, wouldn't it.

There's hope too, because, boring though the thought of peaceful fiction may be to readers who prefer hostaged submarines or Cold War assassinations, you, dear reader, did pick this book up.

You must have had a reason.

What you're holding is a book about the struggle for peace—about what it means to be human, about how an honest, thoughtful recognition of what we are as human beings can show us the way toward a real peace. Not an easily dreamt peace, no—not one where men and women

3

lie down lobotomized in the garden of Eden with lambs and lions and somehow, in the process, lose their very humanity—but a peace achieved in the face of their humanity . . . apples, serpents, fear, rage, prejudice, and all. Intelligence is the key, of course—but so are trust, compassion, respect, and a very real recognition of the paradoxes, the conflicts within us, that make us human. The struggle isn't easy, but then it shouldn't be: a peace without struggle is no real human victory. Nothing in life is. That's one of the things that makes us human. . . .

When we conceived of this book in 1988, we knew we wanted it to illuminate the two major lies, the illusions, that drive us so often, that have, in fact, undermined peace for millennia now. We also, of course, wanted it to be a celebration of the best within humankind—rationality, respect, social cooperation, and, of course, the ability to dream a better world that the one we've so far made.

What are these two lies—these illusions—that for so long have done their best to keep us from a real peace where we can still remain human? One is certainly *the glory of war*. It offers us cheaply, but with tragic results, a sense of *power* in the face of that 20th Century helplessness and powerlessness we hear so much about. War is about the *power* that *fear* demands of us, isn't it? Power, after all (the lie assures us), is what the world is really about, isn't it? The meek are fools. The reasonable are suckers. If you really believe in your country, your family, your values, you will wage war to protect them—because there is indeed an Enemy out there and the Enemy, like a host of fallen angels, is out to destroy everything you value. By waging war you'll be redeemed by war's very violence, won't you? The consequences of this are of course terrible: The perpetuation of Power Über Alles, of war itself, of the assumption that whether we win or lose our submission to Power redeems us.

The other lie is trickier still. It looks so good to us. It is, very simply, the *daydream of Eden*, and what could possibly be wrong with that (though even an eleven-year-old may see through it when many grown-ups do not)? If we will, in the end, forge a peace, despite the darker regions of our nature, because we dream of peace, what could possibly be wrong with dreaming? A lot. If we daydream—with the help of the religions we may subscribe to, or out of our own sense of powerlessness in the world—a perfect Eden on earth (or everafter), we're able to escape the misery here. If we daydream it, we free ourselves from the here-and-now. The dream fixes everything—like a needle, a pill, a designer opiate. The consequences of this, too, are just as tragic: By daydreaming, by assuming we have no power (or responsibility, or right) to change the world, to work hard at changing it—by assuming all will be made right after this life, at the hand of Someone else, in a Finer Place, or by assuming that the struggle is meaningless (a religion of its own nihilistic kind) we avoid struggling with our own humanity, with our own contradictions, to make something better here on earth. We tell ourselves by the daydream that we're good, but we do nothing to reach the dream. By daydreaming—by relinquishing the power we do have, through intelligence and reason and commitment, in the world—we avoid earning the very thing we have wanted so very much, for so very long, in our finest dreams.

Which is the more evil lie? It's very hard to tell. But unless we look them both squarely in the face, we'll never beat them.

* * *

Introduction

Thanks to the storytelling gifts and brains of some of the best science fiction writers today—the Big Names we all grew up with as well as the newer, gifted, award-winning writers who will take their places in the decades to come—Harry and I are indeed able to give the very book we'd hoped for . . . and then some. Ferocious satires by Isaac Asimov, Robert Sheckley, William Tenn, Gregory Frost, Nicholas Emmett, Ratislav Durman and Frederik Pohl. Economic warfare—*and* peace-making—stories by Charles Stross, Jack C. Haldeman II, and Timothy Zahn. Mythic fantasies by Jack McDevitt and Marc Laidlaw. An alternate universe by Kim Stanley Robinson. *Human* stories by Nancy Collins, George Zebrowski, J. G. Ballard, James Morrow, and Joe Haldeman. An international collection as varied as you'll find. Eighteen visions of what we are and what we might become, on our way through war (and our own human nature) . . . toward a real Peace. A celebration of what makes us human—at our best. And a warning of the pitfalls that have always done their best to keep us from what we might, out of our best dreams, make of this world.

And no, it won't be boring. Like human nature itself, the best science fiction never is.

—Bruce McAllister

Frustration

Isaac Asimov

Herman Gelb turned his head to watch the departing figure. Then he said, "Wasn't that the Secretary—"

"Yes, that was the Secretary of Foreign Affairs. Old man Hargrove. Are you ready for lunch?"

"Of course. What was he doing here?"

Peter Jonsbeck didn't answer immediately. He merely stood up, and beckoned Gelb to follow. They walked down the corridor and into a room that had the steamy smell of spicy food.

"Here you are," said Jonsbeck. "The whole thing has been prepared by computer. Completely automated. Untouched by human hands. And my own programming. I promised you a treat, and here you are."

It *was* good. Gelb could not deny it and didn't want to. Over dessert, he said, "But what was Hargrove doing here?"

Jonsbeck smiled. "Consulting me on programming. What else am I good for?"

"But why? Or is it something you can't talk about?"

"It's something I suppose I *shouldn't* talk about, but it's a fairly open secret. There isn't a computer man in the capital who doesn't know what the poor frustrated simp is up to."

"What is he up to then?"

"He's fighting wars."

Gelb's eyes opened wide. "With whom?"

"With nobody, really. He fights them by computer analysis. He's been doing it for—I don't know how long."

"But why?"

"He wants the world to be the way we are—noble, honest, decent, full of respect for human rights and so on."

"So do I. So do we all. We have to keep up the pressure on the bad guys, that's all."

"And they're keeping the pressure on us, too. They don't think we're perfect."

"I suppose we're not, but we're better than they are. You know that."

Jonsbeck shrugged. "A difference in point of view. It doesn't matter. We've got a world to run, space to develop, computerization to extend. Computerization puts a premium on continued cooperation and there is slow improvement. We'll get along.—It's just that Hargrove doesn't want to wait. He hankers for quick improvement—by force. You know, *make* the bums shape up. We're strong enough to do it."

"By force? By war, you mean. We don't fight wars anymore."

"That's because it's gotten too complicated. Too much danger. We're all too powerful. You know what I mean. Except that Hargrove thinks he can find a way. You punch certain starting conditions into the computer and let it fight the war mathematically and yield the results."

"How do you make equations for war?"

"Well, you try, old man. Men. Weapons. Surprise. Counterattack. Ships. Space stations. Computers. We mustn't forget computers. There are a hundred factors and thousands of intensities and millions of combinations. Hargrove thinks it is possible to find *some* combination of starting conditions and courses of development that will result in clear victory for us and not too much damage to the world, and he labors under constant frustration."

"But what if he gets what he wants?"

"Well, if he can find the combination—if the computer says, 'This is it,' then I suppose he thinks he can argue our government into hitting out and fighting exactly the war the computer has worked out so that, barring random events that upset the indicated course, we'd have what we want."

"There'd be casualties."

"Yes, of course. But the computer will presumably compare the casualties and other damage—to the economy and ecology, for instance—with the benefits that would derive from our control of the world, and if it decides the benefits will outweigh the casualties, then it will give the go-ahead for a 'just war.' After all, it might seem that even the losing nations would benefit by being directed by us, with our stronger economy and stronger moral sense."

Gelb stared his disbelief, and said, "I never knew we were sitting at the lip of a volcanic crater like that. What about the 'random events' you mentioned?"

"The computer program tries to allow for the unexpected, but you never can, of course. So I don't think the go-ahead will come. It hasn't so far, and unless old man Hargrove can present the government with a computer simulation of the war that is totally satisfactory, I don't think there's much chance he can force one."

"And he comes to you, then, for what reason?"

"To improve the program, of course."

"And you help him?"

"Yes, certainly. There are big fees involved, Herman."

Gelb shook his head, "Peter! Are you going to try to arrange a war, just for money?"

"There won't be a war. There's no realistic combination of events that would make the computer decide on war. Computers place a greater value on human lives than human beings themselves do, and what will seem bearable to Secretary Hargrove, or even to you and me, will never be passed by a computer."

"How can you be sure of that?"

"Because I'm a programmer and I don't know of any way of programming a computer in such a way as to give it what is most needed to start any war, any persecution, any deviltry, and to ignore any harm that may be done in the process. And because it lacks what is most needed, the computers will always give Hargrove, and all others who hanker for war, nothing but frustration."

"What is it that a computer doesn't have, then?"

"Why, Gelb. It totally lacks a sense of self-righteousness."

Known But to God
and Wilbur Hines

James Morrow

My keeper faces east, his gaze lifting above the tree-tops and traveling across the national boneyard clear to the glassy Potomac. His bayonet rises into the morning sky, as if to skewer the sun. In his mind he ticks off the seconds, one for each shell in a twenty-one gun salute.

Being dead offers certain advantages. True, my pickled flesh is locked away inside this cold marble box, but my senses float free, as if they were orbiting satellites beaming back snippets of the world. I see the city, dense with black citizens and white marble. I smell the Virginia air, the ripe grass, the river's scum. I hear my keeper's boots as he pivots south, the echo of his heels coming together: two clicks, always two clicks, like a telegrapher transmitting an eternal *I*.

My keeper pretends not to notice the crowd—the fifth graders, Rotarians, garden clubbers, random tourists. Occasionally he catches a cub scout's bright yellow bandanna or a punker's pink mohawk. "Known but to God,"

11

it says on my tomb. Not true, for I'm known to myself as well. I understand Wilbur Simpson Hines perfectly.

Thock, thock, thock goes my keeper's Springfield as he transfers it from his left shoulder to his right. He pauses, twenty-one seconds again, then marches south twenty-one paces down the narrow black path, protecting me from the Bethesda Golden Age Society and the Glen Echo Lions Club.

I joined the army to learn how to kill my father. An irony: the only time the old man ever showed a glimmer of satisfaction with me was when I announced I was dropping out of college and enlisting. He thought I wanted to make the world safe for democracy, when in fact I wanted to make it safe from him. I intended to sign up under a false name. Become competent with a rifle. Then one night, while my father slept, I would sneak away from basic training, press the muzzle to his head—Harry Hines the failed and violent Pennsylvania farmer, Harry Hines the wife abuser and son beater, laying into me with his divining rods till my back was freckled with slivers of hazelwood—and blast him to Satan's backyard while he dreamed whatever dreams go through such a man's mind. You see how irrational I was in those days? The tomb has smoothed me out. There's no treatment like this box, no therapy like death.

Click, click, my keeper faces east. He pauses for twenty-one seconds, watching the morning mist hovering above the river.

"I want to be a Doughboy," I told them at the Boals-burg Recruiting Station. They parceled me. Name: Bill Johnson. Address: Bellefonte YMCA. Complexion: fair. Eye color: blue. Hair: red.

"Get on the scales," they said.

They measured me, and for a few dicey minutes I feared that, being short and scrawny—my father always detested the fact that I wasn't a gorilla like him—I'd flunk out, but the sergeant just winked at me and said, "Stand on your toes, Bill."

I did, stretching to the minimum height.

"You probably skipped breakfast this morning, right?" said the sergeant. Another wink. "Breakfast is good for a few pounds."

"Yes, sir."

My keeper turns: click, click, left face. Thock, thock, thock, he transfers his rifle from his right shoulder to his left. He pauses for twenty-one seconds then marches north down the black path. Click, click, he spins toward the Potomac and waits.

It's hard to say exactly why my plans changed. At Camp Sinclair they put me in a crisp khaki uniform and gave me a mess kit, a canteen, and a Remington rifle, and suddenly there I was, Private Bill Johnson of the American Expeditionary Forces, D Company, 18th U.S. Infantry, 1st Division. And, of course, everybody was saying what a great time we were going to have driving the Heinies into the Baltic and seeing gay Paree. The Yanks were coming, and I wanted to be one of them— Bill Johnson *nee* Wilbur Hines wasn't about to risk an A.W.O.L. conviction and a tour in the brig while his friends were off visiting *la belle France* and its French belles. After my discharge, there'd be plenty of time to show Harry Hines what his son had learned in the army.

They're changing the guard. For the next half-hour, an African-American PFC will protect me. We used to call them Coloreds, of course. Niggers, to tell you the truth. Today this particular African-American has a fancy job patrolling my tomb, but when they laid me here in 1921 his people weren't even allowed in the regular divisions. The 365th, that was the Nigger regiment, and when they finally reached France, you know what Pershing had them

13

do? Dig trenches, unload ships, and bury white Dough-boys.

But my division—*we'd* get a crack at glory, oh yes. They shipped us over on the British tub *Magnolia* and dropped us down near the front line a mile west of a jerkwater Frog village, General Robert Bullard in charge. I'm not sure what I expected from France. My buddy Alvin Platt said they'd fill our canteens with red wine every morning. They didn't. Somehow I thought I'd be in the war without actually *fighting* the war, but suddenly there we were, sharing a four-foot trench with a million cooties and dodging *Mieniewaffers* like some idiots you'd see in a newsreel at the Ziegfeld with a Fairbanks picture and a Chaplin two-reeler, everybody listening for the dreaded cry "Gas attack!" and waiting for the order to move forward. By April of 1918 we'd all seen enough victims of Boche mustard—coughing up blood, shitting their gizzards out, weeping from blind eyes—that we clung to our gas masks like little boys hugging their Ted-dies.

My keeper marches south, his bayonet cutting a straight incision in the summer air. I wonder if he's ever used it. Probably not. I used mine plenty in '18. "If a Heinie comes toward you with his hands up yelling 'Ka-merad,' don't be fooled," Sergeant Fiskejohn told us back at Camp Sinclair. "He's sure as hell got a potato masher in one of those hands. Go at him from below, and you'll stop him easy. A long thrust in the belly, then a short one, then a butt stroke to the chin if he's still on his feet, which he won't be."

On May 28th the order came through, and we climbed out of the trenches and fought what's now call the Battle of Cantigny, but it wasn't really a battle, it was a grind-ing push into the German salient with hundreds of men on both sides getting hacked to bits like we were a bunch of steer haunches hanging in our barns back home. Evidently the Boche caught more than we did, because after forty-five minutes that town was ours, and we waltzed down the gunky streets singing our favorite ditty.

The mademoiselle from gay Paree, parlez-vous?
The mademoiselle from gay Paree, parlez-vous?
The mademoiselle from gay Paree,
She had the clap and she gave it to me,
Hinky Dinky, parlez-vous?

I'll never forget the first time I drew a bead on a Heinie, a sergeant with a handlebar moustache flaring from his upper lip like antlers. I aimed, I squeezed, I killed him, just like that: now he's up, now he's down—a man I didn't even know. I thought how easy it was going to be shooting Harry Hines, a man I hated.

For the next three days the Boche counterattacked, and then I did learn to hate them. Whenever somebody lost an arm or a leg to a potato masher, he'd cry for his mother, in English mostly but sometimes in Spanish and sometimes Yiddish, and you can't see that happen more than once without wanting to shoot every Heinie in Europe, right up to the Kaiser himself. I did as Fiskejohn said. A boy would stumble toward me with his hands up—"Komerad! Komerad!"—and I'd go for his belly. There's something about having a Remington in your grasp with that lovely slice of steel jutting from the bore. I'd open the fellow up left to right, like I was underlining a passage in the sharpshooter's manual, and he'd spill out like soup. It was interesting and legal. Once I saw a sardine. On the whole, though, Fiskejohn was wrong. The dozen boys I ripped weren't holding potato mashers or anything else.

I switched tactics. I took prisoners. "Komerad!" Five

at first. "Komerad!" Six. "Komerad!" Seven. Except that seventh boy in fact had a masher, which he promptly lobbed into my chest.

Lucky for me, it bounced back.

The Heinie caught enough of the kick to get his face torn off, whereas I caught only enough to earn myself a bed in the field hospital. For a minute I didn't know I was wounded. I just looked at that boy who had no nose, no lower jaw, and wondered whether perhaps I should use a grenade on Harry Hines.

Click, click, my keeper turns to the left. Thock, thock, thock, he transfers his rifle, waits. The Old Guard—the 3rd U.S. Infantry—never quits. Twenty-four hours a day, seven days a week: can you imagine? Three A.M. on Christmas morning, say, with snow tumbling down and nobody around except a lot of dead veterans, and here's this grim, silent sentinel strutting past my tomb? It gives me the creeps.

The division surgeons spliced me together as best they could, but I knew they'd left some chips behind because my chest hurt like hell. A week after I was taken off the critical list, they gave me a month's pay and sent me to Bar-le-Duc for some rest and relaxation, which everybody knew meant cognac and whores.

The whole village was a red light district, and if you had the francs you could find love around the clock, though you'd do well to study the choices and see who had that itchy look a lady acquires when she's got the clap. And so it was that on the 1st of July, as the hot French twilight poured into a cootie-ridden bordello on the Place Vendôme, Wilbur Hines's willy finally put to port after nineteen years at sea. Like Cantigny, it was quick and confusing and over before I knew it. I had six more days coming to me, though, and I figured it would get better.

My keeper heads north, twenty-one paces. The sun beats down. The sweatband of his cap is rank and soggy. Click, click: right face. His eyes lock on the river.

I loved Bar-le-Duc. The citizens treated me like a war hero, saluting me wherever I went. There's no telling how far you'll go in this world if you're willing to bellyrip a few German teenagers.

Beyond the Poilu and the hookers, the cafés were also swarming with Bolsheviks, and I must admit their ideas made sense to me—at least, they did by my fourth glass of Château d'Yquem. After Cantigny, with its flying metal and Alvin Platt walking around with a bloody stump screaming "Mommy!" I'd begun asking the same questions as the Bolshies, such as, "Why are we having this war, anyway?" When I told them my family was poor, the Bolshies got all excited, and I hadn't felt so important since the army took me. I actually gave those fellows a few francs, and they promptly signed me up as a noncom in their organization. So now I held two ranks, PFC in the American Expeditionary Forces and lance corporal in the International Brotherhood of Proletarian Veterans or whatever the hell they were calling themselves.

My third night on the cathouse circuit, I got into an argument with one of the tarts. Fifi—I always called them Fifi—decided she'd given me special treatment on our second round, something to do with her mouth, her *bouche*, and now she wanted twenty francs instead of the usual ten. Those ladies thought every Doughboy was made of money. All you heard in Bar-le-Duc was "les Americains, beaucoup d'argent."

"Dix francs," I said.

"Vingt," Fifi insisted. Her eyes looked like two dead snails. Her hair was the color of Holstein dung.

"Dix."

17

"Vingt—or I tell ze MP you rip me," Fifi threatened. She meant rape.

"Dix," I said, throwing the coins on the bed, whereupon Fifi announced with a tilted smile that she had "a bad case of ze VD" and hoped she'd given it to me.

Just remember, you weren't there. Your body wasn't full of raw metal, and you didn't have Fifi's clap, and nobody was expecting you to maintain a lot of distinctions between the surrendering boys you were supposed to stab and the Frog tarts you weren't. It was hot. My chest hurt. Half my friends had died capturing a pissant hamlet whose streets were made of horse manure. And all I could see were those nasty little clap germs gnawing at my favorite organs.

My Remington stood by the door. The bayonet was tinted now, the color of a turnip; so different from the war itself, that bayonet—no question about its purpose. As I pushed it into Fifi and listened to the rasp of the steel against her pelvis, I thought how prophetic her mispronunciation had been: I tell ze MP you rip me.

I used the fire escape. My hands were wet and warm. All the way back to my room, I felt a gnawing in my gut like I'd been gassed. I wished I'd never stood on my toes in the Boalsburg Recruiting Station. A ditty helped. After six reprises and a bottle of cognac, I finally fell asleep.

The mademoiselle from Bar-le-Duc, parlez-vous?
The mademoiselle from Bar-le-Duc, parlez-vous?
The mademoiselle from Bar-le-Duc,
She'll screw you in the chicken coop,
Hinky Dinky, parlez-vous?

On the sixteenth of July I boarded one of those 40 and 8 trains and rejoined my regiment, now dug in along the Marne. A big fight had already happened there, sometime in '14, and they were hoping for another. I was actually glad to be leaving Bar-le-Duc, for all its wonders and delights. I knew the local gendarmes were looking into the Fifi matter.

Click, click, thock, thock, thock. My keeper pauses, twenty-one seconds. He marches south down the black path.

At the Marne they put me in charge of a Hotchkiss machine gun, and I set it up on a muddy hill, the better to cover the forward trench where they'd stationed my platoon. I had two good friends in that hole, and so when Captain Mallery showed up with orders from *le gé-néral*—we were now part of the XX French Corps—saying I should haul the Hotchkiss a mile downstream, I went berserk.

"Those boys are completely exposed," I protested. The junk in my chest was on fire. "If there's an infantry attack, we'll lose 'em all."

"Move the Hotchkiss, Private Johnson," the captain said.

"That's not a very good idea," I said.

"Move it."

"They'll be naked as jaybirds."

"Move it. *Now.*"

A couple of wars later, of course, attacks on officers by their own men got raised to a kind of art form—I know all about it, I like to read the tourists' newspapers—but this was 1918 and the concept was still in its infancy. I certainly didn't display much finesse as I pulled out my Colt revolver and in a pioneering effort shot Mallery through the heart. It was all pretty crude.

And then, damn, who should happen by but the C.O. himself, crusty old Colonel Horrocks, his eyes bulging with disbelief. He told me I was arrested. He said I'd hang. But by then I was fed up. I was fed up with gas scares and Alvin Platt getting his arm blown off. I was fed up with being an American infantry private and an honorary Bolshevik, fed up with greedy hookers and gonorrhea and the whole dumb, bloody, smelly war. So I ran. That's right: ran, retreated, quit the western front.

Unfortunately, I picked the wrong direction. I'd meant to make my way into Château-Thierry and hide out in the cathouses till the Mallery affair blew over, but instead I found myself heading toward Deutschland itself, oh yes, straight for the enemy line. Stupid, stupid.

When I saw my error, I threw up my hands.

And screamed.

"Komerad! Komerad!"

Bill Johnson *née* Wilbur Hines never fought in the Second Battle of the Marne. He never helped his regiment drive the Heinies back eight miles, capture four thousand of the Kaiser's best troops, and kill God knows how many more. This private missed it all, because the Boche hit him with everything they had. Machine gun fire, grapeshot, rifle bullets, shrapnel. A potato masher detonated. A mustard shell went off. Name: unknown. Address: unknown. Complexion: charred. Eye color: no eyes. Hair: burned off. Weeks later, when they scraped me off the Marne floodplain, it was obvious I was a prime candidate for the Arlington program. Lucky for me, Colonel Horrocks got killed at Soissons. He'd have voted me down.

As I said, I read the newspapers. I keep up. That's how I learned about my father. One week after they put me in this box, Harry Hines cheated at seven-card stud and was bludgeoned to death by the loser with a ball-peen hammer. He made the front page of the *Centre County Democrat*.

It's raining. The old people hoist their umbrellas; the fifth graders glom onto their teacher; the cub scouts march away like a platoon of midgets. Am I angry about

my life? For many years, yes, I was furious, but then the eighties rolled around, mine and the century's, and I realized I'd be dead by now anyway. So I won't leave you with any bitter thoughts. I'll leave you with a pretty song.
  Listen.

The mademoiselle from Is-sur-Tille, parlez-vous?
The mademoiselle from Is-sur-Tille, parlez-vous?
The mademoiselle from Is-sur-Tille,
She can zig-zig-zig like a spinning wheel,
Hinky Dinky, parlez-vous?

My keeper remains, facing east.

The Liberation of Earth

William Tenn

This, then, is the story of our liberation. Suck air and grab clusters. Heigh-ho, here is the tale.

August was the month, a Tuesday in August. These words are meaningless now, so far have we progressed; but many things known and discussed by our primitive ancestors, our unliberated, unreconstructed forefathers, are devoid of sense to our free minds. Still the tale must be told, with all of its incredible place-names and vanished points of reference.

Why must it be told? Have any of you a *better* thing to do? We have had water and weeds and lie in a valley of gusts. So rest, relax and listen. And suck air, suck air.

On a Tuesday in August, the ship appeared in the sky over France in a part of the world then known as Europe. Five miles long the ship was, and word has come down to us that it looked like an enormous silver cigar.

The tale goes on to tell of the panic and consternation

among our forefathers when the ship abruptly materialized in the summer-blue sky. How they ran, how they
shouted, how they pointed!

How they excitedly notified the United Nations, one
of their chiefest institutions, that a strange metal craft of
incredible size had materialized over their land. How they
sent an order *here* to cause military aircraft to surround
it with loaded weapons, gave instructions *there* for hastily grouped scientists, with signaling apparatus, to approach it with friendly gestures. How, under the great
ship, men with cameras took pictures of it; men with
typewriters wrote stories about it; and men with conces-
sions sold models of it.

All these things did our ancestors, enslaved and unknowing, do.

Then a tremendous slab snapped up in the middle of
the ship and the first of the aliens stepped out in the
complex tripodal gait that all humans were shortly to
know and love so well. He wore a metallic garment to
protect him from the effects of our atmospheric peculiarities, a garment of the opaque, loosely folded type that
these, the first of our liberators, wore throughout their
stay on Earth.

Speaking in a language none could understand, but
booming deafeningly through a huge mouth about halfway up his twenty-five feet of height, the alien discoursed
for exactly one hour, waited politely for a response when
he had finished, and, receiving none, retired into the
ship.

That night, the first of our liberation! Or the first of
our first liberation, should I say? *That* night, anyhow!
Visualize our ancestors scurrying about their primitive
intricacies: playing ice-hockey, televising, smashing atoms, red-baiting, conducting giveaway shows and sign-
ing affidavits—all the incredible minutiae that made the

olden times such a frightful mass of cumulative detail in which to live—as compared with the breathless and majestic simplicity of the present.

The big question, of course, was—what had the alien said? Had he called on the human race to surrender? Had he announced that he was on a mission of peaceful trade and, having made what he considered a reasonable offer—for, let us say, the north polar ice-cap—politely withdrawn so that we could discuss his terms among ourselves in relative privacy? Or, possibly, had he merely announced that he was the newly appointed ambassador to Earth from a friendly and intelligent race—and would we please direct him to the proper authority so that he might submit his credentials?

Not to know was quite maddening.

Since decision rested with the diplomats, it was the last possibility which was held, very late that night, to be most likely; and early the next morning, accordingly, a delegation from the United Nations waited under the belly of the motionless star-ship. The delegation had been instructed to welcome the aliens to the outermost limits of its collective linguistic ability. As an additional earnest of mankind's friendly intentions, all military craft patrolling the air about the great ship were ordered to carry no more than one atom-bomb in their racks, and to fly a small white flag—along with the U.N. banner and their own national emblem. Thus did our ancestors face this, the ultimate challenge of history.

When the alien came forth a few hours later, the delegation stepped up to him, bowed, and, in the three official languages of the United Nations—English, French and Russian—asked him to consider this planet his home. He listened to them gravely, and then launched into his talk of the day before—which was evidently as highly charged with emotion and significance to him as it was completely incomprehensible to the representatives of world government.

Fortunately, a cultivated young Indian member of the secretariat detected a suspicious similarity between the speech of the alien and an obscure Bengali dialect whose anomalies he had once puzzled over. The reason, as we all know now, was that the last time Earth had been visited by aliens of this particular type, humanity's most advanced civilization lay in a moist valley in Bengal; extensive dictionaries of that language had been written, so that speech with the natives of Earth would present no problem to any subsequent exploring party.

However, I move ahead of my tale, as one who would munch on the succulent roots before the dryer stem. Let me rest and suck air for a moment. Heigh-ho, truly those were tremendous experiences for our kind.

You, sir, now you sit back and listen. You are not yet of an age to Tell the Tale. I remember, *well enough do I remember* how my father told it, and his father before him. You will wait your turn as I did; you will listen until too much high land between water holes blocks me off from life.

Then *you* may take your place in the juiciest weed patch and, reclining gracefully between sprints, recite the great epic of our liberation to the carelessly exercising young.

Pursuant to the young Hindu's suggestions, the one professor of comparative linguistics of the world capable of understanding and conversing in this peculiar version of the dead dialect was summoned from an academic convention in New York where he was reading a paper he had been working on for eighteen years: *An Initial Study of Apparent Relationships Between Several Past*

Participles in Ancient Sanscrit and an Equal Number of Noun Substantives in Modern Szechuanese.

Yea, verily, all these things—and more, many more—did our ancestors in their besotted ignorance contrive to do. May we not count our freedoms indeed?

The disgruntled scholar, minus—as he kept insisting bitterly—some of his most essential word lists, was flown by fastest jet to the area south of Nancy which, in those long-ago days, lay in the enormous black shadow of the alien space-ship.

Here he was acquainted with his task by the United Nations delegation, whose nervousness had not been allayed by a new and disconcerting development. Several more aliens had emerged from the ship carrying great quantities of immense, shimmering metal which they proceeded to assemble into something that was obviously a machine—though it was taller than any skyscraper man had ever built, and seemed to make noises to itself like a talkative and sentient creature. The first alien still stood courteously in the neighborhood of the profusely perspiring diplomats; ever and anon he would go through his little speech again, in a language that had been almost forgotten when the cornerstone of the library of Alexandria was laid. The men from the U.N. would reply, each one hoping desperately to make up for the alien's lack of familiarity with his own tongue by such devices as hand-gestures and facial expressions. Much later, a commission of anthropologists and psychologists brilliantly pointed out the difficulties of such physical, gestural communication with creatures possessing—as these aliens did—five manual appendages and a single, unwinking compound eye of the type the insects rejoice in.

The problems and agonies of the professor as he was trundled about the world in the wake of the aliens, trying to amass a usable vocabulary in a language whose peculiarities he could only extrapolate from the limited samples supplied him by one who must inevitably speak it with the most outlandish of foreign accents—these vexations were minor indeed compared to the disquiet felt by the representatives of world government. They beheld the extra-terrestrial visitors move every day to a new site on their planet and proceed to assemble there a titanic structure of flickering metal which muttered nostalgically to itself, as if to keep alive the memory of those faraway factories which had given it birth.

True, there was always the alien who would pause in his evidently supervisory labors to release the set little speech; but not even the excellent manners he displayed, in listening to upward of fifty-six replies in as many languages, helped dispel the panic caused whenever a human scientist, investigating the shimmering machines, touched a projecting edge and promptly shrank into a disappearing pinpoint. This, while not a frequent occurrence, happened often enough to cause chronic indigestion and insomnia among human administrators.

Finally, having used up most of his nervous system as fuel, the professor collated enough of the language to make conversation possible. He—and, through him, the world—was thereupon told the following:

The aliens were members of a highly advanced civilization which had spread its culture throughout the entire galaxy. Cognizant of the limitations of the as-yet-underdeveloped animals who had latterly become dominant upon Earth, they had placed us in a sort of benevolent ostracism. Until either we or our institutions had evolved to a level permitting, say, at least *associate* membership in the galactic federation (under the sponsoring tutelage, for the first few millennia, of one of the older, more widespread and more important species in that federation)—until that time, all invasions of our privacy and ignorance—except for a few scientific expeditions conducted under conditions of great secrecy—had been strictly forbidden by universal agreement.

Several individuals who had violated this ruling—at great cost to our racial sanity, and enormous profit to our reigning religions—had been so promptly and severely punished that no known infringements had occurred for some time. Our recent growth-curve had been satisfactory enough to cause hopes that a bare thirty or forty centuries more would suffice to place us on applicant status with the federation.

Unfortunately, the peoples of this stellar community were many, and varied as greatly in their ethical outlook as in their biological composition. Quite a few species lagged a considerable social distance behind the Dendi, as our visitors called themselves. One of these, a race of horrible, worm-like organisms known as the Troxxt—almost as advanced technologically as they were retarded in moral development—had suddenly volunteered for the position of sole and absolute ruler of the galaxy. They had seized control of several key suns, with their attendant planetary systems, and, after a calculated decimation of the races thus captured, had announced their intention of punishing with a merciless extinction all species unable to appreciate from these object-lessons the value of unconditional surrender.

In despair, the galactic federation had turned to the Dendi, one of the oldest, most selfless, and yet most powerful of races in civilized space, and commissioned them—as the military arm of the federation—to hunt down the Troxxt, defeat them wherever they had gained illegal suzerainty, and destroy forever their power to wage war.

This order had come almost too late. Everywhere the

Troxxt had gained so much the advantage of attack, that the Dendi were able to contain them only by enormous sacrifice. For centuries now, the conflict had careened across our vast island universe. In the course of it, densely populated planets had been disintegrated; suns had been blasted into novae; and whole groups of stars ground into swirling cosmic dust.

A temporary stalemate had been reached a short while ago, and—reeling and breathless—both sides were using the lull to strengthen weak spots in their perimeter.

Thus, the Troxxt had finally moved into the till-then peaceful section of space that contained our solar system—among others. They were thoroughly uninterested in our tiny planet with its meager resources; nor did they care much for such celestial neighbors as Mars or Jupiter. They established their headquarters on a planet of Proxima Centauri—the star nearest our own sun—and proceeded to consolidate their offensive-defensive network between Rigel and Aldebaran. At this point in their explanation, the Dendi pointed out, the exigencies of interstellar strategy tended to become too complicated for anything but three-dimensional maps; let us here accept the simple statement, they suggested, that it became immediately vital for them to strike rapidly, and make the Troxxt position on Proxima Centauri untenable—to establish a base inside their lines of communication.

The most likely spot for such a base was Earth.

The Dendi apologized profusely for intruding on our development, an intrusion which might cost us dear in our delicate developmental state. But, as they explained—in impeccable pre-Bengali—before their arrival we had, in effect, become (all unknowingly) a satrapy of the awful Troxxt. We could now consider ourselves liberated.

We thanked them much for that.

Besides, their leader pointed out proudly, the Dendi were engaged in a war for the sake of civilization itself, against an enemy so horrible, so obscene in its nature, and so utterly filthy in its practices, that it was unworthy of the label of intelligent life. They were fighting, not only for themselves, but for every loyal member of the galactic federation; for every small and helpless species; for every obscure race too weak to defend itself against a ravaging conqueror. Would humanity stand aloof from such a conflict?

There was just a slight bit of hesitation as the information was digested. Then—*"No!"* humanity roared back through such mass-communication media as television, newspapers, reverberating jungle drums, and mule-mounted backwoods messenger. *"We will not stand aloof! We will help you destroy this menace to the very fabric of civilization! Just tell us what you want us to do!"*

Well, nothing in particular, the aliens replied with some embarrassment. Possibly in a little while there might *be* something—*several* little things, in fact—which could be *quite* useful; but, for the moment, if we would concentrate on not getting in their way when they serviced their gunmounts, they would be very grateful, really. . . .

This reply tended to create a large amount of uncertainty among the two billion of Earth's human population. For several days afterward, there was a planet-wide tendency—the legend has come down to us—of people failing to meet each other's eyes.

But then Man rallied from this substantial blow to his pride. He would be useful, be it ever so humbly, to the race which had liberated him from potential subjugation by the ineffably ugly Troxxt. For this, let us remember well our ancestors! Let us hymn their sincere efforts amid their ignorance!

All standing armies, all air and sea fleets, were reorganized into guard-patrols around the Dendi weapons: no human might approach within two miles of the murmuring machinery, without a pass countersigned by the Dendi. Since they were never known to sign such a pass during the entire period of their stay on this planet, however, this loophole-provision was never exercised as far as is known; and the immediate neighborhood of the extra-terrestrial weapons became and remained henceforth wholesomely free of two-legged creatures.

Cooperation with our liberators took precedence over all other human activities. The order of the day was a slogan first given voice by a Harvard professor of government in a querulous radio round table on "Man's Place in a Somewhat Over-Civilized Universe."

"Let us forget our individual egos and collective conceits," the professor cried at one point. "Let us subordinate everything—to the end that the freedom of the solar system in general, and Earth in particular, must and shall be preserved!"

Despite its mouth-filling qualities, this slogan was repeated everywhere. Still, it was difficult sometimes to know exactly what the Dendi wanted—partly because of the limited number of interpreters available to the heads of the various sovereign states, and partly because of their leader's tendency to vanish into his ship after ambiguous and equivocal statements—such as the curt admonition to "Evacuate Washington!"

On that occasion, both the Secretary of State and the American President perspired fearfully through five hours of a July day in all the silk-hatted, stiff-collared, dark-suited diplomatic regalia that the barbaric past demanded of political leaders who would deal with the representatives of another people. They waited and wilted beneath the enormous ship—which no human had ever been invited to enter, despite the wistful hints constantly thrown out by university professors and aeronautical designers—they waited patiently and wetly for the Dendi leader to emerge and let them know whether he had meant the State of Washington or Washington, D. C.

The tale comes down to us at this point as a tale of glory. The capitol building taken apart in a few days, and set up almost intact in the foothills of the Rocky Mountains; the missing Archives, that were later to turn up in the Children's Room of a Public Library in Duluth, Iowa; the bottles of Potomac River water carefully borne westward and ceremoniously poured into the circular concrete ditch built around the President's mansion (from which unfortunately it was to evaporate within a week because of the relatively low humidity of the region)—all these are proud moments in the galactic history of our species, from which not even the later knowledge that the Dendi wished to build no gun site on the spot, nor even an ammunition dump, but merely a recreation hall for their troops, could remove any of the grandeur of our determined cooperation and most willing sacrifice.

There is no denying, however, that the ego of our race was greatly damaged by the discovery, in the course of a routine journalistic interview, that the aliens totaled no more powerful a group than a squad; and that their leader, instead of the great scientist and key military strategist that we might justifiably have expected the Galactic Federation to furnish for the protection of Terra, ranked as the interstellar equivalent of a buck sergeant.

That the President of the United States, the Commander-in-Chief of the Army and the Navy, had waited in such obeisant fashion upon a mere noncommissioned officer was hard for us to swallow; but that the impending Battle of Earth was to have a historical dignity only slightly higher than that of a patrol action was impossibly humiliating.

And then there was the matter of "lendi."

The aliens, while installing or servicing their planet-wide weapon system, would occasionally fling aside an evidently unusable fragment of the talking metal. Separated from the machine of which it had been a component, the substance seemed to lose all those qualities which were deleterious to mankind and retain several which were quite useful indeed. For example, if a portion of the strange material was attached to any terrestrial metal—and insulated carefully from contact with other substances—it would, in a few hours, itself become exactly the metal that it touched, whether that happened to be zinc, gold, or pure uranium.

The stuff—"lendi," men have heard the aliens call it—was shortly in frantic demand in an economy ruptured by constant and unexpected emptyings of its most important industrial centers.

Everywhere the aliens went, to and from their weapon sites, hordes of ragged humans stood chanting—well outside the two-mile limit—"Any lendi, Dendi?" All attempts by law-enforcement agencies of the planet to put a stop to this shameless, wholesale begging were useless—especially since the Dendi themselves seemed to get some unexplainable pleasure out of scattering tiny pieces of lendi to the scrabbling multitude. When policemen and soldiery began to join the trampling, murderous dash to the corner of the meadows wherein had fallen the highly versatile and garrulous metal, governments gave up.

Mankind almost began to hope for the attack to come,

so that it would be relieved of the festering consideration of its own patent inferiorities. A few of the more fanatically conservative among our ancestors probably even began to regret liberation.

They did, children; they did! Let us hope that these would-be troglodytes were among the very first to be dissolved and melted down by the red flame-balls. One cannot, after all, turn one's back on progress!

Two days before the month of September was over, the aliens announced that they had detected activity upon one of the moons of Saturn. The Troxxt were evidently threading their treacherous way inward through the solar system. Considering their vicious and deceitful propensities, the Dendi warned, an attack from these worm-like monstrosities might be expected at any moment.

Few humans went to sleep as the night rolled up to and past the meridian on which they dwelt. Almost all eyes were lifted to a sky carefully denuded of clouds by watchful Dendi. There was a brisk trade in cheap telescopes and bits of smoked glass in some sections of the planet; while other portions experienced a substantial boom in spells and charms of the all-inclusive, or omnibus, variety.

The Troxxt attacked in three cylindrical black ships simultaneously; one in the Southern Hemisphere, and two in the Northern. Great gouts of green flame roared out of their tiny craft; and everything touched by this imploded into a translucent, glass-like sand. No Dendi was hurt by these, however, and from each of the now-writhing gun mounts there bubbled forth a series of scarlet clouds which pursued the Troxxt hungrily, until forced by a dwindling velocity to fall back upon Earth.

Here they had an unhappy after-effect. Any populated area into which these pale pink cloudlets chanced to fall was rapidly transformed into a cemetery—a cemetery, if the truth be told as it has been handed down to us, that had more the odor of the kitchen that the grave. The inhabitants of these unfortunate localities were subjected to enormous increases of temperature. Their skin reddened, then blackened; their hair and nails shriveled; their very flesh turned into liquid and boiled off their bones. Altogether a disagreeable way for one-tenth of the human race to die.

The only consolation was the capture of a black cylinder by one of the red clouds. When, as a result of this, it had turned white-hot and poured its substance down in the form of a metallic rainstorm, the two ships assaulting the Northern Hemisphere abruptly retreated to the asteroids into which the Dendi—because of severely limited numbers—steadfastly refused to pursue them.

In the next twenty-four hours the aliens—*resident* aliens, let us say—held conferences, made repairs to their weapons and commiserated with us. Humanity buried its dead. This last was a custom of our forefathers that was most worthy of note; and one that has not, of course, survived into modern times.

By the time the Troxxt returned, Man was ready for them. He could not, unfortunately, stand to arms as he most ardently desired to do; but he could and did stand to optical instrument and conjurer's oration.

Once more the little red clouds burst joyfully into the upper reaches of the stratosphere; once more the green flames wailed and tore at the chattering spires of lendi; once more men died by the thousands in the boiling backwash of war. But this time, there was a slight difference: the green flames of the Troxxt abruptly changed color after the engagement had last three hours; they became darker, more bluish. And, as they did so, Dendi after Dendi collapsed at his station and died in convulsions.

The call for retreat was evidently sounded. The survivors fought their way to the tremendous ship in which they had come. With an explosion from her stern jets that blasted a red-hot furrow southward through France, and kicked Marseilles into the Mediterranean, the ship roared into space and fled home ignominiously.

Humanity steeled itself for the coming ordeal of horror under the Troxxt.

They were truly worm-like in form. As soon as the two night-black cylinders had landed, they strode from their ships, their tiny segemented bodies held off the ground by a complex harness supported by long and slender metal crutches. They erected a dome-like fort around each ship—one in Australia and one in the Ukraine—captured the few courageous individuals who had ventured close to their landing sites, and disappeared back into the dark craft with their squirming prizes.

While some men drilled about nervously in the ancient military patterns, others pored anxiously over scientific texts and records pertaining to the visit of the Dendi—in the desperate hope of finding a way of preserving terrestrial independence against this ravening conqueror of the star-spattered galaxy.

And yet all this time, the human captives inside the artificially darkened space-ships (the Troxxt, having no eyes, not only had little use for light but the more sedentary individuals among them actually found such radiation disagreeable to their sensitive, unpigmented skins) were not being tortured for information—nor vivisected in the earnest quest of knowledge on a slightly higher level—but educated.

Educated in the Troxxtian language, that is.

The Liberation of Earth

True it was that a large number found themselves utterly inadequate for the task which the Troxxt had set them, and temporarily became servants to the more successful students. And another, albeit smaller, group developed various forms of frustration hysteria—ranging from mild unhappiness to complete catatonic depression—over the difficulties presented by a language whose every verb was irregular, and whose myriads of prepositions were formed by noun-adjective combinations derived from the subject of the previous sentence. But, eventually, eleven human beings were released, to blink madly in the sunlight as certified interpreters of Troxxt.

These liberators, it seemed, had never visited Bengal in the heyday of its millennia-past civilization.

Yes, these *liberators*. For the Troxxt had landed on the sixth day of the ancient, almost mythical month of October. And October the Sixth is, of course, the Holy Day of the Second Liberation. Let us remember, let us revere. (If only we could figure out which day it is on our calendar!)

The tale the interpreters told caused men to hang their heads in shame and gnash their teeth at the deception they had allowed the Dendi to practice upon them.

True, the Dendi had been commissioned by the Galactic Federal to hunt the Troxxt down and destroy them. This was largely because the Dendi *were* the Galactic Federation. One of the first intelligent arrivals on the interstellar scene, the huge creatures had organized a vast police force to protect them and their power against any contingency of revolt that might arise in the future. This police force was ostensibly a congress of all thinking life forms throughout the galaxy; actually, it was an efficient means of keeping them under rigid control.

Most species thus-far discovered were docile and tractable, however; the Dendi had been ruling from time immemorial, said they—very well, then, let the Dendi continue to rule. Did it make that much difference?

But, throughout the centuries, opposition to the Dendi grew—and the nuclei of the opposition were the protoplasm-based creatures. What, in fact, had come to be known as the Protoplasmic League.

Though small in number, the creatures whose life cycles were derived from the chemical and physical properties of protoplasm varied greatly in size, structure, and specialization. A galactic community deriving the main wells of its power from them would be a dynamic instead of a static place, where extra-galactic travel would be encouraged, instead of being inhibited, as it was at present because of Dendi fears of meeting a superior civilization. It would be a true democracy of species—a real biological republic—where all creatures of adequate intelligence and cultural development would enjoy a control of their destinies at present experienced by the silicon-based Dendi alone.

To this end, the Troxxt—the only important race which had steadfastly refused the complete surrender of armaments demanded of all members of the Federation—had been implored by a minor member of the Protoplasmic League to rescue it from the devastation which the Dendi intended to visit upon it, as punishment for an unlawful exploratory excursion outside the boundaries of the galaxy.

Faced with the determination of the Troxxt to defend their cousins in organic chemistry, and the suddenly aroused hostility of at least two-thirds of the interstellar peoples, the Dendi had summoned a rump meeting of the Galactic Council; declared a state of revolt in being; and proceeded to cement their disintegrating rule with the blasted life-forces of a hundred worlds. The Troxxt, hopelessly outnumbered and out-equipped, had been able to continue the struggle only because of the great ingenuity and selflessness of other members of the Protoplasmic League, who had risked extinction to supply them with newly developed secret weapons.

Hadn't we guessed the nature of the beast from the enormous precautions it had taken to prevent the exposure of any part of its body to the intensely corrosive atmosphere of Earth? Surely the seamless, barely translucent suits which our recent visitors had worn for every moment of their stay on our world should have made us suspect a body chemistry developed from complex silicon compounds rather than those of carbon?

Humanity hung its collective head and admitted that the suspicion had never occurred to it.

Well, the Troxxt admitted generously, we were extremely inexperienced and possibly a little too trusting. Put it down to that. Our naiveté, however costly to them—our liberators—would not be allowed to deprive us of that complete citizenship which the Troxxt were claiming as the birthright of all.

But as for our leaders, our probably corrupted, certainly irresponsible leaders . . .

The first executions of U.N. officials, heads of states, and pre-Bengali interpreters as "Traitors to Protoplasm"—after some of the lengthiest and most nearly-perfectly-fair trials in the history of Earth—were held a week after G-J Day, the inspiring occasion on which—amidst gorgeous ceremonies—Humanity was invited to join, first the Protoplasmic League and thence the New and Democratic Galactic Federation of All Species, All Races.

Nor was that all. Whereas the Dendi had contemptuously shoved us to one side as they went about their business of making our planet safe for tyranny, and had—in all probability—built special devices which made the very touch of their weapons fatal for us, the Troxxt—with the sincere friendliness which had made their name a byword for democracy and decency wherever living creatures came together among the stars—our Second Liberators, as we lovingly called them, actually *preferred* to have us help them with the intensive, accelerating labor of planetary defense.

So men's intestines dissolved under the invisible glare of the forces used to assemble the new, incredibly complex weapons; men sickened and died, in scrabbling hordes, inside the mines which the Troxxt had made deeper than any we had dug hitherto; men's bodies broke open and exploded in the undersea oil-drilling sites which the Troxxt had declared were essential.

Children's schooldays were requested, too, in such collecting drives as ''Platinum Scrap for Procyon'' and ''Radioactive Debris for Deneb.'' Housewives also were implored to save on salt whenever possible—this substance being useful to the Troxxt in literally dozens of incomprehensible ways—and colorful posters reminded: *''Don't salinate—sugarfy!''*

And over all—courteously caring for us like an intelligent parent—were our mentors, taking their giant supervisory strides on metallic crutches, while their pale little bodies lay curled in the hammocks that swung from each paired length of shining leg.

Truly, even in the midst of a complete economic paralysis caused by the concentration of all major productive facilities on other-worldly armaments, and despite the anguished cries of those suffering from peculiar industrial injuries which our medical men were totally unequipped to handle, in the midst of all this mind-wracking disorganization, it was yet very exhilarating to realize

that we had taken our lawful place in the future government of the galaxy and were even now helping to make
the Universe Safe for Democracy.

But the Dendi returned to smash this idyll. They came
in their huge, silvery space-ships and the Troxxt, barely
warned in time, just managed to rally under the blow
and fight back in kind. Even so, the Troxxt ship in the
Ukraine was almost immediately forced to flee to its base
in the depths of space. After three days, the only Troxxt
on Earth were the devoted members of a little band
guarding the ship in Australia. They proved, in three or
more months, to be as difficult to remove from the face
of our planet as the continent itself; and since there was
now a state of close and hostile siege, with the Dendi on
one side of the globe, and the Troxxt on the other, the
battle assumed frightful proportions.

Seas boiled; whole steppes burned away; the climate
itself shifted and changed under the gruelling pressure of
the cataclysm. By the time the Dendi solved the problem,
the planet Venus had been blasted from the skies in the
course of a complicated battle maneuver, and Earth had
wobbled over as orbital substitute.

The solution was simple: since the Troxxt were too
firmly based on the small continent to be driven away,
the numerically superior Dendi brought up enough fire-
power to disintegrate all Australia into an ash that mud-
died the Pacific. This occurred on the twenty-fourth of
June, the Holy Day of First Reliberation. A day of reck-
oning for what remained of the human race, however.

How could we have been so naive, the Dendi wanted
to know, as to be taken in by the chauvinistic pro-
protoplasm propaganda? Surely, if physical characteris-
tics were to be the criteria of our racial empathy, we
would not orient ourselves on a narrow chemical basis!

41

The Dendi life-plasma was based on silicon instead of carbon, true, but did not vertebrates—*appendaged* vertebrates, at that, such as we and the Dendi—have infinitely more in common, in spite of a *minor* biochemical difference or two, than vertebrates and legless, armless, slime-crawling creatures who happened, quite accidentally, to possess an identical organic substance?

As for this fantastic picture of life in the galaxy . . . *Well!* The Dendi shrugged their quintuple shoulders as they went about the intricate business of erecting their noisy weapons all over the rubble of our planet. Had we ever seen a representative of these protoplasmic races the Troxxt were supposedly protecting? No, nor would we. For as soon as a race—animal, vegetable or mineral— developed enough to constitute even a *potential* danger to the sinuous aggressors, its civilization was systematically dismantled by the watchful Troxxt. We were in so primitive a state that they had not considered it at all risky to allow us the outward seeming of full participation.

Could we say we had learned a single useful piece of information about Troxxt technology—for all of the work we had done on their machines, for all of the lives we had lost in the process? No, of course not! We had merely contributed our mite to the enslavement of far-off races who had done us no harm.

There was much that we had cause to feel guilty about, the Dendi told us gravely—once the few surviving interpreters of the pre-Bangali dialect had crawled out of hiding. But our collective onus was as nothing compared to that borne by "vermicular collaborationists"—those traitors who had supplanted our martyred former leaders. And then there were the unspeakable human interpreters who had had linguistic traffic with creatures destroying a two-million-year-old galactic peace! Why, killing was almost too good for them, the Dendi murmured as they killed them.

When the Troxxt ripped their way back into possession of Earth some eighteen months later, bringing us the sweet fruits of the Second Reliberation—as well as a complete and most convincing rebuttal of the Dendi—there were few humans found who were willing to accept with any real enthusiasm the responsibilities of newly opened and highly paid positions in language, science, and government.

Of course, since the Troxxt, in order to reliberate Earth, had found it necessary to blast a tremendous chunk out of the northern hemisphere, there were very few humans to be found in the first place. . . .

Even so, many of these committed suicide rather than assume the title of Secretary General of the United Nations when the Dendi came back for the glorious Re-Reliberation, a short time after that. This was the liberation, by the way, which swept the deep collar of matter off our planet, and gave it what our forefathers came to call a pear-shaped look.

Possibly it was at this time—possibly a liberation or so later—that the Troxxt and the Dendi discovered the Earth had become far to eccentric in its orbit to possess the minimum safety conditions demanded of a Combat Zone. The battle, therefore, zig-zagged coruscatingly and murderously away in the direction of Aldebaran.

That was nine generations ago, but the tale that has been handed down from parent to child, to child's child, has lost little in the telling. You hear it now from me almost exactly as *I* heard it. From my father I heard it as I ran with him from water puddle to distant water puddle, across the searing heat of yellow sand. From my mother I heard it as we sucked air and frantically grabbed at clusters of thick green weed, whenever the planet beneath us quivered in omen of a geological spasm that might bury us in its burned-out body, or a cosmic gyration threatened to fling us into empty space.

Yes, even as we do now did we do then, telling the same tale, running the same frantic race across miles of unendurable heat for food and water; fighting the same savage battles with the giant rabbits for each others' carrion—and always, ever and always, sucking desperately at the precious air, which leaves our world in greater quantities with every mad twist of its orbit.

Naked, hungry, and thirsty came we into the world, and naked, hungry, and thirsty do we scamper our lives out upon it, under the huge and never-changing sun.

The same tale it is, and the same traditional ending it has as that I had from my father and his father before him. Suck air, grab clusters, and hear the last holy observation of our history:

"Looking about us, we can say with pardonable pride that we have been about as thoroughly liberated as it is possible for a race and a planet to be!"

Valkyrie

Jack McDevitt

We still get together once a month at the VFW. We drink too much and play shuffleboard and leer at Bess and talk about the old days. And we always get around to how different things are now: everybody out for himself, everybody on dope. Kids today just aren't worth a damn and we all know it. God help us if we ever need them to defend the country. Brad Conner always makes the same remark: when the Russians land at Virginia Beach the only people out there to meet them will be us.

I get scared when I hear that. It's a joke that prompts laughter and raised glasses from Herman and Cuff and the rest. And a knowing wink from Bess. Because it's the truth, we would be alone. But nobody seriously believes anymore that the Russians might really come. *Glasnost* and all that.

Maybe. But somebody's coming. Unless whatever controls these things has changed its mind, they're coming.

I'm not like some of the guys, refusing to talk about the war, or even think about it. But I've never told anyone about what I saw the first night of the Tet Offensive, except occasionally when I've had too much to drink and nobody listens anyhow.

The attack caught me in Quangngai, in a downtown bar. I got out the back about the time a grenade came through a window. The streets were swarming with packs of armed men, some moving with military precision, others not much more than mobs. They shot down a few people for laughs. And they hauled a man out of a newspaper office and beat him to death, and then killed a woman who objected.

Hard to tell whose side they were on. Not that it mattered.

A Cobra ranged overhead early in the evening, spraying the attackers with heavy machine guns. But other than that, and a burned-out tank, I saw no sign of the Army.

The tank was in the middle of the street in front of a bicycle shop. The bicycle shop was pretty well blown apart too. I stood in the shadows and watched the tank smolder, until I realized I wasn't alone. Movement somewhere. Metal clicking softly. Get off the street: I climbed through the shattered front window into the shop, and crawled behind a counter, intending to wait things out. Nearby explosions shook dust out of the rafters. Squads of Cong riflemen appeared, and moved down both sides of the street. The fire glittered on their weapons. A few of them appeared on a rooftop opposite and set up a 50-caliber machine gun. The 50-calibers were heavy and loud, and they were hell on choppers.

The Cobra kept hammering away. Missile tracks raced toward it, wire-thin tracers hurtling over the city. The gunship dropped low, out of sight, and then rolled in, pumping rockets and 30mm shells into the clapboard streets. I heard screams.

A bright yellow moon, big and peaceful, floated over the scene.

They answered with the 50-caliber. The chopper veered off, and the street fell silent. Then it came back, running at roof top level. But Charlie must have got a couple more of the big machine guns up. They erected a goddam solid wall of steel and I wanted the chopper to back off, but he was committed by then so he kept coming and ripped by me, firing everything he had, churning down the center of the street, blowing dust in all directions.

Something hit it: it shuddered, and pulled up trailing smoke. Charlie kept firing. One of the rotor blades blew away. Moments later, the Cobra exploded.

Almost simultaneously, a brilliant white light erupted above the blast. It filled the sky, threw the street into sudden daylight, faded, and brightened again. I covered my eyes with my hands and cringed. For a moment, for a single bottomless moment, I thought: nuke.

It lasted only a few seconds. Then it was gone, and when I looked again, I saw only a blazing blue-white flare plunging down the sky. It was almost directly overhead.

Another gunship, maybe. Something.

The gunners concentrated their fire on it. A piece of the thing broke off, and spurted away to the southeast, in the direction of the Pacific. It might have been a rocket misfire.

The rest of the object continued to drop. It burned furiously, utterly silent.

But it wasn't quite falling anymore. Not under control, exactly, but it seemed to be slowing down. Leveling off. It drifted toward the rooftops, pursued by streams of tracers.

It sliced across the night, a brilliant cobalt star, and plowed into the roof of a four-story office building in the next block. The walls exploded, and the structure leaned toward the street, and collapsed. A cloud of gas and steam rose.

Fires broke out up and down the street. The gunners cheered.

Windows in adjoining buildings let go like gunshots. Then, in the steam and smoke and rubble, I saw something moving.

A human figure.

A woman.

She stumbled out, clothes smoking, face and hair burned black. She staggered halfway across the street, and went down, one fist clenched in agony.

I looked at her, glanced back toward the shadows (filled with the dark figures of the Cong, just watching, not moving), and did the dumbest thing of my life: I ran into the middle of the street and charged toward her.

There was no point trying to keep close to the buildings. I was silhouetted against moonlight and fire no matter where I was, so I made what use I could of the tank. Charlie was slow to react: I covered about forty yards and got across the intersection before the first shot whistled over my head.

The woman looked up. She was afire: the flames ate at her clothing, enveloped her. She should have been rolling in the street, the night should have filled with her screams. Instead she only watched me come.

Charlie opened up in earnest. Bullets flew through the thick air, shattered wood, bounced off the tank, buried themselves in the street. One tore away a piece of my shoulder.

I ran with clumsy terror. The woman got up on one

knee, took a deep breath, and struggled to her feet. She watched me come, eyes filled with pain.

Her jacket burst into flame. She ripped it off and hurled it away.

I stumbled toward her, lost my balance, ran a few more steps, arms and legs flailing, fell, rolled over, and came up in full stride. In all, it was a hell of a performance.

She shook her head no. And waved me away.

No time to argue. I plowed into her, knocking her over. But I kept going and got us both off the street and into a storefront.

She held onto a post, trying to steady herself. I'd got the fire out, but her clothes were steaming, and her face was scorched. She stared at me out of angry black eyes.

I kicked the door open. "Inside." I pointed into the store.

Her nostrils widened slightly, and I saw something that scared me more than all the goddam shooting: she smiled.

Then she stepped through. The interior was dark, il-luminated only by spasms of firelight, slicing through a bank of cross-hatched windows along the front wall. We were in a big room, and shadowy objects hung from the ceiling. From the smell of things, it was easy to guess what. We were in a tannery.

"They'll be right behind us," I said, trying to see through to the back of the building. She rubbed a knee, and rotated one shoulder, wincing. I got the impression that I was looking up at her. Ridiculous. The flickering light distorted everything. "Are you okay?" I asked.

She looked through a window, and pointed out. The Cong were coming. I realized about then that I was leak-ing blood from my shoulder. My right sleeve was drenched, and I felt wobbly.

She cast a long shadow. She was tall, taller even than

I, which put her at six-two or -three. Slim. Athletic. Black hair cut short. And despite her size she was Asiatic.

I reached for her, intending to draw her away from the window, and make for the rear entrance. "Just go," she said. "I will be behind you." It was the precise accent of one who has learned English from formal instruction.

I pushed the front door shut, secured it as best I could, and started back. Strips of leather dangled in my face. I barged almost immediately into a table. "Be careful," she said. "There are floor drains too."

It was getting hard to breathe. Probably the stench of the hides and the tanning fluid. Maybe loss of blood. Whatever. The room started to rotate. Gunfire ripped through the windows. Leather strips fluttered.

And, in the dark, a curious thing happened. I couldn't be sure, but I thought she moved to place herself between me and the Cong. Whatever. I grabbed for her wrist and hit the deck. But I didn't quite get hold of her. She slid free. "Down," I snarled.

The shooting went on and on.

She knelt beside me. "You can't stay here."

Not *we. You.*

The floor was wet and slippery. It smelled vaguely of formaldehyde. "Okay," I said. I found her in the dark and pulled her after me.

Abruptly the gunfire stopped.

There was a door in the rear wall. I pushed it open and we shoved through out onto a loading dock. A truck with no wheels was parked outside. I glanced up: the tannery was located in a three-story building. A staircase mounted along the wall to the second floor, where there was a wooden landing and a door. Other buildings crouched nearby. Occasional bursts of sparks fell among them. "This way," I said, climbing down into the street. "We might just have time to get clear."

She shook her head. No. "I don't travel in alleys," she said.

I opened my mouth to tell her she was crazy. If I could have got hold of her, I'd have dragged her along. But she stepped back, and studied the stairway. Flickers of red light glowed in her eyes. Without a word, she started up.

I hesitated. "They'll trap us." You dumb bitch. I thought it. But I didn't say it.

She stopped at the upper level and tried the door. It opened and she disappeared back into the tannery.

Goddamn it.

I started up, and got halfway when a blast took out the lower room. She'd left the door open for me, and I was howling mad when I caught up with her. "They'll burn this goddamn place down around our ears," I said.

She stopped, and turned toward me. "Courage, Anderson," she said.

Anderson? Had I told her my name?

"There are more stairs here," she added, coolly. "Toward the center of the building. I believe they go all the way to the roof."

She was moving among walls and offices.

With all chance of escape now cut off, I took the sensible course. I followed. "Who are you?" I asked.

Behind us there were shouts, running footsteps, occasional shots. Shadows danced outside.

Voices. In French. Already on the lower staircase.

They fired a couple of bursts through the door.

She waited for me, and led the way up to the third floor. I moved as quietly as I could. The woman had been gasping occasionally, peering at her burned flesh, holding up her arms and rotating them against the air, as though she derived a cooling effect from the motion. She paused in the darkness at the top of the staircase, pushed through a wooden door, and strode into a dusty corridor lined with storerooms. She looked up, murmured something. But I caught a sense of satisfaction. Then, to me: "Skylight."

I could see it, dark, stained, rusted, padlocked. Out of reach. "Nice move," I said.

There was confusion below. They didn't know where we were. But that condition wouldn't last long. Worse: I didn't feel good. I was sweating heavily, and the stairs felt slippery. The night felt slippery.

Something creaked, broke, and I was looking out at a rooftop.

She was silhouetted momentarily against the smoking sky.

"Hurry," she said. Her voice sounded far away.

The stars grew dim.

She reached down, took my hand.

It was the last thing I felt as darkness closed in.

When I came out of it, she was standing with her back to me, gazing over the city. The building shook under the whine and whomp of incoming mortars and distant artillery. Automatic fire clattered in the streets, and screams spilled into the night. Long plumes of smoke drifted across the face of the moon. "It never ends," she said.

I wondered how she'd known I was awake. "Yeah," I said. "It never does."

She turned. Her features were composed, calm, masked. Her eyelids were half-closed, her lips parted revealing sharp white teeth. Most of the soot was gone. "You have no idea, Anderson."

That was the second time she'd used my name. "Who are you?" I asked. "Do I know you?"

"No," she said.

I was propped against a chimney, and my shoulder ached. I moved cautiously, but something spasmed and

I gasped. She was gazing toward the horizon, and gave no sign she'd heard. Lights were moving high in the sky. Helicopters. "Are you from Quangngai?" I asked.

Her eyes clouded. And she smiled. But it was a smile composed of shadow and empty spaces. "I'm from Austerlitz," she said. "And Cannae. And Lepanto and Gettysburg." The voice was controlled. Resigned. Weary.

"I don't think I understand." I was chilled.

"No." She was watching something in the street. "You don't."

There was a doorway in the center of the roof. Heavy. Ribbed with iron bands. The door was closed, braced by a timber. "Is that the way we came?"

"No," she said.

"Where are they?"

"Everywhere on the lower floors. And in the street. They were trying to ambush some of your friends." Again that stab of pain in her eyes. "They had some success."

"Sons of bitches."

I could hear footsteps on the stairs. The door was rusted, bent, splintered. But it looked solid. The Cong were laughing, sliding their bolts forward.

The knob rattled.

"Have no fear," said the woman. "You're safe with me." Another chill.

I heard them retreating. Then the door blew out, and flame belched from the stairway. Six men stepped onto the roof.

She watched them without emotion. They leveled rifles at us. "I'm sorry," I said to her. "They may let you go."

She came silently from the roof's edge, and stood by my side.

They watched in angry silence. An officer came out

behind them. He was bullwhip lean, efficient, alert. His movements were crisply economical. "ID," he said to me.

Without hesitation, I pulled it out of my wallet and handed it over. He glanced at it, and lost interest. Only a corporal. His gaze traveled to the woman. He slid his pistol out of its holster and used it to signal her to get away from me.

She didn't move.

The weapon was a Czech automatic of the kind commonly carried by NVA officers. He caressed his jaw with the barrel, and brought the gun up until I was looking into the front sights.

Then she stepped directly in front of me.

I couldn't see his face. He spoke to her in French. The tone was hard and cold. Annoyed. He would not warn her again.

A sudden hot wind blew across the rooftop.

The officer shrugged. His finger tightened on the trigger.

But something in her face caught his eyes. He stared at her. She stood quietly. Sweat stood out on his brow. I started to move, to get out from behind her, but she reached back and seized my shoulder, held me still.

A pulse appeared in his throat. His soldiers seemed frozen, staring into her face as their captain did. Then one broke free, the youngest of the group. He shook himself, as though awakening suddenly in an unfamiliar place. His eyes glittered with hard cold fear. But he advanced nonetheless, forcing himself forward, and stood with his captain.

The others, perhaps released by his movement, began to back away. Weapons sagged.

The officer's breath was coming in short hard gasps.

He struggled with his gun, trying (I thought) to pull the trigger. But it was no longer aimed at me.

He took a step back. And one by one, they retreated into the stairway until only the young soldier was left. He held tight to his AK-47, and stared at her with stricken eyes. She spoke to him in Vietnamese, gently, and then he too was gone.

"Who the hell are you?"

"Do you really not know?" Her face had taken on the tint of the smoldering sky. "After all this time, after all the killing, do you really not know?" Her gaze swept the rooftop, and locked on the city. Savagery flickered in her eyes. "Your fathers knew me. At Troy, at Port Arthur, at the Coral Sea, they knew me. Pray that your sons do not."

I don't know how to describe that moment. I was terrified, as I had not been at any other time during that fearful evening. She stood full in the moonlight, breast heaving, voice thick with emotion. "You've come for me," I said in a hoarse whisper.

Her expression softened. "No. Not for you."

"Then why are you here?" I was drenched with sweat.

"I was careless."

And I thought: the pilot. The Cobra pilot. I must have said it aloud.

Something swirled within that dark shape. "No. Rather, the soldier who tried to challenge me a few moments ago. The young one. Within the hour, he will sacrifice his life for a comrade."

"My God," I said. "One of those bastards? You came for one of those bastards?"

"Yes," she said. "One of those bastards." The words were brittle. Flat. They hung on the night air, dull with impotent rage. "I am concerned only with courage, Anderson. Not with politics."

"What about the pilot? And his gunner?" I demanded.

"I am not alone." Her eyes slid shut. "Tonight we fill the skies of this wretched peninsula!"

"I'm sorry," I said, not sure exactly what I meant.

"We all are." She inhaled, deeply, sadly. "It is not permitted that the valiant should perish. But who comes for the ordinary man? Who stands with him when the shells rain down? Who speaks to him in the moment of terror? We are too few.

"You are children, Anderson. Have you any idea how many will die tonight?" Her eyes raked the stars, and she raised a fist at the moon. "How many more battlefields can this pitiful world support?"

I can close my eyes now and see that rooftop and smell burning tar. And hear her final words. Her voice was warm and rich, lovely and terrible. "Anderson, we do not come for all who die in combat. But we will come for you. You will have your hour, and I will be with you."

You will have your hour.

Hell, I'm over 40 years old. I do actuarial tabulations for Northwestern Insurance. A desk job. I don't walk very well. I'm thirty pounds overweight. And I have three kids. The Army will never have any use for me.

I think sometimes about her, and I wonder if she was wrong. And I think about the kind of war that would need my services.

It's why I don't like to hear Brad Conner joke about him and me holding off invaders at Virginia Beach.

SEAQ and Destroy

Charles Stross

Day 1

NewsBurst: **11:43 G.M.T.**

The Third World War began this morning with a Russian dawn raid on the City of London. Bombs exploded all over the Docklands Enterprise Zone, disrupting the white-hot core of European industrial asset-stripping; the follow-up raids involved extensive use of lethal virus weapons and tactical assault units. Casualties included Larry Steinberg, a systems analyst for BSF:

Video intercut:

Steinberg: "It was terrible. They must have infiltrated those time bombs weeks ago, but there was no sign of them. They began going off at nine-thirteen this morning, bringing down whole systems. One entire block just crumbled . . . it was terrible, I tell you. We lost SEAQ for starters and then it all went to hell. There were casualties everywhere . . . I saw this young dealer, she was crying and pulling her hair out over her colleague, he'd copped it but bad, flat on the floor . . ."

Voice-over: "Barclays de Stoat Fader is just one of the large financial houses to suffer at the hands of the *spetznaz* assault this morning. Other large institutions affected include Country NatWest and the European desks of Drexel Burnham.
"Casualty figures are high, possibly running into tens of thousands of city workers and billions of ECU's of damage. Further video updates will follow."

Viral attack was largely confined to peripheral dealer desks where data throughput was limited to those personnel who had time to play a pirated game of Strip Poker which was being passed around. The virus was triggered by a date check, which suggests that the assault has been prepared far in advance. The main network through which it was disseminated appears to have been via SEAQ, the Stock Exchange Automated Quotations system.

BSF have refused to comment on a rumour to the effect that the attack was planned with the assistance of disgruntled employees sacked last year after a securities scandal which led to the company being investigated by the MMC.

The Soviet Embassy in London was unavailable for comment. The US Treasury Department is expected to make a statement later in the day.

NewsBurst: 12:51 G.M.T.

Initial damage caused by the Soviet attack appears to have been limited, and the main clearing banks are switching in their reserve and back-up capacity. About 30% of the damaged dealer desks are up and running from back-ups, but the virus-infected optical discs are still in quarantine with DTI investigators and S&Q Enterprises called in. The attack failed to induce a massive slide, but Snake currencies are shaky and an unscheduled internal adjustment has been announced for this afternoon. Interest rates have not yet been affected, but announcements are expected hourly.

At 12:49 the European Currency Unit stood at 0.92 Roubles, down 23 Kopeks in just three and a half hours. The U.S. Dollar remained stable at 0.89 ECUs, three cents up on yesterday.

A press conference has been scheduled by the Soviet Embassy in nine minutes' time and will be covered by this service.

Just in:

At the press conference in Washington that has just ended, the U.S. Treasury Department spokesman, Mr. John Flatbush, read the following statement but left the platform before he could be asked any questions:

"At nine hundred hours today the Treasury Department's monitoring service became aware of the serious nature of the current Russian attack on London. We are of course monitoring the present scenario in real-time, but we do not believe that there are any grounds for alarm in this country. The days of the great corporate raiders—Icahn and Boesky and the like—are over, thanks to the decisive lead provided by the Jackson administration in restructuring the U.S. economy. There are no grounds to fear a joint Japanese-Soviet attack on our corporate heartland, but in order to prevent any localized slides we are taking action to freeze European assets held in U.S. stocks and bonds. These shares will be underwritten by the Federal Reserve Bank for the duration of the—er, instability.

"It falls to me to say—off the record—that any of our boys who go in there deserve the best of luck and our encouragement in fighting the good fight and getting while the getting's good on foreign soil! This could be the offshore investment opportunity of the century."

NewsBurst: 13:27 G.M.T.

At 13:03 today, the Soviet trade attaché, Ms. V. I. Retshuchenko, released the following statement, reproduced in its entirety:

"My friends, this morning forces based within the RFSFR launched an economic attack upon the United States of Europe, with the goal of dominating those states. On behalf of the government of the RFSFR, may I express our sincere sympathy for the victims of this unprecedented offensive; unfortunately we are unable to prevent further incursions. The hostile forces appear to be a secret consortium of Soviet industry, including Mikoyan-Gurevitch design bureau, Glavkosmos, and the First Consolidated Peoples' Bank of Azerbaijan; these corporations appear to be cooperating with extra-national powers of unknown identity.

"As you know, such an attack would have been both impossible and implausible if the RFSFR still retained the old, monolithic industrial centralism of the decadent Lenin-Brezhnev era. Following the marked improvements in international progress and trade of the past decade, however, certain organizations listed on the Moscow stock exchange have decided that the Soviet economy cannot support their investment programs. They appear to have decided that a leveraged buy-out of the entire Western economy would be a suitable way of resolving their balance of payments surplus, and unfortunately the Communist Party of the Soviet Union is unable to restrain them.

"Bluntly, such a sequence of events was not considered possible, and no restraining legislation has been drafted. The Politburo is not sanguine about the consequences, however. We have no desire to return to the isolationist, Cold War mentality of the seventies and eighties, and in any event such a policy will inevitably induce considerable public discontent.

"President Boris Yeltsin has expressed his condolences for the victims of the conflict, and has promised maximum cooperation with the European authorities in an attempt to negotiate an end to the shares war before the G-9 talks are jeopardized.

"Thank you very much indeed for coming here. Goodbye."

NewsBurst: 14:56 G.M.T.

News is coming in of a bloody attack on Wall Street. As trading opened in New York at 13:00 G.M.T. the ailing infotech giant IBM (US) launched a hostile take-over bid for Mercury Telecom PLC in London. Fund transfers to Europe so far total over ten billion dollars, believed to be close to IBM's entire liquid assets. Mercury is the main PSTN and ISDN operator for the London Stock Exchange and handles the Stock Exchange Automated Quotation system, SEAQ. The Monopolies and Mergers Commission have been notified, but no immediate action is possible because inspectors are working at saturation levels elsewhere in the City.

It appears that IBM has been controlled in large measure by shell corporations registered in Colombia and Peru for the past three months. CEO Debbie Beagle has refused to comment on allegations that her corporation is cooperating with the Soviet offensive in an attempt to dismember Western Europe's high-technology industries.

Closer to home, EuroBank has launched a counter-offensive before the close of trading in Moscow, with a bid for shares in the state airline Aeroflot and a back-up investment of ECU 500m in BSF. Amstrad and News International's Sky Channel have announced a consortium bid for BSB in an attempt to consolidate the satellite TV market under one umbrella. Glaxo, Ciba-Geigy, and the NHS Pharmatech division are reported to be entering the fray with a bid for several small Russian pharmaceutical manufacturing units; and the smell of money may drag British Power and even NHS(PLC) into the trade war.

The government remains silent on the issue so far, but

a spokesman for Number Ten Downing Street has reaffirmed the Prime Minister's commitment to the free market. "The share issue for British Monarchy PLC will not be jeopardized," he emphasized. "There is no alternative!"

The Queen was unavailable for comment.

In Europe there has generally been a measured response to the carnage. Fiat, Dassault-Renault, and Airbus Industrie are conducting intensive merger negotiations in conjunction with BMW, Porsche-SEAT and Arianespace, apparently in an attempt to inflate their group capital beyond any credible takeover attempt. The fact that this would automatically be viewed as monopolistic is irrelevant because the move is purely intended as a short-term defensive measure—safety in numbers, and the more zeros on the balance sheet the better.

NewsBurst: 15:45 G.M.T.

In a move that has shocked industry bystanders, IBM (US) has dismissed the entire board of Mercury Telecom and moved a special Emergency Task Group into the boardroom. MT apparently held out for a full twenty-seven minutes under the intensive IBM bidding which raised the price of shares from 198 to 323 in less than half an hour. The price of shares has suddenly slumped into the red, with a post-takeover quotation of 121 delivered five minutes ago by human messenger. The SEAQ service appears to have been overloaded by the rapidity of events, with priority going to financial transactions; many smaller desks are apparently "flying blind" on expert systems alone and praying that their software has no hidden bugs in it.

Judith Richmond, a broker with Copperhouse-Gerbil, had this to say:

> "Things are just going crazy today. It's not a classic meltdown because some shares are going through the roof in real-time, but it's like a shooting war's broken out. *Nothing* is stable any more, and all we small brokers can do is keep our heads down when the big countercurrent exchange laundries go into action. We're spilling a million ECU's a second right now, draining into the Soviet economy; it's sheer havoc. I'm not going to predict what's going to happen tomorrow, but the day *after* tomorrow I expect to see a lot of dealers throwing themselves under BMWs ... or Ladas."

Rumours of a second wave of software bombs tomorrow morning have prompted many dealer rooms to call in the security analysts overnight. There're going to be many sleepless engineers earning their overtime check-summing the operating system files for signs of retrovirus infection.

In Tokyo, the Ministry of Finance announced a suspension of all trading for the next three days, an unprecedented move that echoes Meltdown Monday, October 19th 1987, when Wall Street lost more than a thousand points by closing time as a result of computerized panic-selling. People's Hong Kong and Manila are expected to follow suit.

Barclays Bank, the Midland Bank, and all the leading Merchant Banks announced a rise in interest rates of two percent in one day, to be reviewed as soon as the current crisis is defused. The Chancellor of the Exchequer refused to comment, but an official statement from Downing Street is expected imminently, as is a statement from Brussels.

NewsBurst: 17:03 G.M.T.

In the past ninety-two minutes this service has been overwhelmed by the pace of developments. But first the general market report:

The London FT100 share index closed down 467.3 points at 2891.7, the largest fall on record since Meltdown Monday or the Wall Street Crash of 1929. The ECU was down 43 Kopeks against the Rouble, to an all-time low of 72 Kopeks to the ECU. Two hundred billion ECUs were knocked off shares Europewide in what commentators have been calling "the Greenback War." The Russian surprise attack this morning caused complete havoc, catching virtually every European conglomerate on the hop. Long-term consequences are uncertain, but massive upheavals are expected in every market and a wave of panic-selling cannot be ruled out.

Among the most bizarre developments of today was the attack by IBM (US) on Mercury Telecom, which was hijacked—there is no other word for it—for an outlay estimated conservatively to be triple its market value. Just what strategic priority IBM places on Mercury cannot yet be assessed, but the sheer scale of the offensive, taking place within hours of the Soviet attack, cannot be a coincidence.

In the United States, the Treasury Department commented on allegations of an "unholy alliance" between IBM-Telecom and the computer and communications companies AT&T and DEC:

"All such allegations are specious and utterly untrue. We wish to make it clear that no American corporation would dabble in diabolism—you may remember the rumours concerning Proctor & Gamble's trademark, which was subsequently changed following Moral Majority pressure. Any rumours of an 'unholy alliance' must, a priori, be considered to be malicious gossip and insider scaremongering. Rumours that we are investigating these corporations for monopolism will not be addressed at this date."

There has been no official White House response so far, but a presidential aide has announced that President Jackson will make a substantial statement on the issue tomorrow. It is to be hoped that the President will bring to bear his usual combination of intellectual precision and raw charisma on the issue; at the very least his presence is expected to have a calming effect on the nation. The importance of this speech cannot be underestimated; as the first black president of the Republic, as its leading intellectual and the most popular supreme executive since John F. Kennedy, anything he says may make a decisive impact on the situation. Meanwhile the atmosphere in New York today is one of quiet tension as millions of stockbrokers and company attorneys stay glued to their screens watching the carnage in Europe unfold, and all of them must be asking the same question: "Will it be our turn tomorrow?"

The situation in London this evening is calm but tense, with rumours of imminent government intervention if the situation deteriorates tomorrow. The European multinationals are feverishly negotiating massive mergers which will put them temporarily out of reach of the Russian raiders, even though antitrust legislation will inevitably break them up within a matter of weeks or months; meanwhile, bank interest rates are expected to go through the roof tomorrow. Already estate agents in central London have been offered houses at less than three-quarters of their market value, in the first ripples to spread out into the broader economy.

Several smaller brokers ceased trading this afternoon, with three companies filing for bankruptcy. These firms were unable to invest heavily in ISDN communication systems and artificial-intelligence-based dealing desks; when SEAQ overloaded this afternoon their dealing error margin increased catastrophically until they were caught in the general maelstrom of disinvestment by panicked shareholders.

NewsBurst: 18:09 G.M.T.

Downing Street has announced the resignation of the Chancellor of the Exchequer, and his immediate suicide by hara-kiri over the events of this morning. The announcement from the P.M.'s office confirms rumours which have been circulating since late afternoon. It is believed that Bank of Europe officials informed the Prime Minister that the current rate of disinvestment could drive UK industry into bankruptcy in five days' trading if strict monetarist policies were adhered to; knock-on effects could be expected to devastate the rest of Europe within a week at most. Despite her well-known attitude toward interventionism, the Prime Minister made a statement supporting certain preventative measures at her recent press conference:

    "It has come to my attention that the current catastrophic situation in the markets is the result of a complacent attitude towards foreign investment and trade, coupled with a very aggressive, not to say unprincipled, foreign assault on our entire industrial capacity.

"May I take this opportunity to say how deeply concerned I am that, while British industry must stand on its own two feet, this is *not* a normal situation; this is a perfidious attack upon all things British. It would be tantamount to ignoring our national honour were we to refuse aid to our gallant companies in their time of need. Such aid will be forthcoming when it is required. We are fully pursuing all possible diplomatic channels with President Yeltsin, and I am confident that a negotiated settlement will be arrived at shortly.

"Due to a difference of opinion over interest rates, the Chancellor has offered me his resignation, effective as of tonight. I have accepted it. (The terms of his resignation are classified under the Official Secrets Act and any of you reptiles who tries to get hold of it is going in the slammer so fast your feet won't touch the ground. Understood?) In view of the impracticality of appointing a replacement at this short notice, I will be occupying this post until a suitable candidate can be coerced.

"There is no change in our long-term policies of de-nationalization and rolling back the nanny state. We cannot, and *will* not, permit small-minded and vindictive attacks to divert us from the grand sweep of history. British industry must, indeed *is*, learning to die on its own two feet, and will continue to do so for as long as I remain Head of State of these isles. As a standard of our determination, we have decided to proceed with the share issues of British Monarchy Group and British Justice PLC, regardless of the current market situation. (I can assure you that the Japs and the Arabs are going to go for these issues, which will add further weight to our balance of payments and cut off some more dry wood in the process).

"It is to be hoped that our friends in Europe will take note of the situation here, and take steps to ensure that economic cohesion triumphs over narrow-minded national isolationism in the hour of our trial. As I have said before, there is no alternative!"

Day 2

NewsBurst: 09:04 G.M.T.

Following yesterday's spectacular events, massive counter-attacks took place in the Moscow stock exchange during the night. While Tokyo and Hong Kong remained closed, GEC-Plessey moved into Moscow with a vengeance, buying up shares in the Samizdata-Krokodil electronic publishing group and Glavkosmos space enterprises. Details are uncertain, and it remains to be seen whether Glavkosmos will succumb to the British counter-offensive, but as the major intermediary in the Soviet consortium Glavkosmos is an obvious target for retaliation.

American neutrality was called into question when, late last night in Washington D.C., President Jackson issued a brief statement supporting IBM and equating the takeover of Mercury Telecom with "Mom and Apple Pie and Coca-Cola." It is not clear whether this implies that the Cola Corporation is backing intervention in Europe; more information is expected following his speech later today. Ex-Secretary of State Henry Kissinger announced that a radical policy study was under way into the impact of the trade war on the Far East; he is believed to be especially concerned with rumours of Vietnamese infiltration of the Hong Kong stock exchange.

Fears of a second wave of computer viruses failed to materialize overnight, with many dealing rooms going back on-line at full capacity. EuroBank is today expected to make a general announcement concerning interest rates; rumours of massive inflationary measures cannot yet be discounted, despite the Prime Minister's known hatred of such techniques.

The mood at many desks in the City can best be described as tense, verging on overwound. Collars are unbuttoned, ties are forgotten, and there are hollows under every eye this morning at the thought of a repetition of the events of yesterday. Dealers at Citibank were issued notification of an imminent 50% pay cut as an alternative to instant dismissal; this was promoted as a necessary fluidity-conservation tactic. Small bank and building society branches around the nation will remain closed today until the situation resolves. Meanwhile, rumours that Army Intelligence Corps and GCHQ systems analysts have been called in to help run BSF's investment net have not yet been confirmed.

NewsBurst: 10:16 G.M.T.

EuroBank has just announced an across-the-board ten percent increase in the bank base lending rates. This has prompted sighs of relief from all the major fund clearing houses, but is expected to provoke an angry response in the House of Commons, and subsequently in the European Parliament, where it is perceived as a gamble with political suicide. The increase will be the first result of the crisis that the public at large have experienced, and will affect almost ten million mortgage-holders immediately, with repayment increases in excess of 200% likely within days.

The announcement comes on top of panic-selling of GEC-Plessey shares on the basis of rumours that the electronics giant had overextended itself in the Soviet market and was about to come under threat again from a Gorki-based consortium. Suggestions of an alliance with British Aerospace or Amstrad have been discounted by spokespersons for those companies.

Shares fell sharply from their opening prices, but recovered slightly half an hour into trading when buying programs were activated by unprecedentedly low prices. The DTI has not yet released details of its Emergency Economic Rescue Package, but an announcement from Downing Street is expected this afternoon.

In Moscow, the Politburo released a sharply critical statement, accusing several Soviet-based multinationals of placing personal gain ahead of the public good, and of forgetting their socialist origins. None of the companies concerned had anything to say in response to this accusation.

NewsBurst: 11:25 G.M.T.

Catastrophe has struck the Stock Exchange in the past hour, with the revelation that IBM is definitely cooperating with the Soviet MGF consortium and Cola Corporation. Following the IBM takeover of Mercury, the company responsible for running the SEAQ dealer network, confidence in the very medium of trade has collapsed. It is considered likely that details of confidential bids are being piped direct to hostile corporate computers. While this "outsider dealing" is definitely in breach of the law, it cannot yet be proven and by the time DTI inspectors and Scotland Yard have established the facts, many companies will be in receivership.

It is reported that the main Tandem fault-tolerant mainframes in use by Barclays de Stoat Fader have become infected by a virus which is systematically downloading all their files into SEAQ. The blatant data piracy has shaken the board of directors, who are expected to announce a suspension of trading by the UK's biggest investment house in less than half an hour's time.

Chaos has hit the international exchange rates, with the ECU falling to 43 Kopeks, a completely unprecedented collapse. The FT100 index at 11:00 G.M.T. stood at 1892, its lowest level in ten years.

President Jackson has scheduled his big speech for 13:00 G.M.T., which will be covered by this data channel.

The initial effect of the rise in interest rates has been a massive drop in the cost of housing. Prices in the high street chains have fallen by up to 60% in one morning, and reports of estate agents engaging in suicide pacts have been coming in. Pedestrians are advised to be careful about venturing out on foot in the Square Mile and the Docklands Enterprise Zone, where eight suicides by jumping have been reported this morning so far. The London Underground's Northern Line was reported to be at a standstill, with a record four bodies on the line in two hours.

The parliamentary Opposition has tabled a vote of no confidence in the government, and is predicting a defection by large numbers of back-bench Thatcherite MPs. Fears of an incoming hard-left government have done nothing to allay share instability in the system; the Opposition remains committed to a massive program of re-nationalisation, wage and price control, and other policies which in the light of the events of this week can be expected to be massively popular with the electorate.

NewsBurst: 12:07 G.M.T.

Amstrad and News International Group have been bought out by Yegor Ligachev Technologies of Novosibirsk, a relatively obscure hydroelectric power project whose fluidity has been massively augmented in the European markets by the behaviour of their commercial big brothers. Rupert Murdock and Alan Sucrose were unavailable for comment, but an unattributable source has stated that Mr. Sucrose is to be offered the Managing Directorship of Sony. With the loss of these two multinationals, the entire UK television industry is now concentrated in the hands of Soviet-owned companies.

A vote of no confidence in the government has been scheduled for 13:30 this afternoon.

Reports are coming in of the lynching of two bank managers in Stoke-on-Trent by customers angered by the rise in mortgage rates. Labour councils in the North-West are said to be considering a general buy-out offer for all mortgage-holders unable to sustain re-payments; in return for title to the properties, the councils are offering to maintain the occupants as sitting tenants in normal council accommodation.

The Trades Union Congress has called for an immediate one-week General Strike in those industries affected by Soviet takeovers, in an attempt to "poison the pill." General Secretary Todt had this to say:

"We're not going to sit around while them Russians take over our—our entire livelihoods. It's not right! People's jobs are at stake and we can't just sit here while the foreigners move in. Europe is one thing, but the Soviet Union, the Americans, they don't care for our way of life. They don't know what it is to be British.

"We say that by striking *now*, we can make our companies so unattractive that the Russians will 'ave to scarper. But we got to do it now, because if we leave it t'KGB'll be through Congress House like a dose o' salts inside a month, you mark my words. I know them people.

"I call on the government to back our strike. It's not they we're striking against, it's these foreign loan sharks who're buying up t'country. If they use the trades' union legislation they'll be shooting themselves in the foot.

"Strike now, while it's not too late! Strike a blow for British Industry!"

NewsBurst: **13:38 G.M.T.**

President Michael Jackson shocked the world half an hour ago with his announcement that American corporations, with his approval, had signed a joint policy agreement with the Soviet MGF consortium. "This is a major breakthrough in international policy relations," the President sang to a mesmerized audience of his fans. "We have the opportunity to forge a lasting bond with our Russian friends and secure peace in Europe forever. We should not let such a thrilling opportunity slip through our hands. What has Britain ever given us besides George the Third, Hitler, and the discovery of Heroin? My fellow Americans, I call upon you to forget the Cold War, forget the old fears, and embrace the future with open arms. Nothing less than our share portfolios are at stake here, and our Russian friends have just offered us the deal of the century!''

The President then answered questions and sang an encore from *Off the Wall* before leaving in a convoy of carnival floats escorted by a National Guard regiment in pink tutus. Throughout the conference he was surrounded by Secret Service men disguised as zombies and Disney dwarves, presumably to deter enraged British expatriates from attempting to assassinate him.

The entire State Department diplomatic machine ground into gear immediately after the speech, which amounts to a declaration of economic war directed at Europe. This is viewed unhappily in some quarters, for many of the President's fans flocked into stadiums all over the continent for his last concert tour ten years ago. However, in diplomatic circles it is seen as a shrewd move, adding political substance to the de facto hostilities which appear to be on the verge of succeeding. The presidential song and dance routine will certainly boost morale in the boardrooms of corporate America who elected him and stand to gain most from the conflict, and make it highly improbable that their conduct will now be investigated by the FBI. More significantly, the President's known dislike of Mrs. Thatcher now appears to have found a relatively harmless outlet in these corporate outings from his recording studio.

An immediate reaction from the joint European Embassy expressed regret about the President's speech, and warned of possible trade sanctions, specifically an embargo on exports of fresh bananas. It is not expected that Lucky's diet will be affected, however; when he arrived, the President insisted that the White House freezers include a decade's supply of his pets' favourite food.

In the Palace of Westminster, MPs are now taking a vote of no-confidence in the government. A large number of Tory MPs are expected to abstain, raising the possibility that this really is the end of the road for Thatcherism.

Reports of rioting in Eastbourne have been coming in. The rioters are predominantly middle-class home-owners with mortgages. Violence has been confined to the town centre, but Estate Agencies have been looted and set alight, and a building society manager has been lynched. Police riot suppression teams are standing by, but have not yet been used to disperse the crowds.

It is anticipated that trading on the Stock Exchange will be suspended within the next two hours.

NewsBurst: 15:00 G.M.T.

The Thatcher government has fallen. At this afternoon's vote of confidence, more than two hundred Tory MPs abstained, resulting in a rollover victory for the opposition. After more than fifteen years in office, the Prime Minister now has four weeks to vacate Number Ten Downing Street. In the present climate of public opinion, a MORI poll commissioned by the Guardian newspaper this morning shows support for the Labour Party running at 62%, the highest level on record. The party leader, Mr. Ken Livingstone, was unavailable for comment; he is believed to be finalizing his cabinet team.

Trading on SEAQ has been suspended indefinitely, pending DTI and Scotland Yard inspection of irregularities in the affairs of at least twenty major companies, including banks, building societies, investment brokers, and multinational corporations.

A total of 32% of all the FT100 company shares are now held in Soviet hands, and 19% in American hands. An announcement on compulsory nationalization is anticipated as one of the first moves of the incoming left-wing administration.

The outgoing Prime Minister is believed to be seeking asylum with a number of foreign governments. The South African and Paraguayan embassies have indicated that if she makes an application for citizenship it will be well received.

At the suspension of trading, the FT100 index was hovering around the 1600 mark. The number of suicides in the City had risen to twenty-three confirmed with four attempts in intensive care. The ECU was hovering at 41 Kopeks, but showed no signs of making a late recovery.

And finally, we bring you a late announcement from the caretaker government, directed to the Kremlin and the White House:

We surrender, tovaritch.

No Carrier.
Bye.

Iphigenia

Nancy A. Collins

People are always asking me if I like my job or not. Sometimes I wish those reporters and TV people would ask me other things. I get tired of saying the same old stuff over and over again but I always smile and say yes. That's my job.

I don't really mind the reporters asking me things and stuff but I wish one of them would think of something *new*! Being famous is not what I thought it would be back when they started the Contest. I thought being famous was when you got to be on TV and in the paper. I didn't think it could be boring. I was just a little kid back then. The President always laughs when I say that but he looks sad even when he is smiling. He looks sad a lot. I follow him around all the time, that's why I know. That he looks sad, I mean. That's my job.

I'm famous. Everybody knows who I am. I am not bragging or telling lies. I've been on the covers of all kinds of magazines since I got my job. *Time*. *U.S. News*

& *World Report*, *Newsweek*. Even *Weekly Reader*! It was kind of neat, seeing pictures of me with the President and Dr. Ballard. I was even on TV! I bet Marjorie was *really* mad when she saw me on CNN! Marjorie thinks she's hot snot because her dad bought her that pony but she's really cold boogers.

I get to go to Camp David a lot. It's ok but it isn't as fun as Camp Tallyho when I went with Aunt Mimi and got to play with other kids and they gave me a neat T-shirt. I also get to go to all these weird countries with the President. It's part of my job. That's better than some stupid pony!

Even though I'm famous and everybody in the world knows who I am (I got a birthday present from the Queen! She sent me this really neat doll that used to belong to her grandmother. It's real old, so Mama doesn't let me play with it too much, but that's okay, I guess.) I try not to let it make me stuck-up like Marjorie. Mama says I shouldn't get a big head. She's right. I'm real lucky they let her visit me on weekends. At first they said they couldn't let her come and see me but Dr. Ballard made them change their minds. He said it was important that I needed to feel safe. He said other people might not understand taking a kid away from her mom and dad and making her live in the White House for so long. I don't know how he talked them into it, but I'm glad Mama is here on Saturday and Sunday.

Dr. Ballard is a nice man. He's almost as nice as the President. Dr. Ballard spends a lot of time with me and making sure I don't get weird. He looks after me when Mama isn't here. He's the one who came up with this idea. He's real smart. Some people say he's a monster, but they don't know anything. They think it's all a trick, that I don't know what my job is *really* about. They think that because I'm a kid I don't know anything. They must think kids are real *stupid*. Dr. Ballard says they're just scared and I should feel sorry for them.

Dr. Ballard says that I'm a living symbol of life—not just here in the USA but all over the world. My job is to remind the President of that when things get bad.

I understand a lot about symbols. I understand them a lot better than when I first got into the Contest. A lot of people were against the Contest, but then something happened someplace that made them change their minds.

A bunch of doctors with white coats and clipboards came to our school and gave us a bunch of tests and took our pictures. None of us minded because it got us out of class for the day.

I was the only kid picked from my school. Mama took me to the testing center in another city, and I took some more tests and I talked to more people in white coats. There were other kids at the testing center too. Most of them were my age, which was ok, I guess, although there were a couple of big kids, too. The big kids didn't pass the second test for some reason.

That's where I met Dr. Ballard. He was different from the other doctors. He didn't wear a white coat. He wore a baggy old sweater and a pair of jeans. He smiled a lot, but his eyes were sad. Just like the President. He talked to me about my pets and what I did good in at school and who my friends were, and Marjorie and her dumb pony. The kind of stuff you talk to your grandma and granpa about.

Then Dr. Ballard told me about the job. He explained how I was the only kid in the whole USA that passed the tests. He said that the President and I have something called "empathic resonance," which means that the President likes me a lot. He told me all the things I would have to do, but he also told me I had to *volunteer*. No one could make me take the job. Not him, not Mama, not even the President! He told me that if I took the job I could quit when the President quit his job. I'd get lots of money and the Government would pay for my school when I grew up.

He said another kid would take over my job someday, but I would always be the most important, because I would be the *first*. I would be in the history book just like George Washington and Thomas Jefferson and kids in school would have to know my name on tests! He told me I should think about it before saying yes or no.

I was just a dumb little kid back then. I didn't know about *symbols* and how people pay more attention to them than to things that are *real*. But even if I'd known, I'd have still said yes in the end. I like the President.

Being a little kid is scary. You don't know the rules of the game that grown-ups play. Sometimes they act like they don't want you to know. Even if you *did* know they wouldn't pay any attention to you anyhow. But I know about The Bomb. All kids know about it.

The first time I heard about The Bomb I got scared and had bad dreams. Then I found out that grownups were scared of it too and how they don't always understand the rules either. That scared me a lot, but when I talked to Dr. Ballard about it he said sometimes grownups aren't as smart as you think. He said sometimes they get stuck and kids have to help them.

So, I made up my own mind. Not Mama, not Dr. Ballard, and not the President—no matter what the newspapers say. I did it because I owe it to all the little kids in the world, *not* because I would be famous and get in the history books. Dr. Ballard says I'm a *living symbol* that says, ''I want to grow up.'' If I do well at my job, then all the other countries will have kids just like me. That's why I've written all of these essays for Dr. Ballard. Because it's history. Writing is ok but I wish I could go outside and play.

I've had my job two years now. That means I get to *retire* soon. The scar from where they opened me up to put in the *codes* doesn't hurt anymore, but it's still there. Sometimes the reporters ask me if I can feel the metal thing inside me near my heart. I tell them no, but sometimes I can feel it. Or I *think* I can. I talked with Dr. Ballard about it and he thinks it's in my head. I told him no, it's in my chest. That made him laugh. I almost never see him laugh for real anymore.

I wonder how it will feel when they take the briefcase off my wrist. It doesn't really bother me. It isn't heavy at all and the handcuff doesn't bug me anymore, like it did at first. It did take Mama a long time to get used to carrying it around everywhere I went, but now I don't really notice it. I don't think about what's inside it.

I only got to see the knife the day Dr. Ballard put it inside the briefcase and locked it and gave the key to the President.

A lot of things are happening now. The President keeps going to meetings with the generals from the *Pentagon*. I have to sit on a chair near the President where they can see me. I spend most of the time coloring or working in my workbook. I don't understand what the generals say most of the time and it's boring. Mainly I don't like the way they look at me. Dr. Ballard says they just don't want me hanging around. Maybe they think I am a spy or something. That is so dumb! The way they look at me makes me feel real funny, though. When I look back at them, they pretend they weren't staring at me and they get embarrassed. Sometimes they look at me with this real mean look. Like Marjorie, only worse.

I like the President. I always have. He's a nice man.

He's got a granddaughter the same age as me. We even get to play together in the Rose Garden when she comes to visit him. When his dog Tinkerbell has puppies, he said I can have one! He wants me to grow up, he says. I wish his eyes weren't so sad, but maybe Mama will let me keep it.

Sacred Fire

George Zebrowski

*"When the beast stays its hand
from killing, it is as one dead."*

—*Old Saying*

At the age of sixteen, as I prepared to attend my first peace festival, I knew that my father feared my going. I could have gone to the annual displays earlier, but he never went and discouraged me from going alone. We stayed in the family shelter when our area was targeted.

"I didn't want you contaminated with their ideas," he said to me on the day before I was to leave, "—until you could think for yourself." His voice trembled as he shifted in his chair. "But the law says you have to go now." He reached over and turned on the standing light. Its brightness seemed to terrify him for a moment.

He squinted and looked away from me as I sat down

on the floor. "Don't worry," I said. "Maybe I'll learn something."

He scowled and leaned back; there was sweat on his face. "You'll learn what they want you to, and nothing more."

"Don't you trust me?" I asked anxiously, afraid that he thought me a failure, unable to think for myself.

He smiled, but it seemed to me that knives were at his heart as he wiped his forehead. "Try not to believe any of it, even it you're having a good time." I knew that he always missed my mother, but I'd never seen him afraid. "They've got it wrong, son, their way of peace."

I said, "But it's been over seventy years. Doesn't that count for anything?"

He seemed to be struggling with himself. "Anyone has to be able to kill anyone," he said slowly, "—and that's how it should be, always, as an extreme of behavior, not to be tampered with. The peacekeepers are just another genetics cult that wants to do away with our capacity for violence. The trouble with trying to improve us is that we don't know what we are, where we are, what we want to become and where that'll take us. Shut up in their mountain enclaves, they've forgotten what it's like to be a human being."

I'd heard some of this before from him, but never so bitterly. "I've come to suspect," he continued, pushing the words out with painful conviction, "that all these decades of the peace festival have been a preparation for a great change to some new human model. There'll be no going back after that." He leaned forward in his chair. "They'll let things get out of hand, have what looks like a small war and blame it on ordinary human nature showing itself, then push their salvation on us. One or two bombs is all it'll take for the keepers to close their grip on us." He shifted in the chair and gazed into the far corner of the room, as if someone were hiding there, listening to him.

"I can't believe they'd kill people," I said.

He looked exasperated. "What you want to believe has nothing to do with it. They'd do anything to get their way, because they're certain it's right."

I didn't know what to say, except to remind him that he still had me, that he wasn't alone. I looked into his eyes, but he turned away before I could speak.

He couldn't have come with me to the festival. Our area had been targeted, and one person in each household had to stay behind. But I knew that he wouldn't have gone even if he could.

He sat perfectly still. I gazed at him, realizing that he expected to die, and was pushing me away; he didn't want to live in the kind of world he feared was coming; the one he had grown up in seemed bad enough. Maybe he would have been different if my mother had lived. I had a dim memory of a man who had laughed more often, but maybe I was only imagining that.

He looked down at me sadly and said, "I'm sorry, son, that I couldn't give you more."

I saw how damaged he was inside, how useless to himself, realizing that it had always been this way for him. I felt lost.

I packed and readied myself for bed, feeling uneasy and alone, as if I wasn't coming back.

"Good night," I said from the landing above the living room. Something stopped inside me as he glanced up, smiled, and continued reading. I retreated to my room, with feelings of independence stirring beneath my fears of being abandoned.

My father claimed to know a lot about the past that he insisted no one else wanted to discuss. He hadn't tried to hide his hatred of the world from me, yet he always said that he wanted me to find my own way and be happy. But if he was right, that was impossible.

The wars of the past, he had often told me, were always fought for good reasons. Our peace had only buried the truth of justifiable killing, which was a transcendent act, cutting short the slow violence of human affairs, or releasing the inner pressure of lives that had nowhere to go; violence called attention to the world's failures, to its inability to shape itself into something better. But he denied that we would ever be wise enough to shape ourselves and remain human. The peace of the keepers was a tyranny that feared its own death, and had set itself against human nature—against him, it seemed to me as I drifted into sleep, because he took everything personally.

At Festival City in the high desert of California, they gave me a bunk in the boys' dorm. I lay down behind my partition, feeling lost and uneasy. Ernie Yose, the boy next to me, tried to say hello, but I ignored him. The next thing I knew it was morning, and a low, droning voice told us over the intercom that our first lecture would be in Dome One.

As I ate breakfast in the big commons, I told myself that if I believed my father, then the world was beyond hope and there was nothing for me here. He had made me afraid of the future.

"What's wrong with you?" Ernie asked.

"Nothing," I said, trying to hide my doubts.

We went out into the bright sun and found Dome One. The cool inside was a relief. We sat down at desks in the third circle. There were almost a hundred boys and girls my age in the hall, dressed in the same loose-fitting white shorts, collarless shirts, and sandals.

A figure wearing a one-piece sky blue suit walked down into the center, looked around at us, and said, "What you will learn in the next two weeks is how humankind restrained itself." I couldn't tell if the soft tenor voice belonged to a man or a woman. "You will understand the foundation of world peace and how it is maintained, and that will enable you to grasp the full meaning of the final demonstration."

A chill went through me. I felt that something was about to be taken from me; suddenly I didn't want to know anything that would change me. My father's voice whispered a warning as he crouched inside me, ready to mock falsehoods.

"War," the teacher began, "was only the most violent expression of humankind's conflict with itself," and I felt my father's suspicions rising up within me. "Societies regulated their members through codes that were claimed to be of divine origin—to give them a convincing legitimacy—and later through laws that served social ends and could not be tampered with easily by individuals. . . ."

The speaker seemed to be talking about a species to which he or she did not belong.

"When the eco-catastrophes of the 21st century worsened, and it became necessary to forbid the use of fossil fuels, the first defensive shields were used to compel resisting nations to observe the ban, as well as to prevent the use of nuclear weapons among the lesser powers. The big powers of the 20th century had originally built nuclear arsenals so they could cherish the illusory hope that their competitors on Earth might one day be destroyed, which is why the first shields so outraged the human heart—because enemies might now make themselves secure forever. At one time it was feared that Capitalism, aided by super-technologies, might endure in defiance of Marx's laws of history, while totalitarian Communism, behind its shield, completed its mastery of the individual, mimicking the West's economic success through state-run Capitalism. . . .''

This view of the last century and a half reminded me of my father's ideas, except that he would have claimed that it had to be this way, that no amount of good will could overcome human nature. The buried monster in us all was a necessary drive, even if it only functioned according to blind nature; to sever it from our intellect would put us in mortal peril.

"But these fears were set aside," the teacher continued, "when the major blocs realized they could be replaced on the main stage of history by any one of several nations. Beam weapons were deployed to preserve superpower rivalry—and humankind blundered into nuclear peace, even though this outraged the secret self that still longed to savage even a brotherly enemy. . . .''

Evolution's slaughterhouse gave us the will to survive, my father had said to me many times. Human reason was self-serving, rationalizing on our behalf, the obedient hound of our will.

"Ironically," the teacher said, "the new peace made the world safe again for conventional wars. These were tolerated among the lesser nations, but were ended by nuclear threat when they got out of hand. This second era of of conventional wars pushed us closer to our age of peace, as regional conflicts were permitted to work themselves out and became fewer. But as the world struggled through its eco-catastrophes, the old rivalries simmered beneath the restraints placed on the old reptilian brain core. Each major power's secret self still saw itself as Rome, unable to bear the prosperity of Carthage. Time might one day unleash the enemy's progeny from behind his shield, like spiders from a buried egg, to shape history in his own image. This deeply held fear, that futurity would not belong to one's own loins, that even one's children might repudiate their parents, was not something for which we should blame the past. It was a biological program arrived at through evolution, and simply a reflection of the way life developed, the way we were, before we could choose new directions. . . .''

I looked into the teacher's calm gray eyes, and wondered at the intelligence behind them as it described a still unfinished process. Despite my father's warnings, I felt no threat, only wonder and curiosity.

"As an interim measure," the teacher went on, "human nature had to be convinced in its deepest domains that the new peace could not be subverted. The festival demonstration is a physical proof, not an argument or treaty, affirming that peace can be preserved every time it is imperiled. Ours is a renewable peace, and it has endured, even though the old human animal struggles against it. But one day even that inward struggle will end.''

The teacher was speaking about my father, I realized, but I felt only a vague threat.

"Old humanity tried to have it both ways—by arguing that a shield would destabilize the old nuclear deterrence, which implied that it might work, and at the same time that a shield was technically impossible. They neglected to consider that few would wish to test such a system by starting a war. At the very least, it would foil attempts at a decisive first strike. In practice it was completely effective in stopping all enemy missiles—because they would never be launched. And that is what happened.''

Silently, the teacher looked around at us, and I knew suddenly that there was a peace beyond this one.

"Consider these three statements," the teacher continued. "They unmask the old humanity within you all. *We reserve the right to kill living creatures, including human beings, under the appropriate conditions. There can be no peace which abolishes this right.* The second asserts that *The ability to be violent in the name of survival is the sacred fire at the center of every living organism.* And finally, *There must always be the possibility of war, even if war never comes.*"

My father struggled within me. Trembling, I raised my hand and heard him say, "Given enough time, there will be war. Sooner or later, something will always go wrong."

The teacher gazed at me calmly, then nodded. "It would seem so—but many possible things never happen. At first, peace demands a tradition of vigilance. The founder of our peacekeeping order said that *Violence lives in each human being as a small flame, burning always, but flaring only with impatience and anger. It is both their strength and greatest weakness, since it can consume itself. Human hearts will never be at peace. They war with themselves even in sleep. But this heart of fire has never turned on itself decisively. Peace is as possible as war. In time, something even better will be born of our rational faith.* Our festival confirms this understanding, and prepares us for the way ahead."

We saw holos of great cities destroyed in past wars. The broken bodies seemed unreal, and it would never happen again, because the peacekeepers would prevent it.

The last day arrived. We gathered on the flat desert as the stars came out. Facing west, we saw a holo of three giant mushroom clouds swell up with a roar from the sands. Screaming human shapes twisted in the rising fireball, ballooned to massive size, and were torn apart. Torsos, limbs, and entrails fell on cities of cinder. People around me turned away, dropped to their knees and moaned; others clutched their heads and wailed. I gazed into the glow, feeling nothing.

A peacekeeper wearing a blindingly white one-piece

suit stepped out of the roiling clouds of fire, gazed down at us as if we were ants and said, "Welcome to the 98th Peace Festival." His voice was intimate and reassuring. He raised his hand. "The test area today takes in the cities of the west coast, including Los Angeles and New San Francisco. There is one live warhead in the first wave just launched by our partners in peace."

I looked around at the parents with their sons and daughters. My father was in his shelter, in the strike zone, as required.

"The armed warhead," the keeper's figure continued, "is the possibility of war in each of you, but you shall not fear it."

The mushroom cloud winked out. Gazing westward through the giant figure of the peacekeeper into a clear evening sky, I realized that if my father's fears were real, our house would be destroyed in the next few minutes. I was afraid for him, and felt ashamed of my doubts.

"We do not fear!" the great figure intoned, reaching into me with strength and certainty. I waited, held by a new hope, but my stomach tightened as lights blossomed high in the west, and my father's doubts crowded into me. Somehow, a warhead had escaped the beams of the orbital stations. I held my breath and waited in the shelter with my father for the flash that he had expected all his life.

The second wave bloomed and died. Trails of light scratched across the sky beyond the mountains as debris reentered and burned. Cries of joy went up from the gathering as parents embraced their children.

"Our peace is born again!" the keeper cried. "And it is stronger than ever."

The giant figure turned and strode away across the desert, and I knew that my father was wrong.

He had always been wrong.

* * *

Coming home was a return to doubt. "Was there a live warhead?" I asked him. "Would they risk so many lives?"

"They're getting us ready, that's what they are," he said from his chair, glaring up at me bitterly. "A keeper isn't a human being, son. They sleep into the future, tinker with their genes, with no two generations alike. They preach to us about keeping the peace, but they're only buying time for themselves, so they can replace us. We've always had them—people who specialize in telling others how to live. Shamans and priests, then kings and politicians, and psychologists of every stripe—leaders, they always call themselves. But none of them ever helped us to be free and self-directed, because that would make us free of them. But they always helped themselves, stealing everything in the way of goods, pleasures, and privileges. Above all, they stole power."

"But we have peace," I said.

He sighed as his vehemence subsided into a look of pain. "I suppose nuclear terror was more dangerous, if something went wrong, but there are ways around this peace of ours." He seemed moody and strange, out of touch.

I asked, "Did you go to the shelter?"

He nodded, clenching his teeth.

"But you weren't in danger," I insisted, sitting down at his feet. "I saw for myself."

He leaned forward and grasped my head in his hands. "Son—you don't know this world, or what you are. Most everything in our kind of organism is hidden deeply, and you've lived too easily to dig it out. There were clues in old poems, plays, and novels, but the keepers stole them from us. What I know has seeped into me slowly. I've read what I could find . . . and there have been miraculous accidents in my thoughts, since your mother died. The keepers are making a garden for themselves—and for us a desert they call peace." He gripped my head and looked into my eyes. "They're working to be rid of us!" It seemed suddenly that he would crush my skull. "Do you understand?"

I tried to nod, realizing that there was no hope for him now. He let go and fell back, exhausted. "There's no one left to know," he whispered, "what's been lost. . . ." He was silent for a while. "What are you going to do?"

"Join them." I hadn't intended to say it, hadn't even realized that I had come to a decision. I would not be like him, I told myself, expecting angry, frantic words, and maybe even violence, because he would believe it was necessary.

He laughed suddenly and said, "Of course," then shook his head and gazed steadily at me. "I knew you would in the end."

When I joined the keepers, he stopped speaking to me, unable to see the great purpose to which I gave myself. One day he disappeared. I came home to visit, and no one in the area knew where to find him. At first I imagined that he had simply found some patch of wilderness to live out his life with the memory of my mother.

I found his last letter to me. He had written it by hand, and left it, unsigned, in his study, under the holo portrait of my mother and me.

Son,

Your kind is right, in a sense. Mine will never be at peace with itself—because for us violence must always be a matter of choice, to be embraced or rejected, depending on the circumstances. You would make us peaceful, but we would have to become you, and there would be nothing left of us. Perhaps you could leave a few of us in the wild;

you might need us someday, when you have forgotten your origins. I know that, in your view, this is the bomb asking to retain its right to explode, the fire to consume, the beast to kill. You won't live to feel this need within yourself before they change you. A part of me admires your willingness to set out into the unknown, to give up what you were given to be, to discard your humanity along the way. I can't understand it, as once the apes failed to comprehend the humans among them. Transitions to a new state are always sad and disorienting; they require some loss of identity. I cannot imagine what you will have on that alien shore, where there will be nothing living to compete with you, when you have lost yourselves. . . .

I taught at the festivals for ten years before I was accepted by the third transhumans, the very core of the peacekeeping order. My mind opened to the future as I shed memories and prepared for longlife.

We who are changing have known the past and salute the passing makers whose peace enabled us to emerge. Even now a fourth humanity waits within us, poised to escape the last lingering perversities of the old human deep. Somewhere, the changeless still survive, my father among them, singing their ancient song of submission to blind nature, enemies to themselves, hurrying toward death with every tortured breath. There will be no new bodies for them, no ascent through time's renewals, and no penetration of the mysteries. The time will come when we will not remember that these shadows once lived their unknowing lives, joined to death. We who have risen out of their agony and humiliation, stepped out of their swift currents, have purged ourselves of their menace.

We will not remember.

The Lucky Strike

Kim Stanley Robinson

War breeds strange pastimes. In July of 1945 on Tinian Island in the North Pacific, Captain Frank January had taken to piling pebble cairns on the crown of Mount Lasso—one pebble for each B-29 takeoff, one cairn for each mission. The largest cairn had four hundred stones in it. It was a mindless pastime, but so was poker. The men of the 509th had played a million hands of poker, sitting in the shade of a palm around an upturned crate sweating in their skivvies, swearing and betting all their pay and cigarettes, playing hand after hand after hand, until the cards got so soft and dog-eared you could have used them for toilet paper. Captain January had gotten sick of it, and after he lit out for the hilltop a few times some of his crewmates started trailing him. When their pilot Jim Fitch joined them it became an official pastime, like throwing flares into the compound or going hunting for stray Japs. What Captain January thought of the development he didn't say. The others grouped near Captain Fitch, who passed around his battered flask. "Hey, January," Fitch called. "Come have a shot."

January wandered over and took the flask. Fitch laughed at his pebble. "Practicing your bombing up here, eh, Professor?"

"Yah," January said sullenly. Anyone who read more than the funnies was Professor to Fitch. Thirstily January knocked back some rum. He could drink it any way he pleased up here, out from under the eye of the group psychiatrist. He passed the flask on to Lieutenant Matthews, their navigator.

"That's why he's the best," Matthews joked. "Always practising."

Fitch laughed. "He's best because I make him be best, right, Professor?"

January frowned. Fitch was a bulky youth, thick-featured, pig-eyed—a thug, in January's opinion. The rest of the crew were all in their mid-twenties like Fitch, and they liked the captain's bossy roughhouse style. January, who was thirty-seven, didn't go for it. He wandered away, back to the cairn he had been building. From Mount Lasso they had an overview of the whole island, from the harbor at Wall Street to the north field in Harlem. January had observed hundreds of B-29s roar off the four parallel runways of the north field and head for Japan. The last quartet of this particular mission buzzed across the width of the island, and January dropped four more pebbles, aiming for crevices in the pile. One of them stuck nicely.

"There they are!" said Matthews. "They're on the taxiing strip."

January located the 509th's first plane. Today, the first of August, there was something more interesting to watch then the usual Superfortress parade. Word was out that General Le May wanted to take the 509th's mission away from it. Their commander Colonel Tibbets had gone and bitched to Le May in person, and the general had agreed the mission was theirs, but on one condition: one of the general's men was to make a test flight with the 509th, to make sure they were fit for combat over Japan. The general's man had arrived, and now he was down there in the strike plane, with Tibbets and the whole first team. January sidled back to his mates to view the takeoff with them.

"Why don't the strike plane have a name, though?" Haddock was saying.

Fitch said, "Lewis won't give it a name because it's not his plane, and he knows it." The others laughed. Lewis and his crew were naturally unpopular, being Tibbets' favorites.

"What do you think he'll do to the general's man?" Matthews asked.

The others laughed at the very idea. "He'll kill an engine at takeoff, I bet you anything," Fitch said. He pointed at the wrecked B-29s that marked the end of every runway, planes whose engines had given out on takeoff. "He'll want to show that he wouldn't go down if it happened to him."

"Course he wouldn't!" Matthews said.

"You hope," January said under his breath.

"They let those Wright engines out too soon," Haddock said seriously. "They keep busting under the takeoff load."

"Won't matter to the old bull," Matthews said. Then they all started in about Tibbets' flying ability, even Fitch. They all thought Tibbets was the greatest. January, on the other hand, liked Tibbets even less than he liked Fitch. That had started right after he was assigned to the 509th. He had been told he was part of the most important group in the war, and then given a leave. In Vicksburg a couple of fliers just back from England had bought him a lot of whiskies, and since January had spent several months stationed near London they had talked for a good long time and gotten pretty drunk. The two were really curious about what January was up to now, but he had stayed vague on it and kept returning the talk to the blitz. He had been seeing an English nurse, for instance, whose flat had been bombed, family and neighbors killed. . . . But they had really wanted to know. So he had told them he was onto something special, and they had flipped out their badges and told him they were Army Intelligence, and that if he ever broke security like that again he'd be transferred to Alaska. It was a dirty trick. January had gone back to Wendover and told Tibbets so to his face, and Tibbets had turned red and threatened him some more. January despised him for that. The upshot was that January was effectively out of the war, because Tibbets really played his favorites. January wasn't sure he really minded, but during their year's training he had bombed better than ever, as a way of showing the old bull he was wrong to write January off. Every time their eyes had met it was clear what was going on. But Tibbets never backed off no matter how precise January's bombing got. Just thinking about it was enough to cause January to line up a pebble over an ant and drop it.

"Will you cut that out?" Fitch complained. "I swear you must hang from the ceiling when you take a shit so you can practice aiming for the toilet." The men laughed.

"Don't I bunk over you?" January asked. Then he pointed. "They're going."

Tibbets's plane had taxied to runway Baker. Fitch passed the flask around again. The tropical sun beat on them, and the ocean surrounding the island blazed white. January put up a sweaty hand to aid the bill of his baseball cap.

The four props cut in hard, and the sleek Superfortress quickly trundled up to speed and roared down Baker. Three-quarters of the way down the strip the outside right prop feathered.

"Yow!" Fitch crowed. "I told you he'd do it!"

The plane nosed off the ground and slewed right, then pulled back on course to cheers from the four young men around January. January pointed again. "He's cut number three, too."

The inside right prop feathered, and now the plane was pulled up by the left wing only, while the two right props windmilled uselessly. "Holy smoke!" Haddock cried. "Ain't the old bull something?"

They whooped to see the plane's power, and Tibbets' nervy arrogance.

"By God, Le May's man will remember this flight," Fitch hooted. "Why, look at that! He's banking!"

Apparently taking off on two engines wasn't enough for Tibbets; he banked the plane right until it was standing on its dead wing, and it curved back toward Tinian.

Then the inside left engine feathered.

War tears at the imagination. For three years Frank January had kept his imagination trapped, refusing to give it any play whatsoever. The dangers threatening him, the effects of the bombs, the fate of the other participants in the war, he had refused to think about any of it. But the war tore at his control. That English nurse's flat. The missions over the Ruhr. The bomber just below him blown apart by flak. And then there had been a year in Utah, and the vise-like grip that he had once kept on his imagination had slipped away.

So when he saw the number two prop feather, his heart gave a little jump against his sternum and helplessly he was up there with Ferebee, the first team bombardier. He would be looking over the pilots' shoulders. . . .

"Only one engine?" Fitch said.

"That one's for real," January said harshly. Despite himself he *saw* the panic in the cockpit, the frantic rush to power the two right engines. The plane was dropping fast and Tibbets leveled it off, leaving them on a course back toward the island. The two right props spun, blurred to a shimmer. January held his breath. They needed more lift; Tibbets was trying to pull it over the island. Maybe he was trying for the short runway on the south half of the island.

But Tinian was too tall, the plane too heavy. It roared right into the jungle above the beach, where 42nd Street met their East River. It exploded in a bloom of fire. By the time the sound of the explosion struck them they knew no one in the plane had survived.

Black smoke towered into white sky. In the shocked silence on Mount Lasso insects buzzed and creaked. The air left January's lungs with a gulp. He had been with Ferebee there at the end, he had heard the desperate shouts, seen the last green rush, been stunned by the dentist-drill-all-over pain of the impact.

"Oh my God," Fitch was saying. "Oh my God." Matthews was sitting. January picked up the flask, tossed it at Fitch.

"C-come on," he stuttered. He hadn't stuttered since he was sixteen. He led the others in a rush down the hill. When they got to Broadway a jeep careened toward them and skidded to a halt. It was Colonel Scholes, the old bull's exec. "What happened?"

Fitch told him.

"Those damned Wrights," Scholes said as the men piled in. This time one had failed at just the wrong moment; some welder stateside had kept flame to metal a second less than usual—or something equally minor, equally trivial—and that had made all the difference.

They left the jeep at 42nd and Broadway and hiked east over a narrow track to the shore. A fairly large circle of trees was burning. The fire trucks were already there.

Scholes stood besides January, his expression bleak. "That was the whole first team," he said.

"I know," said January. He was still in shock, in imagination crushed, incinerated, destroyed. Once as a kid he had tied sheets to his arms and waist, jumped off the roof and landed right on his chest; this felt like that had. He had no way of knowing what would come of this crash, but he had a suspicion that he had indeed smacked into something hard.

Scholes shook his head. A half-hour had passed, the fire was nearly out. January's four mates were over chattering with the Seabees. "He was going to name the plane after his mother," Scholes said to the ground. "He told me that just this morning. He was going to call it *Enola Gay.*"

At night the jungle breathed, and its hot wet breath washed over the 509th's compound. January stood in the doorway of his Quonset barracks hoping for a real breeze. No poker tonight. Voices were hushed, faces solemn. Some of the men had helped box up the dead crew's gear. Now most lay on their bunks. January gave up on the breeze, climbed onto his top bunk to stare at the ceiling.

He observed the corrugated arch over him. Cricket-song sawed through his thoughts. Below him a rapid conversation was being carried on in guilty undertones, Fitch at its center. "January is the best bombardier left," he said. "And I'm as good as Lewis was."

"But so is Sweeney," Matthews said. "And he's in with Scholes."

They were figuring out who would take over the strike.

January scowled. Tibbets and the rest were less than twelve hours dead, and they were squabbling over who would replace them.

January grabbed a shirt, rolled off his bunk, put the shirt on.

"Hey, Professor," Fitch said. "Where you going?"

"Out."

Though midnight was near it was still sweltering. Crickets shut up as he walked by, started again behind him. He lit a cigarette. In the dark the MPs patrolling their fenced-in compound were like pairs of walking armbands. The 509th, prisoners in their own army. Fliers from other groups had taken to throwing rocks over the fence. Forcefully January expelled smoke, as if he could expel his disgust with it. They were only kids, he told himself. Their minds had been shaped in the war, by the war, and for the war. They knew you couldn't mourn the dead for long; carry around a load like that and your own engines might fail. That was all right with January. It was an attitude that Tibbets had helped to form, so it was what he deserved. Tibbets would *want* to be forgotten in favor of the mission, all he had lived for was to drop the gimmick on the Japs, he was oblivious to anything else, men, wife, family, anything.

So it wasn't the lack of feeling in his mates that bothered January. And it was natural of them to want to fly the strike they had been training a year for. Natural, that is, if you were a kid with a mind shaped by fanatics like Tibbets, shaped to take orders and never imagine consequences. But January was not a kid, and he wasn't going to let men like Tibbets do a thing to his mind. And the gimmick . . . the gimmick was not natural. A chemical bomb of some sort, he guessed. Against the Geneva Convention. He stubbed his cigarette against the sole of his sneaker, tossed the butt over the fence. The tropical night breathed over him. He had a headache.

For months now he had been sure he would never fly a strike. The dislike Tibbets and he had exchanged in their looks (January was acutely aware of looks) had been real and strong. Tibbets had understood that January's record of pinpoint accuracy in the runs over the Salton Sea had been a way of showing contempt, a way of saying *you can't get rid of me even though you hate me and I hate you*. The record had forced Tibbets to keep January on one of the four second-string teams, but with the fuss they were making over the gimmick January had figured that would be far enough down the ladder to keep him out of things.

Now he wasn't so sure. Tibbets was dead. He lit another cigarette, found his hand shaking. The Camel tasted bitter. He threw it over the fence at a receding armband, and regretted it instantly. A waste. He went back inside.

Before climbing onto his bunk he got a paperback out of his footlocker. "Hey, Professor, what you reading now?" Fitch said, grinning.

January showed him the blue cover. *Winter's Tales*, by an Isak Dinesen. Fitch examined the little wartime edition. "Pretty racy, eh?"

"You bet," January said heavily. "This guy puts sex on every page." He climbed onto his bunk, opened the book. The stories were strange, hard to follow. The voices below bothered him. He concentrated harder.

As a boy on the farm in Arkansas, January had read everything he could lay his hands on. On Saturday afternoons he would race his father down the muddy lane to the mailbox (his father was a reader too), grab the *Saturday Evening Post* and run off to devour every word of it. That meant he had another week with nothing new to read, but he couldn't help it. His favorites were the Hornblower stories, but anything would do. It was a way off the farm, a way into the world. He had become a man who could slip between the covers of a book whenever he chose.

But not on this night.

The next day the chaplain gave a memorial service, and on the morning after that Colonel Scholes looked in the door of their hut right after mess. "Briefing at eleven," he announced. His face was haggard. "Be there early." He looked at Fitch with bloodshot eyes, crooked a finger. "Fitch, January, Matthews—come with me."

January put on his shoes. The rest of the men sat on their bunks and watched them wordlessly. January followed Fitch and Matthews out of the hut.

"I've spent most of the night on the radio with General Le May," Scholes said. He looked them each in the eye. "We've decided you're to be the first crew to make a strike."

Fitch was nodding, as if he had expected it.

"Think you can do it?" Scholes said.

"Of course," Fitch replied. Watching him January understood why they had chosen him to replace Tibbets: Fitch was like the old bull, he had that same ruthlessness. The young bull.

"Yes, sir," Matthews said.

Scholes was looking at him. "Sure," January said, not wanting to think about it. "Sure." His heart was pounding directly on his sternum. But Fitch and Matthews looked serious as owls, so he wasn't going to stick out by looking odd. It was big news, after all; anyone would be taken aback by it. Nevertheless, January made an effort to nod.

"Okay," Scholes said. "McDonald will be flying with you as co-pilot." Fitch frowned. "I've got to go tell those British officers that Le May doesn't want them on the strike with you. See you at the briefing.''

''Yes, sir,''

As soon as Scholes was around the corner Fitch swung a fist at the sky. ''Yow!'' Matthews cried. He and Fitch shook hands. ''We did it!'' Matthews took January's hand and wrung it, his face plastered with a goofy grin. ''We did it!''

''Somebody did it, anyway,'' January said.

''Ah, Frank,'' Matthews said. ''Show some spunk. You're always so cool.''

''Old Professor Stoneface,'' Fitch said, glancing at January with a trace of amused contempt. ''Come on, let's get to the briefing.''

The briefing hut, one of the longer Quonsets, was completely surrounded by MPs holding carbines. ''Gosh,'' Matthews said, subdued by the sight. Inside it was already smoky. The walls were covered by the usual maps of Japan. Two blackboards at the front were draped with sheets. Captain Shepard, the naval officer who worked with the scientists on the gimmick, was in back with his assistant Lieutenant Stone, winding a reel of film onto a projector. Dr. Nelson, the group psychiatrist, was already seated on a front bench near the wall. Tibbets had recently sicced the psychiatrist on the group—another one of his great ideas, like the spies in the bar. The man's questions had struck January as stupid. He hadn't even been able to figure out that Easterly was a flake, something that was clear to anybody who flew with him, or even played him in a single round of poker. January slid onto a bench beside his mates.

The two Brits entered, looking furious in their stiff-upper-lip way. They sat on the bench behind January. Sweeney's and Easterly's crew filed in, followed by the other men, and soon the room was full. Fitch and the rest pulled out Lucky Strikes and lit up; since they had named the plane only January had stuck with Camels.

Scholes came in with several men January didn't recognize, and went to the front. The chatter died, and all the smoke plumes ribboned steadily into the air.

Scholes nodded, and two intelligence officers took the sheets off the blackboards, revealing aerial reconnaisance photos.

"Men," Scholes said, "these are the target cities."

Someone cleared his throat.

"In order of priority they are Hiroshima, Kokura, and Nagasaki. There will be three weather scouts: *Straight Flush* to Hiroshima, *Strange Cargo* to Kokura, and *Full House* to Nagasaki. *The Great Artiste* and *Number 91* will be accompanying the mission to take photos. And *Lucky Strike* will fly the bomb."

There were rustles, coughs. Men turned to look at January and his mates, and they all sat up straight. Sweeney stretched back to shake Fitch's hand, and there were some quick laughs. Fitch grinned.

"Now listen up," Scholes went on. "The weapon we are going to deliver was successfully tested stateside a couple of weeks ago. And now we've got orders to drop it on the enemy." He paused to let that sink in. "I'll let Captain Shepard tell you more."

Shepard walked to the blackboard slowly, savoring his entrance. His forehead was shiny with sweat, and January realized he was excited or nervous. He wondered what the shrink would make of that.

"I'm going to come right to the point," Shepard said. "The bomb you are going to drop is something new in history. We think it will knock out everything within four miles."

Now the room was completely still. January noticed that he could see a great deal of his nose, eyebrows, and cheeks; it was as if he were receding back into his body, like a fox into its hole. He kept his gaze rigidly on Shepard, steadfastly ignoring the feeling. Shepard pulled a sheet back over a blackboard while someone else turned down the lights.

'This is a film of the only test we have made,'' Shepard said. The film started, caught, started again. A wavery cone of bright cigarette smoke speared the length of the room, and on the sheet sprang a dead gray landscape: a lot of sky, a smooth desert floor, hills in the distance. The projector went *click-click-click-click*, *click-click-click-click*. ''The bomb is on top of the tower,'' Shepard said, and January focused on the pin-like object sticking out of the desert floor, off against the hills. It was between eight and ten miles from the camera, he judged; he had gotten good at calculating distances. He was still distracted by his face.

Click-click-click-click, click—then the screen went white for a second, filling even their room with light. When the picture returned the desert floor was filled with a white bloom of fire. The fireball coalesced and then quite suddenly it leaped off the earth all the way into the *stratosphere*, by God, like a tracer bullet leaving a machine-gun, trailing a whitish pillar of smoke behind it. The pillar gushed up and a growing ball of smoke billowed outward, capping the pillar. January calculated the size of the cloud, but was sure he got it wrong. There it stood. The picture flickered, and then the screen went white again, as if the camera had melted or that part of the world had come apart. But the flapping from the projector told them it was the end of the film.

January felt the air suck in and out of his open mouth. The lights came on in the smoky room and for a second he panicked, he struggled to shove his features into an accepted pattern, the shrink would be looking around at them all—and then he glanced around and realized he needn't have worried, that he wasn't alone. Faces were bloodless, eyes were blinky or bug-eyed with shock, mouths hung open or were clamped whitely shut. For a few moments they all had to acknowledge what they were doing. January, scaring himself, felt an urge to say, "Play it again, will you?" Fitch was pulling his curled black hair off his thug's forehead uneasily. Beyond him January saw that one of the Limeys had already reconsidered how mad he was about missing the flight. Now he looked sick. Someone let out a long *whew*, another whistled. January looked to the front again, where the shrink watched them, undisturbed.

Shepard said, "It's big, all right. And no one knows what will happen when it's dropped from the air. But the mushroom cloud you saw will go to at least thirty thousand feet, probably sixty. And the flash you saw at the beginning was hotter than the sun."

Hotter than the sun. More licked lips, hard swallows, readjusted baseball caps. One of the intelligence officers passed out tinted goggles like welder's glasses. January took his and twiddled the opacity dial.

Scholes said, "You're the hottest thing in the armed forces, now. So no talking, even among yourselves." He took a deep breath. "Let's do it the way Colonel Tibbets would have wanted us to. He picked every one of you because you were the best, and now's the time to show he was right. So—so let's make the old man proud."

The briefing was over. Men filed out into the sudden sunlight. Into the heat and glare. Captain Shepard approached Fitch. "Stone and I will be flying with you to take care of the bomb," he said.

Fitch nodded. "Do you know how many strikes we'll fly?"

"As many as it takes to make them quit." Shepard stared hard at all of them. "But it will only take one."

War breeds strange dreams. That night January writhed over his sheets in the hot wet vegetable darkness, in that frightening half-sleep when you sometimes know you are dreaming but can do nothing about it, and he dreamed he was walking . . .

. . . *Walking through the streets when suddenly the sun swoops down, the sun touches down and everything is instantly darkness and smoke and silence, a deaf roaring. Walls of fire. His head hurts and in the middle of his vision is a bluewhite blur as if God's camera went off in his face. Ah—the sun fell, he thinks. His arm is burned. Blinking is painful. People stumbling by, mouths open, horribly burned—*

He is a priest, he can feel the clerical collar, and the wounded ask him for help. He points to his ears, tries to touch them but can't. Pall of black smoke over everything, the city has fallen into the streets. Ah, it's the end of the world. In a park he finds shade and cleared ground. People crouch under bushes like frightened animals. Where the park meets the river red and black figures crowd into steaming water. A figure gestures from a copse of bamboo. He enters it, finds five or six faceless soldiers huddling. Their eyes have melted, their mouths are holes. Deafness spares him their words. The sighted soldier mimes drinking. The soldiers are thirsty. He nods and goes to the river in search of a container. Bodies float downstream.

Hours pass as he hunts fruitlessly for a bucket. He pulls people from the rubble. He hears a bird screeching and he realizes that his deafness is the roar of the city burning, a roar like the blood in his ears but he is not deaf, he only thought he was deaf because there are no

*human cries. The people are suffering in silence. Through
the dusky night he stumbles back to the river, pain crash-
ing through his head. In a field men are pulling potatoes
out of the ground that have been baked well enough to
eat. He shares one with them. At the river everyone is
dead—*

—and he struggled out of the nightmare drenched in
rank sweat, the taste of dirt in his mouth, his stomach
knotted with horror. He sat up and the wet rough sheet
clung to his skin. His heart felt crushed between lungs
desperate for air. The flowery rotting jungle smell filled
him and images from the dream flashed before him so
vividly that in the dim hut he saw nothing else. He
grabbed his cigarettes and jumped off the bunk, hurried
out into the compound. Trembling he lit up, started pac-
ing around. For a moment he worried that the idiot psychiatrist might see him, but then he dismissed the idea.
Nelson would be asleep. They were all asleep. He shook
his head, looked down at his right arm and almost
dropped his cigarette—but it was just his stove scar, an
old scar, he'd had it most of his life, since the day he'd
pulled the frypan off the stove and onto his arm, burning
it with oil. He could still remember the round O of fear
that his mother's mouth had made as she rushed in to see
what was wrong. Just an old burn scar, he thought, let's
not go overboard here. He pulled his sleeve down.

For the rest of the night he tried to walk it off, cigarette
after cigarette. The dome of the sky lightened until all
the compound and the jungle beyond it was visible. He
was forced by the light of day to walk back into his hut
and lie down as if nothing had happened.

Two days later Scholes ordered them to take one of Le
May's men over Rota for a test run. This new lieutenant

colonel ordered Fitch not to play with the engines on takeoff. They flew a perfect run. January put the dummy gimmick right on the aiming point just as he had so often in the Salton Sea, and Fitch powered the plane down into the violent bank that started their 150-degree turn and flight for safety. Back on Tinian the lieutenant colonel congratulated them and shook each of their hands. January smiled with the rest, palms cool, heart steady. It was as if his body were a shell, something he could manipulate from without, like a bombsight. He ate well, he chatted as much as he ever had, and when the psychiatrist ran him to earth for some questions he was friendly and seemed open.

"Hello, doc."

"How do you feel about all this, Frank?"

"Just like I always have, sir. Fine."

"Eating well?"

"Better than ever."

"Sleeping well?"

"As well as I can in this humidity. I got used to Utah, I'm afraid." Dr. Nelson laughed. Actually January had hardly slept since his dream. He was afraid of sleep. Couldn't the man see that?

"And how do you feel about being part of the crew chosen to make the first strike?"

"Well, it was the right choice, I reckon. We're the be—the best crew left."

"Do you feel sorry about Tibbets's crew's accident?"

"Yes, sir, I do." You better believe it.

After the jokes and firm handshakes that ended the interview January walked out into the blaze of the tropical noon and lit a cigarette. He allowed himself to feel how much he despised the psychiatrist and his blind profession at the same time he was waving good-bye to the man. Ounce brain. Why couldn't he have seen? Whatever happened it would be his fault. . . . With a rush of smoke out of him January realized how painfully easy it was to fool someone if you wanted to. All action was no more than a mask that could be perfectly manipulated from somewhere else. And all the while in that somewhere else January lived in a *click-click-click* of film, in the silent roaring of a dream, struggling against images he couldn't dispel. The heat of the tropical sun—ninety-three million miles away, wasn't it?—pulsed painfully on the back of his neck.

As he watched the psychiatrist collar their tail-gunner Kochenski, he thought of walking up to the man and saying *I quit.* I don't want to do this. In imagination he saw the look that would form in the man's eye, in Fitch's eye, in Tibbets' eye, and his mind recoiled from the idea. He felt too much contempt for them. He wouldn't for anything give them a means to despise him, a reason to call him coward. Stubbornly he banished the whole complex of thought. Easier to go along with it.

And so a couple of disjointed days later, just after midnight of August 9th, he found himself preparing for the strike. Around him Fitch and Matthews and Haddock were doing the same. How odd were the everyday motions of getting dressed when you were off to demolish a city, to end a hundred thousand lives! January found himself examining his hands, his boots, the cracks in the linoleum. He put on his survival vest, checked the pockets abstractedly for fish-hooks, water kit, first aid package, emergency rations. Then the parachute harness, and his coveralls over it all. Tying his bootlaces took minutes; he couldn't do it when watching his fingers so closely.

"Come on, Professor!" Fitch's voice was tight. "The big day is here."

He followed the others into the night. A cool wind

113

was blowing. The chaplain said a prayer for them. They took jeeps down Broadway to runway Able. *Lucky Strike* stood in a circle of spotlights and men, half of them with cameras, the rest with reporter's pads. They surrounded the crew; it reminded January of a Hollywood premiere. Eventually he escaped up the hatch and into the plane. Others followed. Half an hour passed before Fitch joined them, grinning like a movie star. They started the engines, and January was thankful for their vibrating, thought-smothering roar. They taxied away from the Hollywood scene and January felt relief for a moment, until he remembered where they were going. On runway Able the engines pitched up to their twenty-three hundred rpm whine, and looking out the clear windscreen he saw the runway paintmarks move by ever faster. Fitch kept them on the runway till Tinian had run out from under them, then quickly pulled up. They were on their way.

When they got to altitude January climbed past Fitch and McDonald to the bombardier's seat and placed his parachute on it. He leaned back. The roar of the four engines packed around him like cotton batting. He was on the flight, nothing to be done about it now. The heavy vibration was a comfort, he liked the feel of it there in the nose of the plane. A drowsy, sad acceptance hummed through him.

Against his closed eyelids flashed a black eyeless face and he jerked awake, heart racing. He was on the flight, no way out. Now he realized how easy it would have been to get out of it. He could have just said he didn't want to. The simplicity of it appalled him. Who gave a damn what the psychiatrist or Tibbets or anyone else thought, compared to this? Now there was no way out.

It was a comfort, in a way. Now he could stop worrying, stop thinking he had any choice.

Sitting there with his knees bracketing the bombsight January dozed, and as he dozed he daydreamed his way out. He could climb the step to Fitch and McDonald and declare he had been secretly promoted to Major and ordered to re-direct the mission. They were to go to Tokyo and drop the bomb in the bay. The Jap war cabinet had been told to watch this demonstration of the new weapon, and when they saw that fireball boil the bay and bounce into heaven they'd run and sign surrender papers as fast as they could write, kamikazes or not. They weren't crazy, after all. No need to murder a whole city. It was such a good plan that the generals back home were no doubt changing the mission at this very minute, desperately radioing their instructions to Tinian, only to find out it was too late . . . so that when they returned to Tinian January would become a hero for guessing what the generals really wanted, and for risking all to do it. It would be like one of the Hornblower stories in the *Saturday Evening Post*.

Once again January jerked awake. The drowsy pleasure of the fantasy was replaced with desperate scorn. There wasn't a chance in hell that he could convince Fitch and the rest that he had secret orders superseding theirs And he couldn't go up there and wave his pistol around and *order* them to drop the bomb in Tokyo Bay, because he was the one who had to actually drop it, and he couldn't be down in front dropping the bomb and up ordering the others around at the same time. Pipe dreams.

Time swept on, slow as a second hand. January's thoughts, however, matched the spin of the props; desperately they cast about, now this way now that, like an animal caught by the leg in a trap. The crew was silent. The clouds below were a white scree on the black ocean.

January's knee vibrated against the squat stand of the bombsight. He was the one who had to drop the bomb. No matter where his thoughts lunged they were brought up short by that. He was the one, not Fitch or the crew, not Le May, not the generals and scientists back home, not Truman and his advisors. Truman—suddenly January hated him. Roosevelt would have done it differently. If only Roosevelt had lived! The grief that had filled January when he learned of Roosevelt's death reverberated through him again, more strongly than ever. It was unfair to have worked so hard and then not see the war's end. And FDR would have ended it differently. Back at the start of it all he had declared that civilian centers were never to be bombed, and if he had lived, if, if, if. But he hadn't. And now it was smiling bastard Harry Truman, ordering *him*, Frank January, to drop the sun on two hundred thousand women and children. Once his father had taken him to see the Browns play before twenty thousand, a giant crowd—"I never voted for you," January whispered viciously, and jerked to realize he had spoken aloud. Luckily his microphone was off. And Roosevelt would have done it differently, he *would have*.

The bombsight rose before him, spearing the black sky and blocking some of the hundreds of little cruciform stars. *Lucky Strike* ground on toward Iwo Jima, minute by minute flying four miles closer to their target. January leaned forward and put his face in the cool headrest of the bombsight, hoping that its grasp might hold his thoughts as well as his forehead. It worked surprisingly well.

His earphones crackled and he sat up. "Captain January." It was Shepard. "We're going to arm the bomb now, want to watch?"

"Sure thing." He shook his head, surprised at his own duplicity. Stepping up between the pilots, he moved stiffly to the roomy cabin behind the cockpit. Matthews was at his desk taking a navigational fix on the radio signals from Iwo Jima and Okinawa, and Haddock stood beside him. At the back of the compartment was a small circular hatch, below the larger tunnel leading to the rear of the plane. January opened it, sat down and swung himself feet first through the hole.

The bomb bay was unheated, and the cold air felt good. He stood facing the bomb. Stone was sitting on the floor of the bay; Shepard was laid out under the bomb, reaching into it. On a rubber pad next to Stone were tools, plates, several cylindrical blocks. Shepard pulled back, sat up, sucked a scraped knuckle. He shook his head ruefully: "I don't dare wear gloves with this one."

"I'd be just as happy myself if you didn't let something slip," January joked nervously. The two men laughed.

"Nothing can blow till I change those green wires to the red ones," Stone said.

"Give me the wrench," Shepard said. Stone handed it to him, and he stretched under the bomb again. After some awkward wrenching inside it he lifted out a cylindrical plug. "Breech plug," he said, and set it on the mat.

January found his skin goose-pimpling in the cold air. Stone handed Shepard one of the blocks. Shepard extended under the bomb again. "Red ends toward the breech." "I know." Watching them January was reminded of auto mechanics on the oily floor of a garage, working under a car. He had spent a few years doing that himself, after his family moved to Vicksburg. Hiroshima was a river town. One time a flat-bed truck carrying bags of cement powder down Fourth Street hill had lost its brakes and careened into the intersection with River Road, where despite the driver's efforts to turn it smashed into a passing car. Frank had been out in the yard playing, had heard the crash and saw the cement dust rising. He had been one of the first there. The woman and child in the passenger seat of the model T had been killed. The woman driving was okay. They were from Chicago. A group of folks subdued the driver of the truck, who kept trying to help at the Model T, though he had a bad cut on his head and was covered with white dust.

"Okay, let's tighten the breech plug." Stone gave Shepard the wrench. "Sixteen turns exactly," Shepard said. He was sweating even in the bay's chill, and he paused to wipe his forehead. "Let's hope we don't get hit by lightning." He put the wrench down and shifted onto his knees, picked up a circular plate. Hubcap, January thought. Stone connected wires, then helped Shepard install two more plates. Good old American know-how, January thought, goose-pimples rippling across his skin like cat's-paws over water. There was Shepard, a scientist, putting together a bomb like he was an auto mechanic changing oil and plugs. January felt a tight rush of rage at the scientists who had designed the bomb. They had worked on it for over a year down there in New Mexico, had none of them in all that time ever stopped to think what they were doing?

But none of them had to drop it. January turned to hide his face from Shepard, stepped down the bay. The bomb looked like a big long trashcan, with fins at one end and little antennae at the other. Just a bomb, he thought, damn it, it's just another bomb.

Shepard stood and patted the bomb gently. "We've got a live one now." Never a thought about what it would do. January hurried by the man, afraid that hatred would crack his shell and give him away. The pistol strapped to his belt caught on the hatchway and he imagined shooting Shepard—shooting Fitch and McDonald and plunging the controls forward so that *Lucky Strike* tilted and spun down into the sea like a spent tracer bullet, like a plane broken by flak, following the arc of all human ambition. Nobody would ever know what had happened to them, and their trashcan would be dumped at the bottom of the Pacific where it belonged. He could even shoot everyone and parachute out, and perhaps be rescued by one of the Superdumbos following them. . . .

The thought passed and remembering it January squinted with disgust. But another part of him agreed that it was a possibility. It could be done. It would solve his problem. His fingers explored his holster snap.

"Want some coffee?" Matthews asked.

"Sure," January said, and took his hand from the gun to reach for the cup. He sipped: hot. He watched Matthews and Benton tune the loran equipment. As the beeps came in Matthews took a straightedge and drew lines from Okinawa and Iwo Jima on his map table. He tapped a finger on the intersection. "They've taken the art out of navigation," he said to January. "They might as well stop making the navigator's dome," thumbing up at the little plexiglass bubble over them.

"Good old American know-how," January said.

Matthews nodded. With two fingers he measured the distance between their position and Iwo Jima. Benton measured with a ruler.

"Rendezvous at five thirty-five, eh?" Matthews said. They were to rendezvous with the two trailing planes over Iwo.

Benton disagreed: "I'd say five-fifty."

"What? Check again, guy, we're not in no tugboat here."

"The wind—"

"Yah, the wind. Frank, you want to add a bet to the pool?"

"Five thirty-six," January said promptly.

They laughed. "See, he's got more confidence in me," Matthews said with a dopey grin.

January recalled his plan to shoot the crew and tip the plane into the sea, and he pursed his lips, repelled. Not for anything would he be able to shoot these men, who, if not friends, were at least companions. They passed for friends. They meant no harm.

Shepard and Stone climbed into the cabin. Matthews offered them coffee. "The gimmick's ready to kick their ass, eh?" Shepard nodded and drank.

January moved forward, past Haddock's console. Another plan that wouldn't work. What to do? All the flight engineer's dials and gauges showed conditions were normal. Maybe he could sabotage something? Cut a line somewhere?

Fitch looked back at him and said, "When are we due over Iwo?"

"Five forty, Matthews says."

"He better be right."

A thug. In peacetime Fitch would be hanging around a pool table giving the cops trouble. He was perfect for war. Tibbets had chosen his men well—most of them, anyway. Moving back past Haddock January stopped to stare at the group of men in the navigation cabin. They joked, drank coffee. They were all a bit like Fitch: young toughs, capable and thoughtless. They were having a good time, an adventure. That was January's dominant impression of his companions in the 509th; despite all the bitching and the occasional moments of overmastering fear, they were having a good time. His mind spun forward and he saw what these young men would grow up to be like as clearly as if they stood before him in businessmen's suits, prosperous and balding. They would be tough and capable and thoughtless, and as the years passed and the great war receded in time they would look back on it with ever-increasing nostalgia, for they would be the survivors and not the dead. Every year of this war would feel like ten in their memories, so that the war would always remain the central experience of their lives—a time when history lay palpable in their hands, when each of their daily acts affected it, when moral issues were simple, and others told them what to do—so that as more years passed and the survivors aged, bodies falling apart, lives in one rut or another, they would unconsciously push harder and harder to thrust the world into war again, thinking somewhere inside themselves that if they could only return to world war then they would magically be again as they were in the last one—young, and free, and happy. And by that time they would hold the positions of power, they would be capable of doing it.

So there would be more wars, January saw. He heard it in Matthews' laughter, saw it in their excited eyes. "There's Iwo, and it's five thirty-one. Pay up! I win!" And in future wars they'd have more bombs like the gimmick, hundreds of them no doubt. He saw more planes, more young crews like this one, flying to Moscow no doubt or to wherever, fireballs in every capital, why not? And to what end? To what end? So that the old men could hope to become magically young again. Nothing more sane than that.

They were over Iwo Jima. Three more hours to Japan. Voices from *The Great Artiste* and *Number 91* crackled on the radio. Rendezvous accomplished, the three planes flew northwest, toward Shikoku, the first Japanese island in their path. January went aft to use the toilet. "You okay, Frank?" Matthews asked. "Sure. Terrible coffee, though." "Ain't it always." January tugged at his baseball cap and hurried away. Kochenski and the other gunners were playing poker. When he was done he returned forward. Matthews sat on the stool before his maps, readying his equipment for the constant monitoring of drift that would now be required. Haddock and Benton were also busy at their stations. January maneuvered between the pilots down into the nose. "Good shooting," Matthews called after him.

Forward it seemed quieter. January got settled, put his headphones on and leaned forward to look out the ribbed plexiglass.

Dawn had turned the whole vault of the sky pink. Slowly the radiant shade shifted through lavender to blue, pulse by pulse a different color. The ocean below was a glittering blue plane, marbled by a pattern of puffy pink cloud. The sky above was a vast dome, darker above than on the horizon. January had always thought that dawn was the time when you could see most clearly how big the earth was, and how high above it they flew. It seemed they flew at the very upper edge of the atmosphere, and January saw how thin it was, how it was just a skin of air really, so that even if you flew up to its top the earth still extended away infinitely in every direction. The coffee had warmed January, he was sweating. Sunlight blinked off the plexiglass. His watch said six. Plane and hemisphere of blue were split down the middle by the bombsight. His earphones crackled and he listened in to the reports from the lead planes flying over the target cities. Kokura, Nagasaki, Hiroshima, all of them had six-tenths cloud cover. Maybe they would have to cancel the whole mission because of weather. "We'll look at Hiroshima first," Fitch said. January peered down at the fields of miniature clouds with renewed interest. His parachute slipped under him. Readjusting it he imagined putting it on, sneaking back to the central escape hatch under the navigator's cabin, opening the hatch . . . he could be out of the plane and gone before anyone noticed. Leave it up to them. They could bomb or not but it wouldn't be January's doing. He could float down onto the world like a puff of dandelion, feel cool air rush around him, watch the silk canopy dome hang over him like a miniature sky, a private world.

An eyeless black face. January shuddered; it was as though the nightmare could return any time. If he jumped nothing would change, the bomb would still fall—would he feel any better, floating on his Inland Sea? Sure, one part of him shouted; maybe, another conceded; the rest of him saw that face. . . .

Earphones cracked. Shepard said, "Lieutenant Stone has now armed the bomb, and I can tell you all what we are carrying. Aboard with us is the world's first atomic bomb."

Not exactly, January thought. Whistles squeaked in his earphones. The first one went off in New Mexico. Splitting atoms: January had heard the term before. Tremendous energy in every atom, Einstein had said. Break one, and—he had seen the result on film. Shepard was talking about radiation, which brought back more to January. Energy released in the form of X-rays. Killed by X-rays! It would be against the Geneva Convention if they had thought of it.

Fitch cut in. "When the bomb is dropped Lieutenant Benton will record our reaction to what we see. This recording is being made for history, so watch your language." Watch your language! January choked back a laugh. Don't curse or blaspheme God at the sight of the first atomic bomb incinerating a city and all its inhabitants with X-rays!

Six twenty. January found his hands clenched together on the headrest of the bombsight. He felt as if he had a fever. In the harsh wash of morning light the skin on the backs of his hands appeared slightly translucent. The whorls in the skin looked like the delicate patterning of waves on the sea's surface. His hands were made of atoms. Atoms were the smallest building block of matter, it took billions of them to make those tense, trembling hands. Split one atom and you had the fireball. That meant that the energy contained in even one hand . . . he turned up a palm to look at the lines and the mottled flesh under the transparent skin. A person was a bomb that could blow up the world. January felt that latent power stir in him, pulsing with every hard heart-knock. What beings they were, and in what a blue expanse of a world!—And here they spun on to drop a bomb and kill a hundred thousand of these astonishing beings.

When a fox or raccoon is caught by the leg in a trap, it lunges until the leg is frayed, twisted, perhaps broken, and only then does the animal's pain and exhaustion force it to quit. Now in the same way January wanted to quit. His mind hurt. His plans to escape were so much crap—stupid, useless. Better to quit. He tried to stop thinking, but it was hopeless. How could he stop? As long as he was conscious he would be thinking. The mind struggles longer in its traps than any fox.

Lucky Strike tilted up and began the long climb to bombing altitude. On the horizon the clouds lay over a green island. Japan. Surely it had gotten hotter, the heater must be broken, he thought. Don't think. Every few minutes Matthews gave Fitch small course adjustments. "Two seventy-five, now. That's it." To escape the moment January recalled his childhood. Following a mule and plow. Moving to Vicksburg (rivers). For a while there in Vicksburg, since his stutter made it hard to gain friends, he had played a game with himself. He had passed the time by imagining that everything he did was vitally important and determined the fate of the world. If he crossed a road in front of a certain car, for instance, then the car wouldn't make it through the next intersection before a truck hit it, and so the man driving would be killed and wouldn't be able to invent the flying boat that would save President Wilson from kidnappers—so he had to wait for that car because everything afterward depended on it. Oh damn it, he thought, damn it, think of something *different*. The last Hornblower story he had read—how would *he* get out of this? The round O of his mother's face as she ran in and saw his arm—The Mississippi, mud-brown behind its levees—Abruptly he shook his head, face twisted in frustration and despair, aware at last that no possible avenue of memory would serve as an escape for him now, for now there was no part of his life that did not apply to the situation he was in, and no matter where he cast his mind it was going to shore up against the hour facing him.

Less than an hour. They were at thirty thousand feet, bombing altitude. Fitch gave him altimeter readings to dial into the bombsight. Matthews gave him windspeeds. Sweat got in his eye and he blinked furiously. The sun rose behind them like an atomic bomb, glinting off every corner and edge of the Plexiglas, illuminating his bubble compartment with a fierce glare. Broken plans jumbled together in his mind, his breath was short, his throat dry. Uselessly and repeatedly he damned the scientists, damned Truman. Damned the Japanese for causing the whole mess in the first place, damned yellow killers, they had brought this on themselves. Remember Pearl. American men had died under bombs when no war had been declared; they had started it and now it was coming back to them with a vengeance. And they deserved it. And an invasion of Japan would take years, cost millions of lives—end it now, end it, they deserved it, they deserved it steaming river full of charcoal people silently dying damned stubborn race of maniacs!

"There's Honshu," Fitch said, and January returned to the world of the plane. They were over the Inland Sea. Soon they would pass the secondary target Kokura, a bit to the south. Seven thirty. The island was draped more heavily than the sea by clouds, and again January's heart leaped with the idea that weather would cancel the mission. But they did deserve it. It was a mission like any other mission. He had dropped bombs on Africa, Sicily, Italy, all Germany. . . . He leaned forward to take a look through the sight. Under the X of the crosshairs was the sea, but at the lead edge of the sight was land. Honshu. At two hundred and thirty miles an hour that gave them about a half hour to Hiroshima. Maybe less. He wondered if his heart could beat so hard for that long.

Fitch said, "Matthews, I'm giving over guidance to you. Just tell us what to do."

"Bear south two degrees," was all Matthews said. At last their voices had taken on a touch of awareness, even fear.

"January, are you ready?" Fitch asked.

"I'm just waiting," January said. He sat up, so Fitch could see the back of his head. The bombsight stood between his legs. A switch on its side would start the bombing sequence; the bomb would not leave the plane immediately upon the flick of the switch, but would drop after a fifteen-second radio tone warned the following planes. The sight was adjusted accordingly.

"Adjust to a heading of two sixty-five," Matthews said. "We're coming in directly upwind." This was to make any side-drift adjustments for the bomb unnecessary. "January, dial it down to two hundred and thirty-one miles per hour."

"Two thirty-one."

Fitch said, "Everyone but January and Matthews, get your goggles on."

January took the darkened goggles from the floor. One needed to protect one's eyes or they might melt. He put them on, put his forehead on the headrest. They were in the way. He took them off. When he looked through the sight again there was land under the crosshairs. He checked his watch. Eight o'clock. Up and reading the papers, drinking tea.

"Ten minutes to AP," Matthews said. The aiming point was Aioi Bridge, a T-shaped bridge in the middle of the delta-straddling city. Easy to recognize.

"There's a lot of cloud down there," Fitch noted. "Are you going to be able to see?"

"I won't be sure until we try it," January said.

"We can make another pass and use radar if we need to," Matthews said.

Fitch said, "Don't drop it unless you're sure, January."

"Yes, sir."

Through the sight a grouping of rooftops and gray roads was just visible between broken clouds. Around it green forest. "All right," Matthews exclaimed, "here we go! Keep it right on this heading, Captain! January, we'll stay at two thirty-one."

"And same heading," Fitch said. "January, she's all yours. Everyone make sure your goggles are on. And be ready for the turn."

January's world contracted to the view through the bombsight. A stippled field of cloud and forest. Over a small range of hills and into Hiroshima's watershed. The broad river was mud brown, the land pale hazy green, the growing network of roads flat gray. Now the tiny rectangular shapes of buildings covered almost all the land, and swimming into the sight came the city proper, narrow islands thrusting into a dark blue bay. Under the crosshairs the city moved island by island, cloud by cloud. January had stopped breathing, his fingers were rigid as stone on the switch. And there was Aioi Bridge. It slid right under the crosshairs, a tiny T right in a gap in the clouds. January's fingers crushed the switch. Deliberately he took a breath, held it. Clouds swam under the crosshairs, then the next island. "Almost there," he said calmly into his microphone. "Steady." Now that he was committed his heart was humming like the Wrights. He counted to ten. Now flowing under the crosshairs were clouds alternating with green forest, leaden roads. "I've turned the switch, but I'm not getting a tone!" he croaked into the mike. His right hand held the switch firmly in place. Fitch was shouting something—Matthews' voice cracked across it—"Flipping it b-back and forth," January shouted, shielding the bombsight with his body from the eyes of the pilots. "But *still*—wait a second—"

He pushed the switch down. A low hum filled his ears. "That's it! It started!"

"But where will it land?" Matthews cried.

"Hold steady!" January shouted.

Lucky Strike shuddered and lofted up ten or twenty feet. January twisted to look down and there was the bomb, flying just below the plane. Then with a wobble it fell away.

The plane banked right and dove so hard that the centrifugal force threw January against the plexiglass. Several thousand feet lower Fitch leveled it out and they hurtled north.

"Do you see anything?" Fitch cried.

From the tailgun Kockenski gasped "Nothing." January struggled upright. He reached for the welder's goggles, but they were no longer on his head. He couldn't find them. "How long has it been?" he said.

"Thirty seconds," Matthews replied.

January clamped his eyes shut.

The blood in his eyelids lit up red, then white.

On the earphones a clutter of voices: "Oh my God. Oh my God." The plane bounced and tumbled, metallically shrieking. January pressed himself off the plexiglass. "Nother shockwave!" Kockenski yelled. The plane rocked again, bounced out of control, this is it, January thought, end of the world, I guess that solves my problem.

He opened his eyes and found he could still see. The engines still roared, the props spun. "Those were the shockwaves from the bomb," Fitch called. "We're okay now. Look at that! Will you look at that sonofabitch go!"

January looked. The cloud layer below had burst apart, and a black column of smoke billowed up from a core of red fire. Already the top of the column was at their height. Exclamations of shock clattered painfully in January's ears. He stared at the fiery base of the cloud, at the scores of fires feeding into it. Suddenly he could see past the cloud, and his fingernails cut into his palms. Through a gap in the clouds he saw it clearly, the delta, the six rivers, there off to the left of the tower of smoke: the city of Hiroshima, untouched.

"We missed!" Kockenski yelled. "We missed it!"

January turned to hide his face from the pilots; on it was a grin like a rictus. He sat back in his seat and let the relief fill him.

Then it was back to it. "God damn it!" Fitch shouted down at him. McDonald was trying to restrain him. "January, get up here!"

"Yes, sir." Now there was a new set of problems.

January stood and turned, legs weak. His right fingertips throbbed painfully. The men were crowded forward to look out the plexiglass. January looked with them.

The mushroom cloud was forming. It roiled out as if

it might continue to extend forever, fed by the inferno and the black stalk below it. It looked about two miles wide, and half a mile tall, and it extended well above the height they flew at, dwarfing their plane entirely. "Do you think we'll all be sterile?" Matthews said.

"I can taste the radiation," McDonald declared. "Can you? It tastes like lead."

Bursts of flame shot up into the cloud from below, giving a purplish tint to the stalk. There it stood: lifelike, malignant, sixty thousand feet tall. One bomb. January shoved past the pilots into the navigation cabin, over-whelmed.

"Should I start recording everyone's reactions, Captain?" asked Benton.

"To hell with that," Fitch said, following January back. But Shepard got there first, descending quickly from the navigation dome. He rushed across the cabin, caught January on the shoulder, "You bastard!" he screamed as January stumbled back. "You lost your nerve, coward!"

January went for Shepard, happy to have a target at last, but Fitch cut in and grabbed him by the collar, pulled him around until they were face to face—

"Is that right?" Fitch cried, as angry as Shepard. "Did you screw up on purpose?"

"No," January grunted, and knocked Fitch's hands away from his neck. He swung and smacked Fitch on the mouth, caught him solid. Fitch staggered back, re-covered, and no doubt would have beaten January up, but Matthews and Benton and Stone leaped in and held him back, shouting for order. "Shut up! Shut up!" McDonald screamed from the cockpit, and for a moment it was bedlam, but Fitch let himself be restrained, and soon only McDonald's shouts for quiet were heard. January retreated to between the pilot seats, right hand on his pistol holster.

"The city was in the crosshairs when I flipped the switch," he said. "But the first couple of times I flipped it nothing happened—"

"That's a lie!" Shepard shouted. "There was nothing wrong with the switch, I checked it myself. Besides, the bomb exploded *miles* beyond Hiroshima, look for yourself! That's *minutes*." He wiped spit from his chin and pointed at January. "You did it."

"You don't know that," January said. But he could see the men had been convinced by Shepard, and he took a step back. "You just get me to a board of inquiry, quick. And leave me alone till then. If you touch me again," glaring venomously at Fitch and then Shepard, "I'll shoot you." He turned and hopped down to his seat, feeling exposed and vunerable, like a treed raccoon.

"They'll shoot *you* for this," Shepard screamed after him, "Disobeying orders—treason—" Matthews and Stone were shutting him up.

"Let's get out of here," he heard McDonald say. "I can taste the lead, can't you?"

January looked out the plexiglass. The giant cloud still burned and roiled. One atom. . . . Well, they had really done it to that forest. He almost laughed but stopped himself, afraid of hysteria. Through a break in the clouds he got a clear view of Hiroshima for the first time. It lay spread over its islands like a map, unharmed. Well, that was that. The inferno at the base of the mushroom cloud was eight or ten miles around the shore of the bay, and a mile or two inland. A certain patch of forest would be gone, destroyed—utterly blasted from the face of the earth. The Japs would be able to go out and investigate the damage. And if they were told it was a demonstration, a warning—and if they acted fast—well, they had their chance. Maybe it would work.

The release of tension made January feel sick. Then he recalled Shepard's words and he knew that whether his plan worked or not he was still in trouble. In trouble! It was worse than that. Bitterly he cursed the Japanese, he even wished for a moment that he *had* dropped it on them. Wearily he let his despair empty him.

A long while later he sat up straight. Once again he was a trapped animal. He began lunging for escape, casting about for plans. One alternative after another. All during the long grim flight home he considered it, mind spinning at the speed of the props and beyond. And when they came down on Tinian he had a plan. It was a long shot, he reckoned, but it was the best he could do.

The briefing hut was surrounded by MPs again. January stumbled from the truck with the rest and walked inside. He was more than ever aware of the looks given him, and they were hard, accusatory. He was too tired to care. He hadn't slept in more than thirty-six hours, and had slept very little since the last time he had been in the hut, a week before. Now the room quivered with the lack of engine vibration to stabilize it, and the silence roared. It was all he could do to hold on to the bare essentials of his plan. The glares of Fitch and Shepard, the hurt incomprehension of Matthews, they had to be thrust out of his focus. Thankfully he lit a cigarette.

In a clamor of question and argument the others described the strike. Then the haggard Scholes and an intelligence officer led them through the bombing run. January's plan made it necessary to hold to his story: ". . . and when the AP was under the crosshairs I pushed down the switch, but got no signal. I flipped it up and down repeatedly until the tone kicked in. At that point there was still fifteen seconds to the release.''

"Was there anything that may have caused the tone to start when it did?''

"Not that I noticed immediately, but—''

"It's impossible," Shepard interrupted, face red. "I checked the switch before we flew and there was nothing wrong with it. Besides, the drop occurred over a minute—''

"Captain Shepard," Scholes said. "We'll hear from you presently.''

"But he's obviously lying—''

"Captain Shepard! It's not at all obvious. Don't speak unless questioned.''

"Anyway," January said, hoping to shift the questions away from the issue of the long delay, "I noticed something about the bomb when it was falling that could explain why it stuck. I need to discuss it with one of the scientists familiar with the bomb's design.''

"What was that?" Scholes asked suspiciously.

January hesitated. "There's going to be an inquiry, right?''

Scholes frowned. "This is the inquiry, Captain January. Tell us what you saw.''

"But there will be some proceeding beyond this one?''

"It looks like there's going to be a court-martial, yes, Captain.''

"That's what I thought. I don't want to talk to anyone but my counsel, and some scientist familiar with the bomb.''

"*I'm* a scientist familiar with the bomb," Shepard burst out. "You could tell me if you really had anything, you—''

"I said I need a scientist!" January exclaimed, rising to face the scarlet Shepard across the table. "Not a

G-God damned mechanic." Shepard started to shout, others joined in and the room rang with argument. While Scholes restored order January sat down, and he refused to be drawn out again.

"I'll see you're assigned counsel, and initiate the court-martial," Scholes said, clearly at a loss. "Meanwhile you are under arrest, on suspicion of disobeying orders in combat." January nodded, and Scholes gave him over to MPs.

"One last thing, " January said, fighting exhaustion. "Tell General Le May that if the Japs are told this drop was a warning, it might have the same effect as—"

"I told you!" Shepard shouted. "I told you he did it on purpose!"

Men around Shepard restrained him. But he had convinced most of them, and even Matthews stared at him with surprised anger.

January shook his head wearily. He had the dull feeling that his plan, while it had succeeded so far, was ultimately not a good one. "Just trying to make the best of it." It took all of his remaining will to force his legs to carry him in a dignified manner out of the hut.

His cell was an empty NCO's office. MPs brought his meals. For the first couple of days he did little but sleep. On the third day he glanced out the office's barred window, and saw a tractor pulling a tarpaulin-draped trolly out of the compound, followed by jeeps filled with MPs. It looked like a military funeral. January rushed to the door and banged on it until one of the young MPs came.

"What's that they're doing out there?" January demanded.

Eyes cold and mouth twisted, the MP said, "They're making another strike. They're going to do it right this time."

"No!" January cried. "No!" He rushed the MP, who knocked him back and locked the door. *"No!"* He beat the door until his hands hurt, cursing wildly. "You don't *need* to do it, it isn't *necessary.*" Shell shattered at last, he collapsed on the bed and wept. Now everything he had done would be rendered meaningless. He had sacrificed himself for nothing.

A day or two after that the MPs led in a colonel, an iron-haired man who stood stiffly and crushed January's hand when he shook it. His eyes were a pale, icy blue.

"I am Colonel Dray," he said. "I have been ordered to defend you in court-martial." January could feel the dislike pouring from the man. "To do that I'm going to need every fact you have, so let's get started."

"I'm not talking to anybody until I've seen an atomic scientist."

"I am your *defense* counsel—"

"I don't care who you are," January said. "Your defense of me depends on you getting one of the scientists *here*. The higher up he is, the better. And I want to speak to him alone."

"I will have to be present."

So he would do it. But now January's counsel, too, was an enemy.

"Naturally," January said. "You're my counsel. But no one else. Our atomic secrecy may depend on it."

"You saw evidence of sabotage?"

"Not one word more until that scientist is here."

Angrily the colonel nodded and left.

Late the next day the colonel returned with another man. "This is Dr. Forest."

"I helped develop the bomb," Forest said. He had a crew-cut and dressed in fatigues, and to January he looked more Army than the colonel. Suspiciously he stared back and forth at the two men.

"You'll vouch for this man's identity on your word as an officer?" he asked of Dray.

"Of course," the colonel said stiffly, offended.

"So," Dr. Forest said. "You had some trouble getting it off when you wanted to. Tell me what you saw."

"I saw nothing," January said harshly. He took a deep breath; it was time to commit himself. "I want you to take a message back to the scientists. You folks have been working on this thing for years, and you must have had time to consider how the bomb should have been used. You know we could have convinced the Japs to surrender by showing them a demonstration—"

"Wait a minute," Forest said. "You're saying you didn't see anything? There wasn't a malfunction?"

"That's right," January said, and cleared his throat. "It wasn't *necessary*, do you understand?"

Forest was looking at Colonel Dray. Dray gave him a disgusted shrug. "He told us he saw evidence of sabotage."

"I want you to go back and ask the scientists to intercede for me," January said, raising his voice to get the man's attention. "I haven't got a chance in that courtmartial. But if the scientists defend me than maybe they'll let me live, see? I don't want to get shot for doing something every one of you scientists would have done."

Dr. Forest had backed away. Color rising, he said, "What makes you think that's what we would have done? Don't you think we considered it? Don't you think men better qualified than you made the decision?" He waved a hand—"God damn it—what made you think you were competent to decide something as important as that!"

January was appalled at the man's reaction; in his plan it had gone differently. Angrily he jabbed a finger at Forest. "Because *I* was the man doing it, *Doctor* Forest. You take even one step back from that and suddenly you can pretend it's not your doing. Fine for you, but I *was there*."

At every word the man's color was rising. It looked like he might pop a vein in his neck. January tried once more. "Have you ever tried to imagine what one of your bombs would do to a city full of people?"

"I've had enough!" the man exploded. He turned to Dray. "I'm under no obligation to keep what I've heard here confidential. You can be sure it will be used as evidence in Captain January's court-martial." He turned and gave January a look of such blazing hatred that January understood it. For these men to admit he was right would mean admitting that they were wrong—that every one of them was responsible for his part in the construction of the weapon January had refused to use. Understanding that, January knew he was doomed.

The bang of Dr. Forest's departure still shook the little office. January sat on his cot, got out a smoke. Under Colonel Dray's cold gaze he lit one shakily, took a drag. He looked up at the colonel, shrugged. "It was my best chance," he explained. That did something—for the first and only time the cold disdain in the colonel's eyes shifted to a little, hard, lawyerly gleam of respect.

The court-martial lasted two days. The verdict was guilty of disobeying orders in combat, and of giving aid and comfort to the enemy. The sentence was death by firing squad.

For most of his remaining days January rarely spoke, drawing ever further behind the mask that had hidden him for so long. A clergyman came to see him, but it was the 509th's chaplain, the one who had said the prayer blessing the *Lucky Strike*'s mission before the took off. Angrily January sent him packing.

Later, however, a young Catholic priest dropped by. His name was Patrick Getty. He was a little pudgy man, bespectacled and, it seemed, somewhat afraid of January. January let the man talk to him. When he returned the next day January talked back a bit, and on the day after that he talked some more. It became a habit.

Usually January talked about his childhood. He talked of plowing mucky black bottom land behind a mule. Of running down the lane to the mailbox. Of reading books by the light of the moon after he had been ordered to sleep, and of being beaten by his mother for it with a high-heeled shoe. He told the priest the story of the time his arm had been burnt, and about the car crash at the bottom of Fourth Street. "It's the truck driver's face I remember, do you see, Father?"

"Yes," the young priest said. "Yes."

And he told him about the game he had played in which every action he took tipped the balance of world affairs. "When I remembered that game I thought it was dumb. Step on a sidewalk crack and cause an earthquake—you know, it's stupid. Kids are like that." The priest nodded. "But now I've been thinking that if everybody were to live their whole lives like that, thinking that every move they made really was important, then . . . it might make a difference." He waved a hand vaguely, expelled cigarette smoke. "You're accountable for what you do."

"Yes," the priest said. "Yes, you are."

"And if you're given orders to do something wrong, you're still accountable, right? The orders don't change it."

"That's right."

"Hmph." January smoked a while. "So they say, anyway. But look what happens." He waved at the office.

"I'm like the guy in a story I read—he thought everything in books was true, and after reading a bunch of westerns he tried to rob a train. They tossed him in jail." He laughed shortly. "Books are full of crap."

"Not all of them," the priest said. "Besides, you weren't trying to rob a train."

They laughed at the notion. "Did you read that story?"

"No."

"It was the strangest book—there were two stories in it, and they alternated chapter by chapter, but they didn't have a thing to do with each other! I didn't get it."

". . . Maybe the writer was trying to say that everything connects to everything else."

"Maybe. But it's a funny way to say it."

"I like it."

And so they passed the time, talking.

So it was the priest who was the one to come by and tell January that his request for a Presidential pardon had been refused. Getty said awkwardly, "It seems the President approves the sentence."

"That bastard," January said weakly. He sat on his cot.

Time passed. It was another hot, humid day.

"Well," the priest said. "Let me give you some better news. Given your situation I don't think telling you matters, though I've been told not to. The second mission—you know there was a second strike?"

"Yes."

"Well, they missed too."

"What?" January cried, and bounced to his feet. "You're kidding!"

"No. They flew to Kokura, but found it covered by clouds. It was the same over Nagasaki and Hiroshima, so they flew back to Kokura and tried to drop the bomb using radar to guide it, but apparently there was a—a genuine equipment failure this time, and the bomb fell on an island.''

January was hopping up and down, mouth hanging open, "So we n-never—''

"We never dropped an atom bomb on a Japanese city. That's right.'' Getty grinned. "And get this—I heard this from my superior—they sent a message to the Japanese government telling them that the two explosions were warnings, and that if they didn't surrender by September first we would drop bombs on Kyoto and Tokyo, and then wherever else we had to. Word is that the Emperor went to Hiroshima to survey the damage, and when he saw it he ordered the Cabinet to surrender. So. . . .''

"So it worked,'' January said. He hopped around, "It worked, it worked!''

"Yes.''

"Just like I said it would!'' he cried, and hopping before the priest he laughed.

Getty was jumping around a little too, and the sight of the priest bouncing was too much for January. He sat on his cot and laughed till the tears ran down his cheeks.

"So—'' he sobered quickly. "So Truman's going to shoot me anyway, eh?''

"Yes,'' the priest said unhappily. "I guess that's right.''

This time January's laugh was bitter. "He's a bastard, all right. And proud of being a bastard, which makes it worse.'' He shook his head. "If Roosevelt had lived. . . .''

"It would have been different,'' Getty finished. "Yes. Maybe so. But he didn't.'' He sat beside January. "Cigarette?'' He held out a pack, and January noticed the white wartime wrapper. He frowned.

"You haven't got a Camel?''

"Oh. Sorry.''

"Oh well. That's all right." January took one of the Lucky Strikes, lit up. "That's awfully good news." He breathed out. "I never believed Truman would pardon me anyway, so mostly you've brought good news. Ha. They *missed*. You have no idea how much better that makes me feel."

"I think I do."

January smoked the cigarette.

". . . So I'm a good American after all. I *am* a good American," he insisted, "no matter what Truman says."

"Yes," Getty replied, and coughed. "You're better than Truman any day."

"Better watch what you say, Father." He looked into the eyes behind the glasses, and the expression he saw there gave him pause. Since the drop every look directed at him had been filled with contempt. He'd seen it so often during the court-martial that he'd learned to stop looking; and now he had to teach himself to see again. The priest look at him as if he were . . . as if he were some kind of hero. That wasn't exactly right. But seeing it. . . .

January would not live to see the years that followed, so he would never know what came of his action. He had given up casting his mind forward and imagining possibilities, because there was no point to it. His planning was ended. In any case he would not have been able to imagine the course of the post-war years. That the world would quickly become an armed camp pitched on the edge of atomic war, he might have predicted. But he never would have guessed that so many people would join a January Society. He would never know of the effect the Society had on Dewey during the Korean crises, never know of the Society's successful campaign for the test ban treaty, and never learn that thanks in part to the Society and its allies, a treaty would be signed by the great powers that would reduce the number of atomic bombs year by year, until there were none left.

Frank January would never know any of that. But in that moment on his cot looking into the eyes of young Patrick Getty, he guessed an inkling of it—he felt, just for an instant, the impact on history.

And with that he relaxed. In his last week everyone who met him carried away the same impression, that of a calm, quiet man, angry at Truman and others, but in a withdrawn, matter-of-fact way. Patrick Getty, a strong force in the January Society ever after, said January was talkative for some time after he learned of the missed attack on Kokura. Then he became quieter and quieter, as the day approached. On the morning that they woke him at dawn to march him out to a hastily constructed execution shed, his MPs shook his hand. The priest was with him as he smoked a final cigarette, and they prepared to put the hood over his head. January looked at him calmly. "They load one of the guns with a blank cartridge, right?"

"Yes," Getty said.

"So each man in the squad can imagine he may not have shot me?"

"Yes. That's right."

A tight, unhumorous smile was January's last expression. He threw down the cigarette, ground it out, poked the priest in the arm. "But I *know*." Then the mask slipped back into place for good, making the hood redundant, and with a firm step January went to the wall. One might have said he was at peace.

Brains on the Dump

Nicholas Emmett

A small boy named John balanced the rock on the edge of an orange-coloured balcony. It was heavy, and he was tired. Searching for it on the dump had not been easy, nor had the struggle up the four flights of stairs, and he thinking, and thinking, about Willie Byrne.

If Willie had only gone away after hitting him on the nose. Why did Willie force him down, rub his face into the cow dung that lay on the street, and stand there while the others laughed. Maybe if Willie had not made him look ridiculous he would not—.

His fingers tightened on the rough edge of rock, while directly below him, sleeping peacefully in a large green pram, lay the white swathed bundle of Willie's baby sister.

John was nineteen when the gelignite blew him to pieces. How cold and wet he had been, as he prepared the booby

143

trap for the expected jeep. How suddenly the charge exploded in his hands, causing that vague sense of identity that had been him to break into little bits.

One bit, his brain, landed on the edge of a footpath, and there considered the course of events that had brought it to its present undignified position. There had been the man he had met at the bus stop in Dublin, and the agreement reached that something should be done for one's country. A large bare room had been entered, and his decision to join the organization accepted. And there had been the training in the use of explosives.

Here the brain tittered to itself, as the thought occurred that either the training or the gelignite had been faulty.

A late afternoon sunshine slanted painfully through the dusty streets when the machine came along. Efficiently, a shovellike mechanism shot from the side, scooped up John's brain, and deposited it with a lot of other brains.

Trundle, trundle, it went into the approaching gloom, until it came to a broad river. Even now it did not stop, but trundled into the darkened water, for by now night was soaking darkly into everything.

After some time there was a thud, and he knew he and the other brains had been dropped through an opening onto the ground. Not that he cared, such an eventful day, such tiredness, and now drifting into sleep.

Strong sunlight woke him, and he looked around. What a strange place, what a big dump, all those miles of lavatory and industrial waste, all shimmering, stinking, fermenting, and bubbling in the sun.

Brains on the Dump

* * *

"Still it's life, insecty life, wormy life, germy life, but still life," said a voice behind John.

John spun his jellied remains around, and saw thousands and thousands of brains, all basking in the sunlight. The one speaking was a large purple specimen, and now it was speaking again.

"I am foreman here. I will tell you as economically as possible our situation."

"First our comrades. They come from many places. Some were good Jews fighting the baddy Arabs, some baddy Jews fighting the goody Arabs, some were good protestants fighting the baddy catholics, some baddy protestants fighting the goody catholics, some were goody, or baddy, Viet Cong, black or white, etc, etc, etc, etc, etc, etc, etc, etc, etc, etc, etc, etc, etc, etc.

"We did not eat what we killed, we did not need it for food, or to feed our young, or to use in any way towards the increase of life.

"Life, friend, that is the word. It is not the empty space between the stars, nor the unconscious mineral. But rather the movement from single cell, towards a jellied fish, bronzed weapon, space ship potential.

"Now, comrade, you enter a sun-bathed botanical garden, and you have life seeding, increasing, screaming its multi-coloured challenge towards the universe. We on the other hand, resting on this unperfumed site, are the shrinking of life, on the way to the greatest horror of all, the nonconsciousness.

* * *

"And you, friend, and all our fellow members have offended. We stopped life without purpose, we stopped a cell on its journey from sea to star."

John began to laugh, his jellied blob shaking and shaking and shaking, with merriment, and all the other brains began to laugh, until a great big gale of rusty laughter, went round and round, and round, the dump.

Beachhead

Joe Haldeman

It was too nice a day for this. The morning sun was friendly warm, still early, not yet hot in the tropical sky. Salt air, sound of the gentle breakers ahead; if you closed your eyes you could picture girls and picnics. Riding waves, playing. The girls in their wet clinging suits, hinting mysteries, that's the kind of day it should have been.

Curious sea birds creaked and cawed, begging, as they followed the craft wallowing its way toward shore. Its motor was silent, as was its cargo of boys. Quiet tick and clack as bits of metal swung and tapped in the swaying craft.

The salt tang not quite as strong as the smell of lubricant. Duncan opened his eyes and for the hundredth time rubbed the treated cloth along the exposed metal parts of his weapon. Take care of this weapon, boy, the sergeant had said, over and over; take care of it and it will take care of you. This weapon's all that's between you and dying.

The readout by the sight said 125. Ten dozen people he could fry before recharging.

A soft triple snick of metal as the boy next to him clicked his bayonet into place over the muzzle of the weapon. Others looked at him but nobody said anything. You weren't supposed to put the bayonet on until you were on the beach. Someone might get hurt in the charge. That was almost funny.

"You're not supposed to do that," Duncan said, just above a whisper.

"I know," the boy said. "I'll be careful." They really hadn't had that much training. Three years before, they'd been pulled out of school and sent to the military academy. But until the last month it had been just like regular school, except that you lived in a dorm instead of at home. Then some quick instruction in guns and knives and they were on their way to the Zone.

The surf grew louder and the pitching of the boat more pronounced as they surged in through the breakers. Someone spattered vomit inside the craft, not daring to raise his head above the heavy metal shielding of the sides, and then two more did the same; so much for the fragrance of the sea. Duncan's breakfast was sour in his throat and he swallowed it back. Someone cried softly, sobbing like a girl. A boy tried to quiet him with a silly harsh insult. Someone admonished him, with no conviction, to save it for the enemy. It was all so absurd. Like dying on a day like this. Even for real soldiers, dying on a day like this would be absurd.

The bow of the craft ground to a halt on coral sand. Duncan lurched to his feet, weapon at port arms, ready to rush out. Warm air from the beach wafted in with a new smell, a horrible smell: burning flesh.

He didn't think he could kill anyone. It was all a dreadful mistake. He was sixteen years old and at the top of his class in calculus and Latin. Now he was going to step off this boat into a firestorm of lasers and die.

"This is crazy." The large boy loomed over the counselor's desk, nearly as tall as the adult and outbulking him by ten kilograms of muscle. "It has to be the tests. They screwed up on my brother three years ago and now they screwed up on me."

"Please watch your language." The boy glared at him and then blushed and nodded. "Do you have any idea how often this happens, Eric? You think that because Duncan didn't want to go to the Zone and you did, the tests would necessarily reflect your wishes. Your own evaluation of yourselves. But people at thirteen don't really know themselves very well. That's no crime. It's just a fact of life."

"Look, Professor. It ain't just my *opinion*. Ask anybody! Anybody who knows us both." He counted out points on his fingers. "Duncan never wanted to play soldier when he was a kid. I always did. He never went out for sports; I'm captain of the two teams. He used to read books, I mean all the time, and I don't unless it's for school. He never once got into a fight in school, and I—"

"And you took the tests. And the tests don't lie."

"Maybe they don't. But they make mistakes in the office all the time. That's gotta be what happened. They took the test results and got Duncan's and mine switched."

"You weren't even ten when Duncan took his last one."

"Yeah, but I'd took 'em twice by the time I was ten. They could of gotten mixed up."

The man shrugged. "All right; I'll show you." He unfolded himself out of the chair and stepped over to a bank of filing cabinets. He took out two adjacent folders and threw them on the desk. Sitting down, he typed something on his keyboard and turned the monitor around to face Eric.

The boy's brow was furrowed as he looked from one test to another. "So it's these red numbers. Duncan got a 68 and I got a 92." He looked up with a skeptical expression. "Usually it's the other way around."

"It's not an intelligence test. It's a test for antisocial aggressive potential. How easy it would be for you to kill somebody." He pointed at the monitor. "You know what a bell-shaped curve is."

"Yeah, like for grades." Red lines showed where he and his brother stood in relation to the average, Eric well to the right of the graph's shoulder and Duncan on the extreme left.

"For grades and for a lot of things. You can chart a bunch of people's height or weight and they come out this way. Or ask them on a scale of one to ten 'Do you like cheddar cheese?'—and this is what you get."

"So?"

"So the attitude test you took didn't come right out and say 'How would you like to get the enemy in your sights and fry him?' Most people in their right mind would say—"

"But I *would*!" His eyes actually glittered. "I mean I've really thought about it a lot! What it would look like and all."

"What it would feel like."

He smiled. "Yeah."

The counselor tapped three times on the test packet. "That's in here, all right. But it's just boyish enthusiasm. Playing soldier. You're going to be a solid citizen. A peaceable, well-adjusted man who makes a real contribution to society. You're the lucky one."

He shook his head slowly. "But Duncan—"

"Duncan was a true psychopath, a born killer who hid it so well he fooled even his brother. That 68 is about as low as I've ever seen. Don't envy him. He's probably dead by now. If he's not dead, he's going through hell."

Eric kept shaking his head and stuffed his hands into his pockets. "He was a nice guy, though."

"Jack the Ripper was probably a nice guy."

"Well . . . thanks. Better get to class." He paused at the door. "But I might see him again. I mean, like, *you* came back."

"That's right. Counselors are all people who've been sent to the Zone. People who lived long enough to change."

"Well. Maybe."

"We can hope." He watched the boy trudge away, deep in thought, and suppressed a grin. Sometimes the satisfactions of this job were not at all subtle.

The front of the landing craft unhooked and slapped forward with a blinding spray of foam. The boys charged out, terrified, frantic, into the smell of roasting flesh—

The first ones on the beach stopped dead. The next ones piled up behind them, and the boy who had fixed his bayonet just missed skewering Duncan.

Twenty meters up the beach, under a red and white striped awning, four pretty girls in brief bathing suits tended a suckling pig that turned over coals, roasting. Tubs of ice with cold drinks.

An older man in a bathing suit held up a drink, toasting them. Duncan didn't recognize him at first, without coat and tie. It was Ian Johnson, the counselor who had condemned him to this place. "Welcome to the Zone," he called out. "War's hell."

Like a number of the others, Duncan pointed his

weapon at the sky and pulled the trigger. Nothing happened.

The girls laughed brightly.

That night, sitting around a bonfire, they learned the actual way of the world. The Zone *was* the real world, and the island nation where they had gone through childhood and most of their early schooling was actually a prison without walls. Or a zoo without bars, where the zookeepers mingled unnoticed with the specimens.

The Enemy did not exist; there was no war. It was only a ruse to explain why people couldn't leave, unless they left in uniform. Children like Eric stayed on the island, constantly monitored by observers from the real world, until they trained themselves out of aggressiveness and were allowed to leave. Or they grew up, lived, and died there, their options restricted for everyone's sake. Their world was a couple of centuries out of date, necessarily, since in the real world everyone had access to technologies that could be perverted into weapons of mass destruction.

It had been a truism since the simple atomic age, that the social sciences hadn't been able to keep up with the physical ones; that our ability to control the material world had accelerated without our moral strength increasing to accommodate our powers.

There was a war that had to be the last one, and the few survivors put together this odd construct to protect themselves and their descendents *from* themselves and their descendents.

They still couldn't change human nature, but they could measure aspects of it with extraordinary reliability. And they could lie about the measurements, denying to a large minority of the population a freedom that they did not know existed.

For some years Duncan went down to the beach on

Beachhead

Invasion Day, looking for his brother Eric in the dumb-founded battalions that slogged through the surf into the real world. Then one year he was too busy, and the rest of the years just had the office computer automatically check the immigration lists.

In the other real world, Eric sometimes wondered if his brother was still alive.

Author's note:

Twenty years ago, my wife had her first real full-time job, teaching Spanish in a rural Florida high school that had recently, reluctantly, become integrated. The students had taken language aptitude tests and only those with high potential were allowed into her classroom.

Predictably, the elite students—most of whom, surprisingly, had gone through the "inferior" black primary school system—threw themselves into the work with enthusiasm, learning fast, doing extra work, having a good time at it. They were a joy to teach.

About a year later, my wife found out that the office had made a fundamental error. Everyone who *took* the test, pass or fail, had been allowed into the class. Some of them had language aptitudes far below average.

They were *told* they were special, though, and would succeed. So of course it turned out to be a self-fulfilling prophecy.

There Will Be No War
After This One

Robert Sheckley

Earth is now well known for her peaceful ways. She is a model of good behavior, though she is an extremely impoverished civilization. She has eschewed war forever.

But some people do not realize that it was not always so. There was a time, and not too long ago, when Earth was dominated by some of the worst military bad-asses to be found anywhere. The armed forces, which held power in the last days before The Great Awakening, were almost unbelievably inept in their policies.

It was at this time that Earth, achieving single rule at last under General Gatt and his marshalls, entered interstellar civilization, and, a few short years later, went through the famous incident with the Galactic Effectuator that led them to put war behind them forever. Here is the true story of that encounter.

At dawn on September 18, 2331, General Vargas's Second Route Army came out of the mists around Redlands,

California, and pinned down Wiedermayer's loyalist troops on the San Francisco peninsula. Wiedermayer, last of the old democratic regime generals, the appointee of the discredited Congress of the United States, had been hoping to get his troops to safety by ship, perhaps to Hawaii. He did not know at that time that the Islands had fallen to military rule. Not that it mattered; the expected transports never arrived. Realizing that further resistance was futile, Wiedermayer surrendered. With him fell the last military force on the planet which had supported civilian rule. For the first time in its history, Earth was utterly and entirely in the hands of the warlords.

Vargas accepted Wiedermayer's surrender and sent a messenger to the Supreme Commander, General Gatt, at his North Texas headquarters. Outside his tent, the men of Vargas's army were camped in pup tents across two grassy fields. The quartermasters were already getting ready the feasts with which Vargas marked his victories.

Vargas was a man somewhat shorter than medium height, thickset, with black curly hair on a big round skull. He had a well-trimmed black moustache, and heavy black eyebrows that met in a bar above his nose. He sat on a campstool. A stubby black cigar smouldered on a corner of the field table beside him. Following long-established practice, Vargas was calming himself by polishing his boots. They were genuine ostrich, priceless now that the last of those great birds had died.

Sitting on the cot across the tent from him was his common-law wife, Lupe. She was redheaded, loud-mouthed, with strong features, a strident voice, and an indomitable spirit. They had been fighting these wars together for most of their adult lives. Vargas had risen from the lowly rank of Camp Follower's Assistant to General in command of Supreme General Gatt's Western Forces.

He and Lupe had campaigned in many parts of the world. The Second Route Army was highly mobile, able to pack up its weapons one day in Italy and appear the next day in California or Cambodia or wherever needed.

Now at last Vargas and his lady had a chance to relax. The troops were spread out on the big plain near Los Gatos. Their campfires sent thin wavering streamers of gray smoke into the blue sky. Many of Wiedermayer's surrendered troops had joined the victors. The campaign was over. Maybe all the battles were won; for as far as Vargas could remember, they seemed to have run out of opponents.

It was a good moment. Vargas and Lupe toasted each other with California champagne, and then pushed their gear off the folding double bed in preparation for more earnest celebrating. It was just then that the messenger arrived, tired and dusty from many hours in the helicopter, with a telegram from General Gatt.

Gatt's telegram read,

The last opposition to our New Order has collapsed in North America. Final resistance in Russia and Asia has ended. At last, the world is under a single unified command! Loyal General and Dear Friend, you must come to me at once. All the generals are coming here to help me celebrate our total victory over all those who opposed us. We will be voting on our next procedures and course of action. I very much want for you to be here for that. Also I tell you in strictest confidence, there has been a surprising new development. I cannot even talk about it over the telegram. I want to discuss it with you. This is of greatest importance! Come immediately! I need you!

When the messenger left, Vargas turned to Lupe. "What could be so important that he can't even entrust it to a telegram? Why can't he give me a hint?"

"I don't know," Lupe said. "But it worries me that he wants you to come to him."

"Woman, what are you talking about? It is a compliment!"

"Maybe it is, but maybe he simply wants you in where he can keep an eye on you. You command one of the last of the independent armies. If he has control of you, he has everything."

"You forget," Vargas said, "he has everything anyway. He has personal command of five times as many men as I do. Besides, John Gatt is my friend. We went to school together in East Los Angeles."

"Oh, I know all that," Lupe said. "But sometimes friendship doesn't last long when it's a question of who's going to have the supreme power."

Vargas said, "I have no ambitions for any more power than I got."

"But does Gatt know that?"

"He knows it," Vargas said, and he sounded sure, but not absolutely sure.

"But maybe he doesn't believe it," Lupe said. "After all, power changes a man. You've seen how it's changed some of the other generals."

"Yes, I know. The Russian and Vietnamese independents. But they can't hold out against Gatt. This time the world is going to be under a single command. John Gatt is going to be the first supreme ruler of Earth."

"Is he worthy of that?" Lupe asked.

"It doesn't matter," Vargas said, annoyed. "It's an idea whose time has come. Life has been too crazy with everybody fighting everybody else. One supreme military commander for all Earth is going to work a lot better for everyone."

"Well," Lupe said, "I hope so. So are we going?"

Vargas thought about it. Despite the brave front he had shown to Lupe, he was not without his doubts. Who could tell what Gatt might do? It would not be the first time a victorious general made sure of his position by executing his field generals under pretext of throwing a party. Still, what was the alternative? The men of the Second Route Army were personally loyal to Vargas, but in a showdown battle, Gatt and his fivefold superiority in men and material would have to prevail.

And Vargas had no desire for the supreme command. He was a good field general. But he was not cut out for supreme command and had no desire to it. Gatt ought to know that about him. He had said it often enough.

"I will go see Gatt."

"And me?" Lupe asked.

"You'll be safe here with my troops."

"Don't be ridiculous," Lupe said. "Where you go, I go. That's what a Camp Follower does."

Vargas had been fighting in Italy before Gatt ordered him to airlift his army to California for the showdown with Wiedermayer, so he hadn't much idea of the level of destruction in America. His flight by Air Force jet from San Francisco to Ground Zero, Texas, showed him plenty of burned-out cities and displaced populations.

But Ground Zero itself looked all right. It was a new city which Gatt had created. In the center of it was a big sports palace, larger than the Coliseum or the Astrodome or any of those old-world sports palaces. Here warrior-athletes and cheerleaders from all over the world could assemble for the sports rituals of the military.

Vargas had never seen so many generals (and generals'

ladies) in his life. All of General Gatt's field commanders were there, men who had been fighting the good fight for military privilege all over the world. Everybody was in a good mood, as may be imagined.

Vargas and Lupe checked into the big convention hotel which had been especially built for this occasion. They went immediately up to their hotel room.

"Eh," Lupe said, looking around at the classy furnishings of their suite, "this is ver' nice, ver' nice."

Actually she could speak perfectly good English, but in order to be accepted among the other Camp Followers who hadn't been raised with her advantages, she had decided that she had to speak with a heavy accent of some sort.

Lupe and Vargas had had to carry up their own luggage to the room since the hotel was so new the bellboys didn't have security clearances yet.

General Vargas was still dressed for combat. He wore the sweat-stained black khaki uniform of the 30th Chaco campaign, his most famous victory, and with it the lion insignia of a Perpetual Commander in the Eternal Corps.

He set down the suitcases and dropped into a chair with a *moue* of annoyance: he was a fighting general, not a luggage-carrying general. Lupe was standing nearby gaping at the furniture. She was dressed in her best pink satin whore's gown. She had a naughty square crimson mouth, a sexy cat's face, snaky black hair, and legs that never stop coming above a torso that would not let go. Yet despite her beauty she was a woman as tough in her own way as the general, albeit with skinnier legs.

Vargas was heavyset, unshaven, with a heavy slouchy face and a small scrubby beard that was coming in piebald. He had given up shaving because he didn't think it looked sufficiently tough.

Lupe said to him, "Hey, Xaxi [her own pet name for him], what we do now?"

Vargas snarled at her, "Why you talk in Russian accent? Shut up, you don't know nothing. Later we go to meeting room and vote."

"Vote?" Lupe said. "Who's going to vote?"

"All the generals, dummy."

"I don't get it," Lupe said. "We're fascists; we don't need no stinkin' votes."

"It's lucky for you that I love you," Vargas says, "Because sometimes you're so stupid I could kill you. Listen to me, my baby vulture, even fascists have to vote sometimes, in order to arrive fairly at the decision to keep the vote away from everyone else."

"Ah," Lupe said. "But I thought that part was understood."

"Of course it's understood," Vargas said. "But we can only count on it for sure after there's been a vote among ourselves agreeing that that's how things are going to be. Otherwise we might lose everything we've worked for. The vote is necessary to secure our beloved revisionist counterrevolution."

"I guess that's true," Lupe said, scratching her haunch, then, remembering her manners, quickly scratching Vargas' haunch. She went to the refrigerator and got herself a drink of tequila, champagne, and beer, her favorite mixture.

"Is that all this vote's about?" she asked Vargas.

Vargas was sitting in the living room with his spurred heels up on the coffee table. The coffee table scratched nicely. Vargas knew that they probably put in new coffee tables for each new group of generals who came through. But he enjoyed scratching it anyway. He was a simple man.

"We got also other things we got to vote about," he told her.

"Do I have to vote too?" Lupe said.

"Naah," Vargas said. "You're a woman. Recently we voted to disenfranchise you."

"Good," Lupe said, "voting is a bore."

Just then there was a knock at the door.

"Come in!" Vargas called out.

The door opened and a tall goofy-looking guy, with droopy lips and narrow little eyes, wearing a gray business suit, came in. "You Vargas?" he said.

"Yeah," Vargas said. "And try knocking before you come in next time or I break your back."

"This is business," the guy said. "I've brought the bribe."

"Oh, why didn't you say so?" Vargas asked. "Sit down, have a drink."

The goofy-looking guy took a thick envelope out of an inside jacket pocket and handed it to Vargas. Vargas looked into the envelope. It was stuffed with thousand-eagle double simoleon bills.

"Hell," Vargas said, "you can barge in any old time. What is this for, or shouldn't I ask?"

"I told you; it's a bribe," the guy said.

"I know it's a bribe," Vargas said. "But you haven't told me what, specifically, I'm being bribed for."

"I thought you knew. Later, when the voting starts, we want you to vote yes on Proposition One."

"You got it. But what *is* Proposition One?"

"That civilians should henceforth be barred from the vote until such time as the military high command decides they are reliable."

"Sounds good to me," Vargas said.

After the guy left, Vargas turned to Lupe, grinning. He was very happy about the bribe, even though he would have voted yes on Proposition One anyhow. But bribes were traditional in elections—he knew that from the history books, to say nothing of the oral tradition. Vargas would have felt unliked and neglected if General Gatt had not thought him worth the bother to bribe.

He wanted to explain this to Lupe but she was a little dense, tending not to understand the niceties. But what the hell, she looked great in her pink satin whore's nightgown.

"Come in, old boy, come in!" That was Gatt's voice, booming out into the anteroom. Vargas had just arrived and given his name to the prune-faced clerk in the ill-fitting Battle Rangers uniform, clerical division.

It was gratifying to Vargas that Gatt asked for him so soon after his arrival. He would not have liked to cool his heels out in the waiting room, even though he would have been in good company. General Lin was there, having just secured China and Japan for Gatt's All-Earth Defensive League. General Leopold was there, plump and ridiculous in his complicated uniform copied from some South American general's fantasy. He had completed the conquest of South America as far south as Patagonia. Below that, who cares? Generalissimo Reitan Dagalaigon was present, the grim-faced Extremaduran whose Armada de Gran Destructividad had secured all of Europe west of the Urals. These were famous men whose names would live in history. Yet he, Vargas, was ushered into Gatt's private office before all the rest of them.

John Odoacer Gatt was tall with flashing eyes and a charismatic manner. He showed Vargas to a seat and poured him a drink and laid out two lines for him without even asking. Gatt was known as an imperious entertainer.

"We've won the war, buddy," Gatt said to Vargas. "The whole thing. All of it. Everything. It's the first time in the history of mankind that the entire human race has been under a single command. It is an unprecedented opportunity."

Vargas blinked. "For what?"

"Well," Gatt said, "for one thing, we are finally in a position to bring peace and prosperity to the human race."

"Wonderful ideals, sir."

"Actually," Gatt said, "I'm not so sure how we can turn a profit on this."

"Why do you say that, *mi general*?"

"It has been a long and costly war. Most countries' economies are wrecked. It will be a long time before things can be put straight. Many people will go hungry, maybe even starve. It'll be difficult even for the military to turn a buck."

"But we knew all this," Vargas said. "We discussed this in detail during the war. Of course there will be a difficult period of recovery. How could it be otherwise? It may take a hundred years, or even longer. But we are humans, and under the stable rule of the military we will recover and bring universal prosperity to all."

"That, of course, is our dream," Gatt said. "But suppose we could speed it up? Suppose we could go directly to the next stage? Suppose we could move directly from this, our victory, to prosperity for everyone on Earth? Wouldn't that be splendid, Getulio?"

"Of course, of course," Vargas said. John Odoacer Gatt was getting him a little nervous. He didn't know what this was leading up to. "But how could this be possible?"

"Let's talk more about it after the vote tomorrow," Gatt said.

163

* * *

The delegates' voting room was a large and circular chamber equipped with comfortable chairs and a cluster of overhead lighting. In the center was a circular stage that revolved slowly so that those in the center would by turns be facing all the delegates. On the platform was the steering committee for the first provisional and temporary world military government.

The generals, Vargas included, voted in a brisk and unanimous manner to disenfranchise all civilians outside of those few approved ones already assembled at the delegate hall. The civilians were stripped of the vote, *habeas corpus*, the Bill of Rights, the Constitution, and all other liberal encumbrances until such time as they could be relied upon to vote in a prescribed manner. This was a very important measure because the military had found out long ago that civilians were inherently untrustworthy and even traitorous.

Next the generals faced the serious question of disarmament, or, as they called it, unemployment. Disarmament meant there would be hard times ahead because war on Earth was finished as a business since everybody was now under a unified command and there was no one to fight. None of the generals liked the idea of giving up war entirely, however, and General Gatt said there might be a way around that and promised there would be an announcement about that later.

The conference ended with a good cheer and boisterous camaraderie among the various military satraps. Vargas very much enjoyed the reception afterwards, where Lupe made a big hit in her blue, yellow and red ball gown.

After the reception, General Gatt took Vargas aside and asked to meet him tomorrow morning at eight hundred hours sharp at the Ground Zero Motor Pool.

"I have a proposition to put to you," Gatt said. "I think you will find it of interest.

Vargas, accompanied by Lupe, was at the Ground Zero Motor Pool at the appointed hour. That morning he was wearing his sash of Commander in the Legion of Death, and also his campaign medals from the sacking of New York. He'd come a long way from when he was a mere bandit's apprentice.

Soon they were speeding out of the city into the flat desert countryside. It was a time of blooming, and there were many little wild flowers carpeting the desert floor with delicate colors.

"This is really nice," Vargas said.

"It used to belong to some Indian tribe," the driver said. "I can never remember which one. They're all gone now to Indianola."

"What's that?"

"Indianola is the new industrial suburb in Mississippi where we're relocating all the Indians in America."

"They used to be all scattered around the country, didn't they?" Vargas asked.

"They sure did," the driver said. "But it was sloppy that way."

"Seems a pity, though," Vargas said. "Indians have been in the country a long time, haven't they?"

"They were always griping anyhow," the driver said. "Don't worry, they'll get used to our way of doing things."

The secret installation was in a tangle of hills some thirty miles west of Ground Zero. General Gatt came out of his temporary headquarters to greet Vargas. There was a pretty young woman with him. Gatt had thoughtfully brought along his mistress, a young lady named Lola Montez—not the original one, a relative, these names tend to run in the family—who immediately put her arm in Lupe's and took her away for cigarettes, dope, coffee, bourbon, and gossip. Generals' mistresses are good entertainers and it's traditional for the military to be hospitable.

Once the two generals were alone, they could settle down to business. First some small talk about how the armed forces security groups were successfully doing away with anyone who felt that things should be handled in a different way. Most of these malcontents were quiet now. It was amazing what the Central Committee had been able to do in the way of cleaning things up.

"It's a beginning," General Gatt said. "These ideas of social perfectability have been around as long as there has been a military. But this is the first time we've had all the soldiers on our side."

General Vargas asked, "What are you going to do about local groups who want to do their own thing or worship their own gods—that sort of stuff?"

"If they really want freedom, they can join the military," Gatt said. "Our fighting men enjoy perfect freedom of religion."

"And if they don't want to join the military?"

"We tell them to shut up and go away," Gatt said. "And if they don't, we shoot them. It saves a lot of arguing, and helps us avoid all the cost of keeping prisons and guards."

General Gatt explained that one of the great advantages of universal peace was that world government could finally afford to put some money into worthwhile projects.

"Oh," Vargas said, "you mean like feeding the poor and stuff like that?"

"I don't mean that at all," Gatt said. "That's been tried and it hasn't worked."

"You're right," Vargas said. "They just keep on coming back for more. But what sort of worthwhile project do you mean?"

"Come with me and I'll show you," Gatt said.

They left General Gatt's office and went to the command car. The driver was a short, thickset, Mongolian-looking fellow with long bandit moustaches, wearing a heavy woollen vest in spite of the oppressive heat. The driver saluted smartly and opened the door for the generals. They got into the command car and drove for twenty minutes, stopping at a huge hangerlike building all by itself on the desert. Guards let them through a concertina of barbed wire to a small side door that led inside.

The building was really huge. From the inside it looked even larger. Gazing up toward the ceiling, Vargas noticed several birds fluttering overhead. But amusing as this spectacle was, what he saw next took his breath away, leaving him gasping in amazement.

He said to Gatt, "Is this real, John, or some optical illusion you're projecting?"

General Gatt smiled in his mysterious way that seemed so easy but was not. "It's real enough, Getulio, old boy. Look again."

Vargas looked. What he saw, towering many stories above him, was a spaceship. Lupe had shown him enough drawings and diagrams in newspapers like *The Brazilian Enquirer* and others of that ilk for him to know what it was. It was unmistakably a spaceship, colored a whale gray and with tiny portholes and a dorsal fin.

"It's amazing, sir." Gatt said, "Just amazing."

"Bet you never knew we had this," Gatt said.

"I had no idea," Vargas assured him.

"Of course not," Gatt said. "This has been kept a

secret from everybody except the ruling council. But you're a part of that ruling council now, Getulio old boy, because I'm appointing you a freely-elected member of it as of today.''

"I don't get it," Vargas said. "Why me?''

"Come inside the ship,'' Gatt said. "Let me show you a little more.''

There was a motorized ramp that led up into the interior of the ship. Gatt took Vargas' arm and led him up.

Vargas felt at home almost immediately. The interior of the ship looked exactly like what he had seen on old *Star Trek* reruns. There were large rooms filled with panels of instruments. There were indirect lighting panels of rectangular shape. There were technicians who wore pastel jumpsuits with high collars. There were avocado green wall-to-wall carpets. It was just what Vargas would have expected if he'd thought about it. He expected to see Spock come out of a passageway at any moment.

"No, we don't have Spock here,'' Gatt said in answer to Vargas' unspoken question. "But we've got a lot more important stuff than some pointy-eared alien. Let me give you a little quiz, Vargas, just for fun. What is the first thing a warrior thinks about when he looks over his new battleship?''

Vargas had to give that some serious thought. He wished Lupe were here with him. Although she was stupid and only a woman, she was very good at supplying, through some mysterious feminine intuition, answers which Vargas had on the tip of his tongue but couldn't quite come up with.

Fortunately for him, this time the answer came unbidden. "Guns!'' he said.

"You got it!'' Gatt said. "Come with me and let me show you the guns on this sucker.''

Gatt led him to a small car of the sort used to drive the long distances between points in a ship. Vargas tried to remember if they'd had a car like that on *Star Trek*. He thought not. He thought this ship was larger than the Enterprise. He liked that. He was not afraid of big things.

The little car hummed down the long, evenly lit passageway deep in the interior of the ship. General Gatt was reeling off statistics as they went, explaining how many battalions of men in Darth Vader helmets could be fit into the attack bays, how many tons of rations in the forms of beef jerky and bourbon could be stored in a thousand hundredweights of standard mess kits, and other important details. Soon they reached the area of the ship's primary armament. Vargas looked admiringly at the large projector tubes, the paralysis wavelength radio, the vibratory beamer, which could shake apart a fair-sized asteroid. His fingers itched to get on the controls of the tractor and pressor beams. But General Gatt told him he would have to be patient for a little while longer. There was nothing around to shoot at. And besides, the main armament wasn't quite all hooked up yet.

Vargas was loud in his praise of the work done by the scientists of the military. But Gatt had to set him straight on that.

"We have a lot of good boys, to be sure," Gatt said. "Some of them quite clever. Especially the ones we drafted. This spaceship, however, was not their doing."

"Whose is it then, sir, if I may enquire?" said Vargas.

"It was the work of a special group of civilian scientists, what they call a consortorium. Which simply means a whole bunch of them. It was a joint European-American-Asian effort. And a damned selfish one."

"Why do you say that, sir?"

"Because they were building this ship to get away from us."

"I can hardly believe that, sir," Vargas said.

"It's almost unthinkable, isn't it? They were scared for their puny lives, of course, afraid that they'd all be killed. As it turned out, quite a few of them *did* get killed. I don't know what made them think any respectable military establishment would let them escape from the planet with a valuable spaceship."

"What happened to the scientists, sir?"

"Oh, we drafted them. Put them to work. Their ship was very good but it lacked a few things. Guns, for one. These people had actually thought they could go into outer space without high-powered weaponry. And another problem was that the ships weren't fast enough. We have learned that space is quite a bit larger than some of our previous estimates at the Military College; therefore, we need really fast ships if we're ever to get anywhere."

"Fast ships and strong guns," Vargas mused. "That's just what I would have asked for myself. Did you have any trouble getting those things, general?"

"A little at first," Gatt said. "The scientists kept on saying it was impossible and other downbeat and subversive talk like that. But I handled it. Gave them a deadline, started having executions when our goals weren't met. You'd be amazed how quickly they picked up the pace."

Vargas nodded, having used similar methods himself in his day.

"It's a beautiful ship," Vargas said. "Is it the only one?"

"What you're looking at here," Gatt said, "is the flagship of the fleet."

"You mean there are more ships?" Vargas asked.

"Indeed there are. Or will be soon. We've got the

entire worldwide shipbuilding and automobile industries working on them. We need lots of ships, Getulio.''

''Yessir,'' Vargas said. The trouble was, he couldn't think of anything to use ships for, now that everything was conquered. But he didn't want to come out and say that. He could see there was a little smile on General Gatt's face, so he guessed that he was about to be told something he hadn't known before, but which he would find of considerable interest. He waited for a while, and then decided that Gatt wanted him to ask, so he said, ''Now, about all these ships, sir . . .''

''Yesss?'' said Gatt.

''We need these,'' Vargas hazarded, ''for security—''

Gatt nodded.

''—and to take care of our enemies.''

''Perfectly correct,'' Gatt said.

''The only thing that perplexes me,'' Vargas said, ''is, who exactly *are* our enemies? I mean, sir, that I was under the impression that we don't really *have* any of them left on Earth. Or are there some enemies I haven't heard about?''

''Oh, we don't have any enemies left on *Earth*,'' Gatt said. ''They have gone the way of the buffalo, the cow, the Airedale, and other extinct species. What we have now, General Vargas, is the God-given opportunity to go forth into space, our Earth troops unified for the first time in history, ready and willing to take on anything that comes along.''

''Anything! In space!'' Vargas said, amazed at the size of the idea.

''Yes! Today Earth, tomorrow, the Milky Way, or at least one hell of a good-sized hunk of it.''

''But can we just do that? Take what we want?''

''Why not? If there's anything out there, it's just aliens.''

"It's a wonderful dream, sir. I hope I may be permitted to do my bit for the cause."

Gatt grinned and punched Vargas on the arm.

"I've got a pretty good bit for you, Getulio. How would you like to be my first Marshall of Space, with command of this ship and orders to go forth and check out some new planets for Earth?"

"Me? Sir, you do me too much honor."

"Nonsense, Getulio. You're the best fighting general I've got. And you're the only one I trust. Need I say more?"

Gatt made the announcement to the other generals. First he showed them the spaceship. Then he told them he was going into space on a fact-finding mission, with good old Vargas along to actually run the ship. He and Vargas would take a lot of fighting men along, just in case they ran into anything interesting. Gatt was sure there were new worlds to explore out there, and these new worlds, in the manner of new worlds since the beginning of recorded history, were going to bring in millions.

The generals were enthusiastic about the expansion of Earth military power and the promise of a good return on the military business.

Working night and day, the ship was soon provisioned. Not long after that, the armament was all bolted into place. When they tried it out it worked perfectly, all except for one missile which unaccountably got out of control and took out Kansas City. A letter of regret to the survivors and a posthumous medal for all concerned soon put *that* to rights, however. Shortly afterwards, ten thousand heavily armed shock troops with full equipment marched aboard. It was time for Earth to make its debut in space.

There Will Be No War After This One

* * *

The ship went through its trial runs in the solar system without a problem. Once past Neptune, Vargas told the engineers to open her up. Space was big; there was no time to dawdle. The ship ran up to speed without a tremor.

Lastly, the hyper-space jump control worked perfectly. They popped out of the wormhole into an area rich with star systems, many of which had nice-looking planets.

Time passed. Not too much of it, but enough so you know you've really gone somewhere.

Soon after this passage of time, the communications officer reported a tremble of movement on the indicator of the Intelligence Detector. This recent invention was a long-range beam which worked on something the scientists called Neuronal Semi-Phase Amplification, or NSPA. The Military-Scientific Junta in charge of technology felt that a detector like this would be useful for finding a race that might be worth talking to.

"Where's the signal coming from?"

"One of them planets out there, sir," the communications officer said, gesturing vaguely at the vast display of stars visible through the ship's transparent shield.

"Well, let's go there," Vargas said.

"Have to find what star it belongs to first," the communications officer said. "I'll get right on it."

Vargas noticed Gatt, who, from the luxury of his suite which was supplied with everything a fighting man could want—women, guns, food, booze, dope—told him to carry on.

Vargas gave the orders to carry on at best speed.

The big spaceship drilled onward through the vacuum of space.

DeepDoze technology let the soldiers pass their time in unconsciousness while the ship ate up the parsecs. The special barbarian shock troops were stacked in hammocks eight or ten high. The sound of ten thousand men snoring was enormous but not unexpected. One man from each squad was detailed to stay awake to brush flies off the sleepers.

More time passed, and quite a few light years sped by, when a flash of green light from the instrumentation readout telltale told the duty officer that they were nearing the source of the signal.

He got up and went to the captain's quarters in the quickest way, by express elevator and pneumo tube.

Vargas was in deep sleep when a hand tapped him lightly on the shoulder.

"Hmmmf?"

"Planet ahead, sir."

"Call me for the next one."

"I think you'd better check this out, sir."

Vargas got out of bed grumpily and followed the man down to the Communications Area.

"Something is coming through," the operator of the Intelligence Detector said.

General Vargas looked over his shoulder. "What've you got there, son?"

"I think it's an intelligent bleep," the operator said.

General Vargas blinked several times, but the concept did not come clear. He glared at the operator, sucking his lips angrily until the operator hastily said, "What I'm saying, sir, is that our forward-scanning intelligence-seeking beam has picked up a trace. This may be nothing, of course, but it's possible that our pattern-matching program has found an intelligent pattern which, of course, argues the presence of intelligent life."

"You mean," Vargas said, "that we are about to discover our first intelligent race out in the galaxy?"

"That is probably the case, sir."

"Great," Vargas said, and announced to his crew and soldiers that they should wake up and stand by.

The planet from which the signal had come was a pretty place with an oxygen atmosphere and plenty of water and trees and sunshine. If you wanted some nice-looking real estate, this planet could be a good investment, except that it was a long commute back to Earth. But this was not at all what Vargas and his men had been looking for. The various drone probes sent out from Earth in the last century had already found plenty of real estate. Robot mining in the asteroids had already dropped the price of minerals to unprecedented lows. Even gold was now commonly referred to as yellow tooth-filling material. What the Earthmen wanted was people to conquer, not just another real estate subdivision in deep space.

The Earth ship went into orbit around the planet. General Vargas ordered down an investigation team, backed up by a battle group, it in turn backed up by the might of the ship, to find the intelligent creatures on this planet, which in the planetary catalogue was called Mazzi 32410A.

A quick aerial survey showed no cities, no towns, not even a hamlet. More detailed aerial surveys failed to show the presence of pastoral hunters or primitive farmers. Not even barefooted fruit gatherers could be found. Yet still the intelligence probe on the ship continued to produce its monotonous beep, sure and unmistakable sign that intelligent life was lurking somewhere around. Vargas put Colonel John Vanderlash in charge of the landing party.

* * *

Colonel John Vanderlash brought along a portable version of the Intelligence Detector, for it seemed possible that the inhabitants of this planet had concealed themselves in underground cities.

The portable intelligence beam projector was mounted on an eight-wheeled vehicle capable of going almost anywhere. A signal was soon picked up. Vanderlash, a small man with big shoulders and a pockmarked face, directed his driver to follow it. The crew of the eight-wheeler stood to their guns, since intelligent beings were known to be dangerous. The were ready to retaliate at the first sign of hostile intent, or even sooner.

They followed the beam signal into an enormous cave. As they moved deeper into it, the signal grew stronger, until it approximated Intelligence Level 5.3, the equivalent of a man thinking about doing the *New York Times* crossword puzzle. The driver of the foremost assault vehicle shifted to a lower gear. The vehicle crept forward slowly, Colonel Vanderlash standing in the prow. He figured the intelligent beings had to be around here somewhere, probably just around the corner . . .

Then the operator announced that the signal was fading.

"Stop!" Vanderlash said. "We've lost them! Back up!"

The vehicle backed. The signal came back to strength.

"Stop here!" Vanderlash said, and the eight-wheeler skidded to a stop. They were in the middle of the signal's field of maximum strength.

The men stared around them, fingers on triggers, breaths bated.

"Doesn't anyone see anything?" Vanderlash asked.

There was a low mutter of denial among the men. One of them said, "Ain't nothin' here but them moths, sir."

"Moths?" Vanderlash said. "*Moths?* Where!"

"Right ahead of us, sir," the driver said.

Vanderlash looked at the moths dancing in the vehicle's yellow headlight beam. There were a lot of them. They darted and flashed and turned and cavorted and twirled and sashayed and dodged and danced and fluttered and crepusculated and do-si-doed.

There was a pattern to their movements. As Vanderlash watched, a thought came to him.

"Point the intelligence beam at them," he said.

"At the *moths*, sir?" the intelligence beam operator asked incredulously.

"You heard me, trooper. Do what you're told."

The operator did as he was told. The dial on the intelligence machine immediately swung to 7.9, the equivalent of a man trying to remember what a binomial equation was.

"Either some wise guy aliens are playing tricks on us," Vanderlash said, "or . . . or . . ."

He turned to his second in command, Major Lash LeRue, who was in the habit of filling in his superior officer's thoughts for him when Colonel Vanderlash didn't have time to think them himself.

"Or," Major LaRue said, "the moths on this planet have developed a group intelligence."

It took the Communications Team less than a week to crack the communications code which the moth entity employed. They would have solved it quicker if any of them had thought to compare the moths' dot and dash pattern with that of Morse Code.

"Are you trying to tell me," Vargas said, "that these alien moths are communicating by Morse Code?"

"I'm afraid so, sir," the communications officer said. "But it's not my fault, sir. Furthermore, these moths are acting like a single entity."

"What did the moth entity say to you?"

"It said, 'Take your leader to me.' "

Vargas nodded. That made sense. Aliens were always saying things like that.

"What did you tell it?" Vargas asked.

"I said we'd get back to him."

"You did good," Vargas said. "General Gatt will want to hear about this."

"Hot damn," Gatt said. "Moths, huh? Not exactly what we were looking for, but definitely a beginning. Let's get down there and talk with this—you couldn't call him a guy, could you?"

Down in the cave, Gatt and Vargas were able to communicate with the moth entity with the assistance of the Chief Signalman. It was an eerie moment. The Earthmen's great battle lanterns cast lurid shadows across the rocky floor. In the cave opening, flickering in a ghostly fashion, the moths spun and fluttered, darted and dived, all cooperating to produce Morse signals.

"Hello," Gatt said. "We're from Earth."

"Yes, I know," the Moth entity said.

"How'd you know that?"

"The other creature told me."

"What other creature?"

"I believe he is referring to me," a voice said from deep in the cave.

It startled the Earthmen. Every gun trained on the cave entrance. The soldiers watched, some breathing shallowly and others with bated breath. And then, through the swirling mists and the multi-colored brilliance of the searchlights, a figure like that of a small, oddly-shaped man stepped into the light.

The alien was small and skinny and entirely bald. His ears were pointed and he had small antennae growing out of his forehead. Everybody knew at once that he was an alien. If there was any doubt of that, it was soon expunged when the alien opened his mouth. For out of that rosebud-shaped orifice came words in recognizably colloquial English, the very best kind.

Gatt directed the Telegrapher to ask, "First of all, Alien, how come you speak our language?"

The alien replied, "We have long been in contact with your race, for we are those you refer to as Flying Saucer people. When we first established a presence on your world of Earth, a foolish clerical error led us to believe that Morse was your universal language. By the time we discovered our error, Morse was firmly established in our language schools."

"Oh. That accounts for it, then," Gatt said. "It would have been too much of a coincidence for you people to have developed the English language on your own."

"I quite agree," the alien replied.

"At least we have the language problem out of the way," Gatt said. "We can't go on referring to you as 'The Alien.' What shall we call you?"

"My people are called Magellenics in your language," the Alien said. "And we all have the same last name. So you could either call me Magellenic, which is also the name of my planet, or Hurtevert, which is my first name."

"Hurtevurt Magellenic," Gatt said. "Quite a mouthful. I suppose there's an explanation for why you're called 'Magellenic.' I mean we have a word like that in our own language."

"We borrowed the word from your language," Hurtevert said. "We liked the sound of it better than our previous name for the planet, Hzuüutz-kril."

"Ah. Makes sense. Now, is this planet your home world? If so, where's everybody else?"

"It is not my home world," Hurtevert said. "This is a world populated solely by intelligent moths. It is far from my home world."

"Whatcha doing here? Exploring or something?"

"No, General. I was sent here as a Watcher by the members of my underground. I was watching for your great ship."

"How'd you know we'd be coming?"

"We didn't. We just sent out Watchers in case somebody *does* came along. You see, my people, the Magellenics, are in a whole lot of trouble."

Gatt turned to Vargas and remarked, "You know, it isn't enough we are the first Earthmen in history to contact aliens, these have to be aliens with problems, yet."

"I don't think that possibility was ever forecast," Vargas said.

"Well," Gatt said, "we may as well hear this creature's problems in comfort. This cave is decidedly chilly, and I don't believe we brought along any refreshment." He turned to the alien, and, speaking through his Telegrapher, said, "How about coming aboard my ship and we'll talk it over? I presume you breathe oxygen and drink liquids and all that."

"I have long missed your excellent intoxicants," Hurtevert said. "Yes, lead the way, my leader."

"This is starting out well," Gatt remarked to Vargas as they started back to the ship.

When he was comfortable, with a glass of Irish whiskey in his hand, and a Slim Jim to munch on, Hurtevert said, "Long have we of Planet Magellenic lived as free entities. But now our planet has been conquered by a cruel foe whose customs are not ours."

"Somebody took over your planet, did they?" Gatt remarked. "Tell us about it."

Hurtevert struck an orator's pose and declaimed, "Dank they were and glaucous-eyed, the ugly and bad-smelling Greems who attacked us from a far star-system. They came down in spider-shaped ships, and red ruin followed in their wake. Not content with murder, rapine, and pillage, they humiliated us by making us worship a giant ragwort."

"That's really low," Vargas said.

"All in all it's intolerable. We'd much rather you Earthians took us over."

Hurtevert made an odd smacking sound. Gatt turned to Vargas. "What was that?"

"It sounded to me like a wet kiss," Vargas said.

"That's disgusting," Vargas said, "but it shows a good spirit. Want us to take over your planet, huh?"

"Yes," the alien sang, "we want to be ruled by you, nobody else will do, bo bo padoo. Do you like it? It is a song we sing to keep up our courage in the dark times ahead. You must rescue us. Let me show you pictures of the Greems."

The pictures, made by a process similar to Polaroid, showed creatures who seemed to be a cross between a spider, a crab, and a wolverine.

"Hell," Gatt said, "anyone would want to be rescued from something like that. Tough fighters, are they?"

"Not at all," Hurtevert assured him. "I can assure you that with your brave fighting men and superior weaponry, you will have no trouble defeating them and taking over my planet. It will be easy, for you see, the enemy has withdrawn all of their forces except a local garrison. Once you take them over, the place is yours. And you will find Magellenic is a very good planet, filled with good-looking women who admire military Earthmen, to say nothing of gold and precious things. This, gentlemen, is a planet worth having.''

Gatt said, ''Sounds pretty good, huh Vargas?''

''And we would like to formally invest you, General Gatt, with the hereditary kingship of our planet.''

''Do you hear that?'' Gatt said to Vargas. ''They want to make me king! But forget about the kingship thing. What's really important is the fact that we can take over this whole planet for the profit of Earth. And it'll be one of the easiest wars on record. And what better way of meeting new peoples than by conquering them, eh?''

''You know something?'' Vargas said. ''You've really got something there.''

To the alien, Gatt said, ''OK, son, you've got a deal.''

''That is wonderful,'' the alien said.

Just then a small dot of light appeared in a corner of the room. It grew, and then it expanded.

''Well, rats,'' said Hurtevert. ''Just what I needed.''

''What is it?''

''It's the Galactic Effectuator.''

''Who's that?'' Gatt asked.

''One of the busybodies from Galactic Central come to tell us how to run our lives.''

''You didn't mention anything about Galactic Central.''

''I can't tell you the entire history of the galaxy in an hour, can I? Galactic Central is a group of very ancient civilizations at the core of this galaxy, just as the name implies. The Centerians, as they are called, try to maintain the status quo throughout the galaxy. They want to keep things as they used to be. If they had their way, they'd go back to the Golden Age before the Big Bang, when things were really quiet.''

"They wouldn't let us help you take back your planet?"

Hurtevert shook his head. "The Galactic Arbitrators never OK any change. If they see what you're up to, they'll nix it."

"Are they powerful enough to do that?"

"Baby, you'd better believe it," Hurtevert said.

"So the war's off."

"Not necessarily." Hurtevert took an object from the pouch attached to his waist and opened it. It was a long pole wound with fine wire. He handed it to Vargas.

"Wave that at him before he has a chance to deliver his message. He'll go away and report to his superiors. Galactic Center will figure there was a mistake, since no one would dare zap a Galactic Effectuator. They will send another Effectuator."

"So they do send another Effectuator. Am I supposed to zap that one, too?"

"No. You're allowed only one mistake by Galactic Center. After that, they crush you."

"How does zapping the first one help us?"

"It gives us time. In the time between the first and second Effectuators, you'll be able to occupy our planet and establish your rule. When the second Effectuator comes and learns the situation, he'll confirm you in power."

"Why would the second Effectuator do that when the first one wouldn't?"

"I told you, it's because Galactic Center tries to preserve any political situation its effectuators discover. It's *change* that Galactic Central is opposed to, not any particular instance of it. Trust me, I know about these things. When he comes in, just wave the rod at him."

"We don't want to kill anyone," Gatt said. "Unnecessarily, that is."

"Don't worry," Hurtevert said. "You can't kill an Effectuator."

And then the Galactic Effectuator appeared before them. He was very tall and seemed to be made entirely of metal. That, and his flat, tinny voice, confirmed Vargas's suspicion that the Effectuator was a robot.

"Greetings," said the Effectuator. "I have come from Galactic Center to bring a message . . ."

Gatt gave Vargas a meaningful look.

"Therefore," said the Effectuator, "know all men by these presents—"

"Now?" Vargas asked in a whisper.

"Yes, now," Gatt said.

Vargas waved the pole. The Galactic Effectuator looked startled, then vanished.

"Where did he go?" Vargas asked the alien.

"Into a holding space," the Alien said. "He'll reassemble himself there, then report back to Galactic Center."

"You're sure he's not hurt?"

"I told you, you can't hurt an Effectuator because he's a robot. In fact, only robots are permitted to be Galactic Effectuators."

"Why is that?"

"To ensure that they won't defend themselves if attacked by barbarians such as yourself."

"Well, whatever," Gatt said. "Let's get on with business. Where's this planet of yours we're going to conquer? Excuse me, I mean liberate."

"Take me to your computer," Hurtevert said. "I will program him to take us there."

The Earthship, with its sleeping troopers and its card-playing officers, hurtled on through space. Several time periods passed without event. Vargas wanted to know why it was taking so long. Hurtevert rechecked his calculations and told him they were almost there. Vargas went to report this to Supreme Commander Gatt. While he was reporting, the Intelligence Detector sounded off. The planet Magellenic lay dead ahead.

"Go get 'em, tiger," Gatt said to Vargas.

"But I don't know how," Vargas said. "An entire planet. . . ."

"You remember how we used to sack cities, don't you?"

Vargas grinned and nodded. How could he forget.

"Just go to Magellenic and do the same thing. It's just the scale that changes."

There was really no way of finding out in advance how much armament the alien occupiers of Magellenic might put up against them. Vargas decided to try a bold yet conservative tactic. He'd just go in and take over the joint. What the hell, it had worked for the Hittites.

The great ship from Earth roared down through the atmosphere. Hurtevert pointed out the leading city on the planet, the one from which all power emanated. That made it convenient. Vargas sent out five thousand shock troops armed with horrifying and instantaneous weapons. The remaining five thousand were kept in reserve. As it turned out, they weren't needed.

General Vargas wrote home soon after the successful conquest of Magellenic:

Dear Lupe, I promised to tell you about the invasion. It went very well. So well, in fact, that at first we suspected some sort of treachery. We airdropped a first force of a thousand picked men, armed to the teeth, into the big square in the middle of the main city here, which is called Magellopolis. Our boys landed during a folk dancing festival and there was quite a bit of confusion, as you can imagine, since the population thought our boys were demonstrating war dances. We cleared that up soon enough.

The remaining four thousand troopers of the first wave came down just outside the city, since there was no room to pack them into the town square. The lads marched into Magellopolis in good order, and they got an enthusiastic greeting from the citizens, who seemed delighted to see them.

The Magellenics took in the situation quickly, and had flowers and paper streamers handy to give our boys a proper welcome. There were no unfortunate incidents, aside from several local women getting trampled in their eagerness to show our boys a nice welcome.

Magellenic is a very nice planet, prosperous, and with a nice climate except at the poles where we don't go. We have seen no signs of the alien invaders that Hurtevert told us about. Either they are holed up in the hills, or they all left when our ship approached.

Now it is a week later. We have been very busy and I am writing hastily so this letter can go out with the first load of booty which we're sending to Earth.

Our Art Squads have done a find job of combing the planet. As we promised the men, the first haul is theirs.

Frankly, the stuff doesn't look like much. But we've collected whatever we can find in the way of furniture, postage stamps, silver, and precious stones, and that sort of thing.

It's too bad that we have to ship it all back to Earth at government expense and sell it for the troops. But that's what we promised and otherwise they might mutiny.

We're also sending back some of the local food surpluses. I just hope there's a market for cranko nuts and pubble fruit back on Earth. Personally, I can do without it.

I forgot to mention, we are sending back to Earth our first draft of Magellenic workers. We had no trouble collecting them. A lot of people on this planet have volunteered to do stoop labor in the fields and unskilled crap work in the factories for starvation wages. This is useful because nobody on Earth wants to do that stuff anymore.

I'll write again soon. Much love, my baby vulture.

Six months later, Vargas received the following message from General Gatt, now on Earth fulfilling his duties as Supreme Leader and Total Commander:

Getulio, I'm dashing this off in great haste. We need a total change in policy and we need it fast. My accountants have just brought me the news that our occupation is costing us more than it is bringing in by a factor of ten. I don't know how this happened. I always thought one made a profit out of winning a war. You know I've lived by the motto, "To the victor goes the spoils."

But it isn't working that way here. The art treasures we brought back have brought in very little on Earth's art market. In fact, leading art critics have declared that the Magellenics are in a pre-artistic stage of their development! We can't sell their music, either, and their furniture is both un-

comfortable to sit in, ugly to look at, and tends to break easily.

And as if that isn't bad enough, now we have all these Magellenics on Earth doing cheap labor. How can cheap labor not be cost-efficient? My experts tell me we're putting millions of Earth citizens out of work, and using up all our tax revenue because the first thing a Magellenic does when he gets here is to go on the dole until he finds a really good job.

That's the trouble, you see. They're not content to stay in the cheap labor market. They learn fast and now some of them are in key positions in government, health, industry. I wanted to pass a law to keep them out of the good jobs, but my own advisors told me that was prejudiced and nobody would stand for it.

So listen, Getulio, stop at once from sending any more of them to Earth! Be prepared to take back all the ones I can round up and ship back to you. Prepare an announcement saying that the forces of Earth have succeeded in their goal of freeing the Magellenics from the cruel conquerers who had been pressing their faces into the dirt and now they're on their own.

As soon as you can, sooner if possible, I want you to pull all our troops out, cancel the war, end the occupation, and get yourself and your men home as fast as you can.

I forgot to mention, these Magellenics are unbelievably fertile. The ones here on Earth need only about three months from impregnation to birth. They have a whole lot of triplets and quintuplets, too. Getulio, we have to get rid of these moochers fast, before they take over our planet and eat us out of house and home.

There Will Be No War After This One

Close up and come home. We'll think of something new.

When Vargas told the news to Captain Arnold Stone, his Chief Accountant, he asked for an accounting to show how much profit they had been showing during their stay on Magellenic.

"Profit?" Stone said with a short, sardonic laugh. "We've been running at a loss ever since we got here."

"But what about the taxes we imposed?"

"Imposing is one thing, collecting is another. They never seem to have any money."

"What about the Magellenic workers on Earth? Don't they send back some of their wages?"

Stone shook his head. "They invest every cent of it in Earth tax-free municipal bonds. They claim it's an ancient custom of theirs."

"I never liked them from the start," Vargas said. "I always knew they'd be trouble."

"You got that right," Stone said.

"All right, get someone in Communications to prepare an announcement for the population here. Tell them that we've done what we came here to do, that is, free them from the cruel hand of whoever it was who was oppressing them. Now we're going away and they can do their own thing and lots of luck."

"That's a lot," Stone said. "I'd better get the boys in Intelligence to help with the wording."

"Do that," Vargas said. "And tell somebody to get the ships ready for immediate departure."

That was the idea. But it didn't work out that way.

That afternoon, as Vargas sat in his office playing mumbly-peg with his favorite Philippine bolo knife and dreaming of being back with Lupe, there was a flash of

189

brilliance in the middle of the floor. Vargas didn't hesitate a moment when he saw it. He dived under the desk to avoid what he assumed was an assassination attempt.

It was sort of nice, under the desk, even though it was not a particularly sturdy desk, Magellenic furniture-building being what it was. Still, it gave Vargas a feeling of protection, and time to unholster his ivory-handled laser blaster.

A voice said, "If you try to use that on me, you are going to be very sorry."

Vargas peered out and saw, standing in the middle of his office, the characteristic metal skin and flashing eyes of the Galactic Effectuator.

"Oh, it's you," Vargas said, getting out from under the table with as much dignity as circumstances allowed. He reholstered his firearm, took his seat at his desk again, and said, "Sorry about that, Galactic Effectuator. I thought it might be an assassination team. Can't be too careful, you know. Now, what can I do for you?"

"The first thing," the Galactic Effectuator said, "is not to try zapping me again. We let you get away with it once. Try again and the Galactic Forces will nuke you back to the Stone Age. If you think I'm kidding, take a look out the window."

Vargas looked. The sky was dark with ships. They were big ships, as you'd expect of a Galactic force.

"I want to apologize for zapping you earlier," Vargas said. "I was acting on bad advice. I'm glad you've come. You're just in time to hear me declare the end of Earth's occupation. Maybe you'd like to watch us get out of here and go home."

"I know that is what you are planning," the Effectuator said. "I'm here to tell you it's not going to be quite as easy as that."

"Why not?"

"Galactic policy is to keep the status quo, whatever it is. We were unable to prevent you from declaring war on Magellenic. That is the one mistake you're allowed. You've got this place, now you have to keep it."

"Believe me," Vargas said, "this sort of thing will never happen again. Can't we just apologize and forget it?"

"No," said the Effectuator. "You can't get out of it as easily as that. War was your idea, not ours. Now you're stuck with it."

"But the war's over!"

"According to Galactic Rules, the war is only over when those you attacked say it's over. And I can assure you, the Magellenics are very satisfied with things as they are."

"I'm starting to get the feeling," Vargas said, "that these Magellenics tricked us. That Hurtevert and his story! It reminds me of something to do with a bird. But I can't quite remember what."

"Permit me to refresh your memory," the Effectuator said. "I have made a study of birdlife throughout the galaxy, so I know there is a bird called the cuckoo on your planet. It lays its egg in other birds' nests and they take care of it. That is what the Magellenics have done to you Earth folks."

"What in hell are you talking about?" Vargas said, his voice blustery but shaky.

"They get you to take over their planet. They get you to take their surplus workforce to your own world. Once there, you can't get rid of them. But that's what you get for trying to practice charity without taking thought for the consequences."

"Charity, hell! We were doing war!"

"In the Galactic view," the Effectuator said, "war is a form of charity."

"How do you figure?"

"We believe that war entails a number of selfless and exemplary actions. First there's the duty of rapine, which we define as the willingness to transfer large quantities of your planet's best sperm to a civilization that badly needs it. Your troops have done well that way. Next there's the duty of pillage, which is the act of cleansing the artistic life of a conquered people by carting away vast quantities of their inferior art treasures in order to unblock their creative self-expression and allow them to produce newer, better works. Finally we have the duty of education and self-improvement, which you have performed by taking in large numbers of Magellenic's surplus and idle population to your own planet, where you support them until they are smart enough to put your own people out of work."

Vargas thought for a while, then shrugged and said, "You got it right, Galactic Effectuator. But how do we end it?"

"That's always the difficult part," the Effectuator said. "Maybe, with some luck, you can find some other planet that'll be crazy enough to take over both your planet *and* Magellenic. That's the only way you're going to get off the hook."

That is how, upon entering Galactic Civilization, Earth gave up war forever. And that is why there are Earthmen on all the civilized planets of the galaxy. They can be found on the street corners of dusty alien cities. They speak all languages. They sidle up to you and say, "Listen, Mister, would you like to take over a planet with no trouble at all?"

Naturally, no one pays them the slightest attention. Even the newer civilizations have learned that war costs too much and charity begins at home.

We, the People

Jack C. Haldeman II

The eggs were just the way he liked them. Mark ate slowly, enjoying the luxury of a leisurely breakfast. Outside his window the city was beginning to stir. Rain had been programmed for last night and the streets were still damp. Across the room his cat was curled up in a patch of sunlight on the sofa, his tail swishing back and forth. The apartment was quiet and he dragged breakfast out as long as he could. Finally he got up, set his plate on the floor for the cat to lick, and walked across the room to his desk.

"Good morning," he said automatically.

"GOOD MORNING, MARK. DID YOU SLEEP WELL?"

Mark looked at the words as they danced across the screen. "Kind of a bad night," he said. "My arthritis is acting up again."

"THAT'S TOO BAD, MARK. WAS IT YOUR KNEES?"

"No, just my hands this time." He looked at his swollen knuckles and ran them through his thinning gray hair. There were worse things.

"THAT'S THE THIRD TIME THIS MONTH. DO YOU WANT ME TO FLASH DR. CROMWELL?"

"No, that's okay. I'll be seeing him next week."

"DO YOU KNOW WHAT TODAY IS, MARK?"

"Saturday." It couldn't be his birthday. He'd told the desk to stop reminding him of those several years ago.

"TODAY IS APRIL 15TH."

"So what?"

"THIS IS TAX DAY. WE HAVE TO FILE BY MIDNIGHT."

"I forgot," he said.

"YOU HAVE BEEN PUTTING THIS OFF FOR MONTHS. SHALL WE START?"

Mark looked around the room. The cat was busily licking the plate. He felt old. You could block out birthdays, but not the IRS. "I guess we might as well get it over with," he said.

"THIS IS A PATRIOTIC OBLIGATION, MARK. YOU SHOULD FEEL PRIVILEGED TO DO YOUR PART."

"Can the pep talk. Let's go."

"DO YOU WANT THE SHORT FORM OR THE LONG FORM?"

"Don't be stupid."

"I AM REQUIRED BY LAW TO ASK YOU THAT."

"Does anybody use the short form?"

"CERTAIN CONVICTED FELONS MUST USE THE SHORT FORM, HAVING SACRIFICED FREEDOM OF CHOICE."

"I'm not a convicted felon and I'm not an idiot. Let's have the long form."

"VERY WELL, MARK. BASED ON LAST YEAR'S

INCOME OF $52,753.68 YOU HAVE AN ADJUSTED
TAX OF $4,963.47. WOULD YOU LIKE TO SEE THE
CALCULATIONS?''

''Yes.''

Mark scanned the figures as they rolled by. His income
was higher than he'd thought, but not much more than
comfortable what with the prices these days. Semi-
retired, he did occasional projects for a variety of eco-
logical organizations. He worked at home. He didn't get
out much anymore.

''They look okay,'' he said.

''DO YOU WISH TO ITEMIZE THE ALLOCATION
OF YOUR TAX MONEY?''

''Now you're being stupid again. Why else would I
use the long form? Doesn't everybody?''

''PLEASE DON'T BE HARD ON ME, MARK, I'M
ONLY DOING MY JOB. I HAVE TO ASK YOU THAT.
IN RESPONSE TO YOUR QUESTION, ROUGHLY
99.987% OF THE ELIGIBLE TAXPAYERS USE THE
LONG, ITEMIZED FORM.''

Mark nodded. A person would have to be crazy to pass
up the chance to say how his money would be spent.

''AID TO DEPENDENT CHILDREN.''

Mark was old enough to remember the hungry times,
the children who had grown up without hope. ''One hundred dollars,'' he said.

''OFFSHORE DRILLING SUBSIDY.''

''Zero.'' They were almost all gone now, much to
Mark's relief.

''RE-EMPLOYMENT TRAINING PROGRAM.''

''Fifty.''

''NATIONAL ENDOWMENT FOR THE ARTS.''

''Fifty.'' He tried to imagine a life without music,
without the sculptures and paintings all over town. He
remembered how much Mary had liked the weekly con-

certs by the river and he recalled that day in the park with the kids and the dancers. "Make that seventy-five," he said.

"NEUTRON BOMB RESEARCH AND DEVELOPMENT."

Mark laughed. They tried to slip that old chestnut by every year. "Zero," he said. A bomb that killed people and left buildings intact was crazy, pure and simple. If they could refine it so it only killed generals he might be interested.

Mark relaxed and let the categories roll by. He always put his taxes off until the last minute. A lot of people did.

Alice Thompson was an actress. At forty-three her career was just peaking. She had worked her way up through the ranks from community theater to stage productions to Hollywood, from ingenue roles to character parts. She had a comfortable income, good investment advice, a secure career. She portioned out her calculated tax with good humor: the Actors' Old Folks Home, a theater scholarship at her alma mater, the Playwrights' Association, two summer camps specializing in drama, the National Repertory Theatre. She had little interest in the mundane affairs of state and saw no reason to spend any money on them. She had a little left over.

Erik Hesse was a janitor. He was sixty-three and had been a janitor for over forty years, from the day he got married. It hadn't been a bad life, especially after the union came in. These days it was hard to get someone to do nontechnical work, so he made a pretty decent wage. When the time came, Erik went to a tax preparer to fill out how much money he had to allocate. He put it in off-track betting, weather control (he hated shoveling snow off the sidewalk), the sports cable network, two research projects that concerned beer, and women's gymnastics. Erik had a granddaughter who was into somersaults. Even so, he had a little left over when he finished and no place to put it.

Raymond Montonero was a Supreme Court Justice. There was less and less for him to do, however. People were working their problems out together in an aura of optimism that astounded him. It seemed that the more control people had over the government, the more control they used in their daily lives. He carefully allocated his tax bite to the Congressional Library, scientific research and social programs. He worried over the remaining balance for a long time.

Tom Hanna was a red-dirt farmer in the Oklahoma panhandle. His family had worked the same land for five generations and even though it wasn't a large spread, it was theirs. He was a proud man, and when he came in from the fields that Saturday he took his taxes seriously. He allocated the bulk of it to the Farm Bureau and the County Agriculture Commission. The rest he parceled out to the two state universities for operating expenses. He had a boy down at OU playing football and studying to be a veterinarian. Still, he had a little left over.

And so it went that day, all over the country. People put money into the programs that touched their lives and ignored the rest. They turned out to be excellent judges of the things they needed. The quality of life in the country had improved tremendously since the introduction of the Uniform Tax Act.

It had all started with a box on the tax form to support Presidential campaigns. The next box to come along allocated money for the space program. Within two years the Mars project was completely funded. That unexpected success had lobbyists descending on Washington like a plague. Everyone wanted a special box on the tax form. Eventually they all got it.

Economists predicted chaos but what they got was co-operation. People knew what they wanted and for the first time in history they were able to get it. Unpopular projects came to a grinding halt as money for them was withheld. Politicians were forced to be more in tune with the desires of the public. Control of the purse-strings turned out to be the ultimate democratic tool, even more effective than the ballot.

Times changed. They changed for the better.

Mark's cat had climbed onto his lap and fallen asleep. He relaxed in front of the desk, stroking the cat and responding to the programs almost automatically as they rolled across the screen in the quiet room. They were presented to him randomly. Each taxpayer got them in a different order so that position on the list didn't favor any one program over another.

Mark had been doing tax forms for years, so it didn't take much thought. He remembered his mother's last years and increased his amount for Aid to the Elderly. He allocated money for the school lunch program and aid for the handicapped. He supported environmental programs and medical research. Although solar energy was the norm now, he put a few dollars into geothermal studies. He refused to put any money into bailing out two major oil companies. If they couldn't change with the times that was their problem.

He studied last year's military expenditures carefully. What was the sense in having enough weapons to kill everyone on the face of the Earth six times over? He cut back even further than he had last year. He made up the difference in veteran's benefits. Being one himself, he had a vested interest.

Viet Nam had cut a bloody swath through his family before he was born, but he hadn't managed to escape the oil wars and that fiasco in South America. The jungle had cost him two brothers, a hip and a knee. No amount of aid could bring back his brothers or his friends. It had been such a useless loss.

The words on the screen were blurry and when he blinked his eyes he realized he'd been crying. He softly cursed. He slipped one hand out from beneath the cat and wiped his eyes. The words became clear once more.

"THAT'S THE END OF THE LISTING, MARK. YOU STILL HAVE A BALANCE OF $795.32. WOULD YOU LIKE ME TO RUN THE SCREEN AGAIN?"

"No." The tears were coming again, damn it. He blinked his eyes.

"YOU MUST ALLOCATE ALL YOUR TAX MONEY."

He thought of his brothers and the times they'd had growing up. The days seemed bathed in the warm glow of summer sunshine. They were precious days, gone forever. He knew that every person who had died in any war on any side for any cause had been grieved for just as he was grieving now. It tore at his heart. All that pain, all that suffering.

"WOULD YOU LIKE ME TO RUN THE SCREEN AGAIN?"

"No," he said softly.

"WOULD YOU LIKE TO ADD AN ADDITIONAL CATEGORY?"

"Yes." It was barely a whisper.

"READY. ENTER NEW CATEGORY."

"Peace," he said and his single word floated in the quiet apartment.

"COULD YOU PLEASE BE MORE SPECIFIC, MARK?"

"I said *peace*, damn it," he shouted. *"Everlasting, fucking peace!"*

The cat jumped from his lap at the outburst and Mark

pushed his chair back, leaving the desk. His eyes were still full of tears and he felt like a fool.

If he was a fool, though, he wasn't alone. On that particular April 15 over two hundred million taxpayers added their voices to his.

By Christmas it was an accomplished fact.

Wartorn, Lovelorn

Marc Laidlaw

It was summer in the wine country, in the cleft of a hilly vale steeped in green heat. I had a noseful of dust, pollen and sex. Our sticky bodies separated slowly as we sat back in the remains of our picnic, the white cloth dirty and disheveled. Carcasses of roast game hens and rinds of soft cheeses were strewn about. The dry, greedy earth had drunk most of the vintage from a toppled bottle, and what remained we quickly swallowed.

My companion rose, gathered her cast-off skirt and blouse, and went into the trees while running a hand through her blonde locks and smiling back at me. As I twisted the corkscrew into the mouth of the last bottle, I heard a muted whine, a soft explosion, the beginnings of a scream—all in the shady confidence of the forest.

I called to her without remembering her name. She did not answer.

I started to rise, then remembered my own nakedness. My gun lay out in the dust, tangled in my trousers. As I scrambled over the tablecloth, twigs broke and leaf-mould crackled in the woods. I claimed the gun and turned to face the forest. Where were my guardians?

A shadow moved between the trees in hazy webs of light. I saw a glint of red-gold, like the heart of a forest fire. No one had hair like that except my hosts, the royal family.

"Prince?" I called, thinking that somehow he had discovered my indiscretions with his sister last night; and now, in retaliation, he had murdered the innocent I'd picked up at the edge of the woods.

The figure with the flaming hair stopped behind the tree where my friend had fallen. I heard a low chuckle, and despite the heat I felt a chill. That was not the Prince's laughter.

"Don't move!" I cried, my finger less than steady on the trigger.

Out of the shadows she came, still laughing. The rifle strap cut between her breasts, her weapon holstered so that I knew she did not intend to fire on me. Even so, her eyes were a fury.

"Princess," I said.

She mocked me with a shake of her head. "Dear Prince, whatever will I do with you? Was it only last night you filled my ears with promises of fidelity? This is a poor start."

"You've gone too far," I said. "That girl—"

The Princess took a step into the sunlight and her hair turned molten. "Was she important to you?"

"She was innocent," I said, momentarily blinded by her hair but pretending otherwise, not trusting her for even a moment with the knowledge of my vulnerability.

"Should that have saved her?" she asked, her voice tiptoeing around me through spots of glare. I tried to follow her with my gun; she was toying with me.

"If you've a fight to pick with me—"

"Oh, come now. If my father insulted your mother, would she go out of her way to slap him in the face? Don't be ridiculous. She'd pay her soldiers to fight, and plenty of innocents would die. This little 'love' of yours was in my way."

"I didn't love her," I said. "You needn't have bothered."

As the glare receded, and her face went into shadow, I saw the Princess stoop to snatch a pear from our picnic and take a bite. I lowered my gun and began to dress. She stared at me with a curious smile while the juice ran down her chin, her throat. She was dressed like a huntress, in soft brown leather and tall boots. As I began lacing up my shirt, she stopped me with a touch. "Don't," she said. –

"Are you mad?"

Her grip tightened on my wrist. She clenched her teeth behind her smile. "Will you tell on me? Why not carry on as before? Only I will ever know that once you broke your promise."

I tore my arm away from her. "What do you want? We've had our pleasure but it can never happen again. What if we had been discovered last night?"

She took a step closer, pressing against me, her smell an aphrodisiac. "It would have simplified everything. We would be planning a spectacular wedding now. It's what our parents want: the children of both countries formally wed."

I kicked through the remains of the picnic and fled into the woods, knowing that she was on my heels. A few yards into the shadows I came upon the body of the girl whose sweat and musk still flavored my tongue. Fallen leaves clung to the wreck of her face. As I leaned against a tree trunk, the Princess caught me from behind, her nails cutting into my ribs. She twisted me toward her, biting at my lips. I stumbled against the tree, fighting her off, but she grabbed my hair and we both went down into the loam. She was naked beneath her brief leather skirt.

"I don't want this," I said. My body hinted otherwise.

"We're two of a kind, Prince, and you know it."

I made myself relax. She believed my imitation of submission; her eyelids narrowed, pupils drifting to one side. She wasn't seeing me, though her hands were all over my body. She trembled, already close, so close that I could feel myself being sucked along with her.

Then I looked through the grass and my body went cold. She was looking at the twisted limbs, the torn belly, the sun-browned breasts draped in a bloodied blouse. The tree trunk obscured my view, but I knew the Princess had a clear sight of my dead lover's gory face.

"My God!" I rolled free of her. She lay panting in the grass, her body wracked by spasms. I tore myself away from the sight and ran toward my car and my guardians, toward the borders of home.

My private jet left the Princess's airspace shortly after sunset; it was another hour before we circled and came to earth. That was time enough for her to destroy the old pattern of my life, as I soon discovered.

Instead of the black ultralight carriage that normally awaited my return, an ugly armored vehicle idled on the airstrip. Arqui's car. In constant fear of assassination, he never traveled in anything less secure than a street tank. Inside, Prime Minister Arquinian sat breaking pencils and cleaning his fingertips.

"You've done it now," he said as I took an uncomfortable seat beside him. "Mind telling us what happened over there?"

By "us" he meant himself and the Queen Mother, who watched from a two-way in the roof.

"How much do you know?" I asked, casually opening the wet bar which the P.M. never left behind.

"How much?" I could see he was in a rage. "They've declared war! It's finished now, all the treaties. Five years of my life, you ruin in a pleasure jaunt that was meant to ease tensions."

"It was fate," I said with a shrug.

"Well, what happened?"

"I met the Princess."

"The Princess," Mother said, as if she understood perfectly. She had been a princess herself once. "You two had a fight? A lovers' tiff?"

"Lovers!" Arquinian waxed apoplectic. "My God, and it came to this? The casualties are already past counting. Can't you talk to the girl, reason with her, if she's the cause?"

I shook my head, raised my hands. "There's no reasoning with her, she's in a passion. I'm all she wants."

"Well!" said my mother, trying to hide her improper amusement from the P.M.

"Then it's your fault," said Arquinian.

"I haven't killed a soul."

"You haven't patched things up, either. This is juvenile behavior."

He shook a finger at me, as if I were still a child to be reprimanded—but I seized it and bent it backward, out of view of my mother, watching his face whiten while I whispered.

"You don't know what you're saying, Arq. She's irrational. How can I reason with such a girl?"

"I've reasoned with far worse, young man, and so must you. She must be stopped. This war especially must stop."

I relinquished his finger, now properly sprained, and he took it away without showing his distress. But the blood had drained from his ultimatum:

"If you don't do something, Prince, we might turn you over to her."

"Oh, leave him alone, Arqui," said my mother. "We'll do nothing of the sort."

"Thanks, Mum."

I peeked out the window, saw that we'd reached the city. "Look, there's nothing I can do if her father sends armies on her word. The whole family must be insane. I'm surprised you'd risk me in negotiations. She killed my consort, that's what started it."

"You think I don't know you better than that?" said Arquinian.

"I don't care what you know."

With that, I unlatched the door and leapt to the street. The Prime Minister and my mother, for once in accord, screamed after me, but Arqui didn't dare leave his movable fortress. He ordered the drivers to give pursuit, but a military procession, brass horns blaring, marched in the way and several foot soldiers vanished beneath the tank treads before it could be halted. I ducked into an alley, leaving familial duties behind, and dodged through street after street, thankful to be home again.

All I needed now was a place to stay.

For three days I hid in a garret, writing sentimental battle odes and drinking cheap wine. I could find none of my old slumming companions to drink with me. For all their brave treasonous talk and rebellious posturing, they had conceded quietly enough to military induction and now were soldiers, mired in mud and gulping gas at the front, too stupid to command planes or even to push buttons in proper sequence from the safety of underground bunkers.

My greatest poetry was penned during the endless hours of midnight airstrikes. I was touched by the Princess's persistence in striking at the heart of my land. It suited her twisted sense of the romantic. I hated to think she had inspired me, and I fought the idea with increased quantities of wine and pills, but the constant explosions were anodyne to my melancholy, and for the first time in my life I found myself able to harness my passions. However, waking one sunset to reread my morbid ballads, I began to wonder if she might have been correct in drawing parallels between us. My longest poem was a complex conceit in which ballistic equations were subtly derived from, and thinly concealed, the curves of her figure, the clash of phosphor lightning in the highlights of her hair. It ended on a black battlefield, and by the time I laid down my pen, I was shivering in an erotic fever.

Unable to purchase wine or water, and starving for breakfast, I left the confines of that close little room. The smell of bodies and cordite played a part in sending me out into the streets and back to my family, who had by now moved into the Emergency Palace.

The Emergency Palace was a perfect replica of our usual homestead, except that every one of its ornate windows opened onto nothing but dirt, rock and roots. It held the same temperature year-round, wherefore my mother preferred it to the regular Palace. Her shingles rarely bothered her here.

"I've come not to surrender," I told her as she sat in state among her fawning courtiers and slightly more dignified lapdogs, "but to state my case."

"Really, dear, it's no concern of mine. Shall I tell Arqui you're here?"

The Prime Minister had overheard my announcement. He appeared from behind an electric arras, eyes alight at the words with which I greeted him: "Set it up, Arq."

And so that very night I was flown to the front over what appeared to be a scale model of luminous craters and stalled war machines. Naturally the Princess could not wait for a reasonable hour; but then, I was not interested in waiting. I wanted to see what would come of the affair.

At an underground airfield I was transferred to a war-scarred limousine which was chauffeured up a slight ramp to that perpetual amusement park whose theme is war.

A cease-fire had been called to facilitate negotiations, but plainly the land had been in some upheaval. Fires of hell fried the obsidian sky, leaping above generous mounds of cadavers, the usual battlefield fare. Although it was summer and no rain had fallen for weeks, the earth showed soaked and sprouting a crimson mildew in the headlights. Upturned helmets lay scattered on the road like battered tortoise shells, dippers full of blood. The tangled bodies became less distinct from the muck as we crossed into no-man's-land.

And there in the worst of it, like a neon saloon in a nightmare, the Princess had parked her bus of state. As we pulled alongside, I commanded my aides to wait calmly no matter what happened. I gave thanks for my tall boots as I waded through the massacre to the bus. A chauffeuse was out polishing the windshield while another took a chamois to the chrome fenders. Mangled hands like squashed starfish reached out from under the tires.

Instead of knocking, I pressed my face to the glass folding door and said, "I hope you appreciate this."

She opened the door with a shiny lever and gazed down at me from the plush driver's seat. If I had expected her face to be streaked with tears or otherwise ravaged by my rejection, I would have been disappointed. Her demeanor was military, unperturbed.

As I climbed in, she said, "Before you say a thing, let me assure you that I have considered your desires before my own. I know that you, like myself, might thrive on new pleasures—while retaining certain favorites to which you may return again and again without exhausting their fascination. Therefore, I offer the portable services of my bus. This is only a taste of what awaits you at home."

She pulled aside a curtain that hung across the cabin, unveiling a living gallery of nudes smeared with fluorescent body paints and soaked in ultraviolet light: a lurid spectrum of humanity, displaying a variety of genders, some surgical. I was touched to see she had included a sex-anemone, for my Nanny and first mistress had possessed one such; although while Nanny's had been a graft, moored in her flesh, this anemone was detached, a lonely polyp growing from a pair of fleshy vegetable thighs, devoid of personality. For the Princess, while she might concede to the pleasure-giving powers of many unexpected elements, would never allow any of them to compete for my *intellectual* attentions. Her human slaves, to similar effect, had the dull grins and sunken temples of the lobotomized.

"There should be something here to suit you," she said.

"You overestimate my appetite," I replied. "How can I consider pleasure in this setting?"

I leaned past her and switched on the headlights. A bright swath of charnel horrors appeared before us. It had been there all along.

"What can you offer them?" I asked.

Her body began to shudder, wracked by spasms welling from her womb. Only her eyes remained unmoved, fixed on the scene beyond the windshield. She snagged my wrist in her nails, gasping, "Please, Prince, take me."

"Say 'fuck,' dear. 'Take' isn't your sort of euphemism."

I considered refusing her, as I had refused the offer of her living cargo. But the blood and the sweating night and now this honest show of desire had worked me up to a fine point. I gave her what she asked for, while she stared out the window at the field of death which was all that would ever issue from her womb. I could not look at it myself. I turned my head to the wind-wing and watched the chamois moving slowly back and forth in the hand of a chauffeuse whose doe-like eyes held mine until that trembling instant when, eyes closing, I jerked and forced the Princess into the horn.

The wailing summoned my guardians from the car. They stood before us, knee-deep in bodies, their guns erect but blinded by the headlights.

"Turn out the light," she said, hitching herself back into the seat.

I did so.

"Come home with me, Prince."

"I can't do that. You've been unfortunate enough to meet me at the height of my reckless youth. This is the only time I have to be wild and passionate, to develop the emotional artistry that must serve me in the slow grind of petty politics." I lifted her hand and kissed it. "Should I apologize for winning your heart? It's a skill of mine, honed to perfection—too sharp, I think—but I will put it aside when I put on the crown."

"Why can't you be like other men?" she said, rising from her ultraviolet pout.

I laughed. "Now I understand the devastation on your other borders. You're entrenched in the affections of 'other men.' Would all those wars end if we married?"

"I will always hate the others, but not as I hate you. You're the only one who dared run from me."

Uncomfortable with all those nudes watching us, I pulled the curtain closed again. "I was trying to preserve the landscape."

"Fuck the landscape. You can't pick a bouquet without gouging the earth."

"And you've picked me a lovely bouquet of bloody flesh."

"I? Pick flesh for you? I'm not courting you, Prince."

"What do you call this?"

She sat back and stared haughtily at me. "Negotiation."

"I shouldn't have come."

She smiled. "Are you always so moody after sex? I'm sure you'll feel differently tomorrow. We'll get an early start, take a slow drive through the wine country. . . . "

"There's not much left of it, judging from the photographs I've seen."

"You shouldn't have retaliated. You'll spoil our honeymoon."

"I didn't start this war."

"Yes, you did. By running. Your country can't be too pleased with its Prince. Who'll follow a coward? If you don't give me what I want, this war will go on forever. I'll assassinate my brother—I've been poisoning him slowly anyway—and the power will stay in my hands. I'll never marry. I will destroy you. The generation that grows up beneath you will be born to attrition. Society has a long memory for blame, and they'll lay their lot to your cowardice. It will be your war then."

"My very own personal war?"

"Which you can't fight without approval. The people will count the bodies and weigh them against yours. You have only one, and you'll lose it."

I sat down on the topmost step and rested my chin in

my hands. "I don't know anymore, Princess. You have my mother's approval, don't you?"

Her laughter rang like a cracked bell. "This marriage, my darling, was arranged long ago. I've merely tried to reconcile you to it. I think it's something we could both enjoy. It wasn't my idea, you know. We're so alike that you should have guessed I wouldn't look forward to putting my neck in a yoke, regardless of the partner."

"Not your idea?"

"Do you think that two children would be allowed to plunge their countries into total war? Our parents have let this war come about, prince, in order to draw us together."

My hair prickled. "Who told you this?"

"I discovered it clue by clue, over the years. It's obvious when you comprehend the pattern."

I rose from the steps. "But how can you go along with it, knowing what you do?"

Her eyebrows arched up. "It suits me. By playing along, I get all I desire. Best of all, I get you."

"A lousy trade. You'll sacrifice your freedom and then you won't want me. Not on our parents' terms, you won't."

I was glad to see her considering this.

"Look," I said, "what if I said you can have me? You know that in the only way that matters, I am already yours."

She leaned closer. Her chauffeuse watched us with eyes like moons. "Yes?"

"But I don't want to live in your land, Princess, and admit it, you have no fondness for mine. If we married, you would have to live in my country."

"We can break with custom."

"If you follow it now, even to get what you want, tradition will trap you forever. Listen, my bloody darling. Listen to what I propose."

Her hand slid into mine.

"Pitch the war with all your will," I said. "Drive your

father until he howls. Be a cancer in his heart. Attack, my love, and never stop. Let there be ever newer weaponry, mountains of bodies. Let our love never stagnate in treaties. If we forsake peace, we can slake our lust forever.''

She looked out over the ragged fields, the sloppy graves. I could see my vision playing in her eyes. How easily it would spread, out of the wine lands and over the hills, blighting crops and felling forests, drenching the world in blood.

''And you'll be mine?'' she asked huskily.

''Yes, yours always. We will meet thus, in the midst of death, pretending to discuss the terms of an impossible peace. For as long as we have each other, peace will never come.''

''You *are* mine!''

''And you are mine, Princess. And now there is something we share.''

''A war.''

''*Our* war.''

''Yes.'' Tightening her grip, she pulled me in again. ''*Yes.*''

When I finally descended from the bus, my escorts stood stiffly around the limousine, sucking on perfumed cigarettes. They gasped at the sight of blood on my face and hands, the nail marks and bruises. The Princess's bus roared and lumbered away, grinding through the carnage. I watched it until the taillights vanished, and thought I heard gunfire beginning in the distance. They couldn't know it yet, but the cease-fire had ended.

''There was trouble?'' asked an aide.

I pushed past him to the car, saying brusquely, ''There will be no truce, no compromise. Take me home.''

The Peacemakers

The Peacemakers

Timothy Zahn

The World Peace Accords were signed January 1, 1992, to a flourish of propagandist trumpets from the major powers and almost deafening skepticism from everyone else. Yet in the first year, contrary to popular cynical expectation, no fewer than four major disputes between East and West were resolved peacefully. By year five a half-dozen long-standing Third World brush wars had been brought to a close; by year eight the message that peace implied progress and prosperity had penetrated even the densest of despots and cruelest of cultures.

By the tenth anniversary celebration the pattern was clear. War was well on its way to joining smallpox and the dodo bird in oblivion.

All the architects of the Accords were on hand in Geneva for the big bash, of course. It was unquestionably the media event of the decade, and for a solid week the assembled dignitaries generated enough quotes and photos and interviews to keep even the impossibly ravenous maw of the international media machine comfortably fed.

In all the noise and fury and videotape, no one paid much attention to Andrew Xavier Martin. No one except me.

Not unexpectedly, of course. On the surface, Martin was hardly one of the leading lights of the spectacle—his only official function during the drafting of the Accords had been to act as recorder and occasional pinch-hitting translator. But I had highly placed sources, and from those sources I had heard some highly intriguing whispers. Insubstantial whispers, not solid enough even to qualify as vague rumors. But I'd always been the type to play long odds, especially when the potential payoff was as big as this one was.

I tracked Martin down the evening of the second day, sitting alone in a corner of the hotel restaurant and watching with gentle amusement the attention being lavished on the Soviet delegation across the room. "Mr. Martin?" I asked, stepping up to his table.

He looked up. "Yes," he acknowledged. "And you?"

"My name is Redmond Kelly," I told him, offering my press card for his inspection. "I wonder if I might ask you a few questions."

"Certainly," he said, gesturing me to the chair opposite. "What would you like to know?"

I sat down, glancing around me as I did so. No one was within earshot; and Martin struck me as the sort who would appreciate the blunt approach. "Very simply, sir," I said quietly, "I'd like to know how you did it."

His eyebrows went up a fraction of an inch, and for a long minute he gazed at me thoughtfully. I held my mental breath; and then the faintest wisp of a smile touched his lips. "My friends at the U.N. have mentioned you," he said. "I've often thought that if I was ever ferreted out you would be the one who did it."

I felt my heartbeat pick up. "Then the Peace Accords *were* your brainchild?"

He snorted gently. "Please. All that flowery legal language, those paragraphs and sub-paragraphs, mine? You flatter and insult me in the same breath." He shook his head. "No, Mr. Kelly, I did none of the work drafting the Accords—nor any of the hard work since then that's gone into making them mankind's success story, for that matter. All I contributed was one, simple suggestion."

I licked my upper lip. So the whispers had been right . . . "And that suggestion was . . . ?"

"What ultimately made the whole thing work," he said, with neither false pride nor false modesty. "Tell me, do you have an insurance card on you?"

"Ah—sure," I said, the change of subject throwing me just a little. "Health and auto both."

"Show me."

I dug out the little chip card, thumbed it on and handed it over. "Prudential," he nodded, looking at it. "You know who owns Prudential?"

"Ah . . . I think the Chubb Group bought it a few years ago—"

"And Chubb is owned by . . . ?"

I had to think about that one. "The Anderson Portfolio?"

He nodded. "Owned by?"

I shook my head. "I give up."

"Split right down the middle by Citibank and the Exxon conglomerate. They also own Hartford and Century Casualty, by the way, through other channels. In fact, if you were to trace through the connections, you'd find that *all* the major insurance companies are owned by one or more of the multinationals. Corporations so big that together they control most of the world's re-sources and wealth . . . and a fair number of its govern-ments, as well.''

I nodded. It wasn't exactly a surprising revelation. "All right. And?''

He handed the chip card back. "Pull up the list of exclusions,'' he instructed me.

Wondering where he was going with this, I complied. "Uh . . . expenses not specifically provided for in the policy, pre-existing conditions, self-inflicted injury, con-finement in a federal hospital, treatment covered under Worker's Comp . . .'' I looked up at him, frowning. "And?''

He sighed; a patient, professorial sort of sigh. "Come, now—you're certainly old enough to have had insurance policies ten years ago. So tell me: what's missing?''

I stared at the list again . . . and then it hit me. "Are you saying . . . ?''

He nodded. "Economic forces are the real king in this world of ours, Mr. Kelly,'' he said. "For all their police forces and armies, governments really have very little of their old power left. But they had enough. Enough power to force the statutory elimination of one small phrase from all insurance policy contracts.''

I nodded. "The exclusion of payments,'' I said qui-etly, "for injuries sustained due to war.''

It was unquestioningly the single most momentous in-terview of my entire career. Now, ten years later, the world almost entirely at peace, I still haven't had the nerve to publish it.

The Terminal Beach

J. G. Ballard

At night, as he lay asleep on the floor of the ruined bunker, Traven heard the waves breaking along the shore of the lagoon, reminding him of the deep Atlantic rollers on the beach at Dakar, where he had been born, and of waiting in the evenings for his parents to drive home along the corniche road from the airport. Overcome by this long-forgotten memory, he woke uncertainly from the bed of old magazines on which he slept and ran toward the dunes that screened the lagoon.

Through the cold night air he could see the abandoned Superfortresses lying among the palms, beyond the perimeter of the emergency landing field three hundred yards away. Traven walked through the dark sand, already forgetting where the shore lay, although the atoll was only half a mile in width. Above him, along the crests of the dunes, the tall palms leaned into the dim air like the symbols of some cryptic alphabet. The landscape of the island was covered by strange ciphers.

The Terminal Beach

Giving up the attempt to find the beach, Traven stumbled into a set of tracks left years earlier by a large caterpillar vehicle. The heat released by one of the weapons tests had fused the sand, and the double line of fossil imprints, uncovered by the evening air, wound its serpentine way among the hollows like the footfalls of an ancient saurian.

Too weak to walk any further, Traven sat down between the tracks. With one hand he began to excavate the wedge-shaped grooves from a drift into which they disappeared, hoping that they might lead him toward the sea. He returned to the bunker shortly before dawn, and slept through the hot silences of the following noon.

The Blocks

As usual on these enervating afternoons, when not even the faintest breath of offshore breeze disturbed the dust, Traven sat in the shadow of one of the blocks, lost somewhere within the center of the maze. His back resting against the rough concrete surface, he gazed with a phlegmatic eye down the surrounding aisles and at the line of doors facing him. Each afternoon he left his cell in the abandoned camera bunker and walked down into the blocks. For the first half hour he restricted himself to the perimeter aisle, now and then trying one of the doors with the rusty key in his pocket—he had found it among the litter of smashed bottles in the isthmus of sand separating the testing ground from the airstrip—and then, inevitably, with a sort of drugged stride, he set off into the center of the blocks, breaking into a run and darting in and out of the corridors, as if trying to flush some invisible opponent from his hiding place. Soon he would be completely lost. Whatever his efforts to return to the perimeter, he found himself once more in the center.

Eventually he would abandon the task, and sit down in the dust, watching the shadows emerge from their crevices at the foot of the blocks. For some reason he always arranged to be trapped when the sun was at Zenith—on Eniwetok, a thermonuclear noon.

One question in particular intrigued him: "What sort of people would inhabit this minimal concrete city?"

The Synthetic Landscape

"This island is a state of mind," Osborne, one of the biologists working in the old submarine pens, was later to remark to Traven. The truth of this became obvious to Traven within two or three weeks of his arrival. Despite the sand and the few anemic palms, the entire landscape of the island was synthetic, a man-made artifact with all the associations of a vast system of derelict concrete motorways. Since the moratorium on atomic tests, the island had been abandoned by the Atomic Energy Commission, and the wilderness of weapons, aisles, towers, and blockhouses ruled out any attempt to return it to its natural state. (There were also stronger unconscious motives, Traven recognized, for leaving it as it was: if primitive man felt the need to assimilate events in the external world to his own psyche, twentieth-century man had reversed this process—by this Cartesian yardstick, the island at least *existed*, in a sense true of few other places.)

But apart from a few scientific workers, no one yet felt any wish to visit the former testing ground, and the naval patrol boat anchored in the lagoon had been withdrawn five years before Traven's arrival. Its ruined appearance, and the associations of the island with the period of the Cold War—what Traven had christened the "pre-Third"—were profoundly depressing, an Auschwitz of the soul whose mausoleums contained the mass graves of the still undead. With the Russo-American detente this nightmarish chapter of history had been gladly forgotten.

The Pre-Third

The actual and potential destructiveness of the atomic bomb plays straight into the hands of the Unconscious. The most cursory study of the dream-life and fantasies of the insane shows that ideas of world-destruction are latent in the unconscious mind. Nagasaki destroyed by the magic of science is the nearest man has yet approached to the realization of dreams that even during the safe immobility of sleep are accustomed to develop into nightmares of anxiety.

—Glover: *War, Sadism and Pacifism*

The Pre-Third: the period had been characterized in Traven's mind above all by its moral and psychological inversions, by its sense of the whole of history, and in particular of the immediate future—the two decades, 1945–65—suspended from the quivering volcano's lip of World War III. Even the death of his wife and six-year-old son in a motor accident seemed only part of this immense synthesis of the historical and psychic zero, and the frantic highways where each morning they met their deaths were the advance causeways to the global armageddon.

Third Beach

He had come ashore at midnight, after a hazardous search for an opening in the reef. The small motorboat he had hired from an Australian pearl diver at Charlotte Island subsided into the shallows, its hull torn by the sharp coral. Exhausted, Traven walked through the darkness among the dunes, where the dim outlines of bunkers and concrete towers loomed between the palms.

He woke the next morning into bright sunlight, lying halfway down the slope of a wide concrete beach. This ringed what appeared to be an empty reservoir or target basin, some two hundred feet in diameter, part of a system of artificial lakes built down the center of the atoll. Leaves and dust choked the waste grilles, and a pool of warm water two feet deep lay in the center, reflecting a distant line of palms.

Traven sat up and took stock of himself. This brief inventory, which merely confirmed his physical identity, was limited to little more than his thin body in its frayed cotton garments. In the context of the surrounding terrain, however, even this collection of tatters seemed to possess a unique vitality. The emptiness of the island, and the absence of any local fauna, were emphasized by the huge sculptural forms of the target basins let into its surface. Separated from each other by narrow isthmuses, the lakes stretched away along the curve of the atoll. On either side, sometimes shaded by the few palms that had gained a precarious purchase in the cracked cement, were roadways, camera towers, and isolated blockhouses, together forming a continuous concrete cap upon the island, a functional megalithic architecture as gray and minatory, and apparently as ancient (in its projection into, and from, time future), as any of Assyria and Babylon.

The series of weapons tests had fused the sand in layers, and the pseudogeological strata condensed the brief epochs, microseconds in duration, of the thermonuclear age. "The key to the past lies in the present." Typically the island inverted this geologist's maxim. Here the key to the present lay in the future. The island was a fossil of time future, its bunkers and blockhouses illustrating the principle that the fossil record of life is one of armor and the exoskeleton.

Traven knelt in the warm pool and splashed his shirt and trousers. The reflection revealed the watery image of a thinly bearded face and gaunt shoulders. He had come to the island with no supplies other than a small bar of chocolate, expecting that in some way the island would provide its own sustenance. Perhaps, too, he had identified the need for food with a forward motion in time, and envisioned that with his return to the past, or at most into a zone of nontime, this need would be obviated. The privations of the previous six months, during his journey across the Pacific, had reduced his always thin body to that of a migrant beggar, held together by little more than the preoccupied gaze in his eye. Yet this emaciation, by stripping away the superfluities of the flesh, seemed to reveal an inner sinewy toughness, an economy and directness of movement.

For several hours he wandered about, inspecting one bunker after another for a convenient place to sleep. He crossed the remains of a small landing strip, next to a dump where a dozen B-29's lay across one another like dead reptile birds.

The Corpses

Once he entered a small street of metal shacks, containing a cafeteria, recreation rooms, and shower stalls. A wrecked jukebox lay half-buried in the sand behind the cafeteria, its selection of records still in their rack.

Further along, flung into a small target basin fifty yards from the shacks, were the bodies of what at first he thought were the inhabitants of this ghost town—a dozen life-size plastic models. Their half-melted faces, contorted into bleary grimaces, gazed up at him from the jumble of legs and torsos.

On either side of him, muffled by the dunes, came the sounds of waves, the great rollers on the seaward side breaking over the reefs, and onto the beaches within the lagoon. However, he avoided the sea, hesitating before any rise that might take him within its sight. Everywhere the camera towers offered him a convenient aerial view of the confused topography of the island, but he avoided their rusting ladders.

He soon realized that however confused and random the blockhouses and camera towers might seem, their common focus dominated the landscape and gave to it a unique perspective. As Traven noticed when he sat down to rest in the window slit of one of the blockhouses, all these observation posts occupied positions on a series of concentric perimeters, moving in tightening arcs toward the inmost sanctuary. This ultimate circle, below ground zero, remained hidden beyond a line of dunes a quarter of a mile to the west.

The Terminal Bunker

After sleeping for a few nights in the open, Traven returned to the concrete beach where he had woken on his first morning on the island, and made his home—if the term could be applied to that damp crumbling hovel—in a camera bunker fifty yards from the target lakes. The dark chamber between the thick canted walls, tomblike though it might seem, gave him a sense of physical reassurance. Outside, the sand drifted against the sides, half-burying the narrow doorway, as if crystallizing the immense epoch of time that had lapsed since the bunker's construction. The narrow rectangles of the five camera slits, their shapes and positions determined by the instruments, studded the east wall like cryptic ideograms. Variations of these ciphers decorated the walls of the other bunkers. In the morning, if Traven was awake, he would always find the sun divided into five emblematic beacons.

Most of the time the chamber was filled only by a damp gloomy light. In the control tower at the landing field Traven found a collection of discarded magazines, and used these to make a bed. One day, lying in the bunker shortly after the first attack of beriberi, he pulled out a magazine pressing into his back and found inside it a full-page photograph of a six-year-old girl. This blond-haired child, with her composed expression and self-immersed eyes, filled him with a thousand painful memories of his son. He pinned the page to the wall and for days gazed at it through his reveries.

For the first few weeks Traven made little attempt to leave the bunker, and postponed any further exploration of the island. The symbolic journey through its inner circles set its own times of arrival and departure. He evolved no routine for himself. All sense of time soon vanished; his life became completely existential, an absolute break separating one moment from the next like two quantal events. Too weak to forage for food, he lived on the old ration packs he found in the wrecked Superfortresses. Without any implements, it took him all day to open the cans. His physical decline continued, but he watched his spindling arms and legs with indifference.

By now he had forgotten the existence of the sea and vaguely assumed the atoll to be part of some continuous continental table. A hundred yards away to the north and south of the bunker a line of dunes, topped by the palisade of enigmatic palms, screened the lagoon and sea, and the faint muffled drumming of the waves at night had fused with his memories of war and childhood. To the east was the emergency landing field and the abandoned aircraft. In the afternoon light their shifting rectangular shadows would appear to writhe and pivot. In front of the bunker, where he sat, was the system of target lakes, the shallow basins extending across the center of the atoll. Above him the five apertures looked out upon this scene like the tutelary deities of some futuristic myth.

The Lakes and the Specters

The lakes had been designed originally to reveal any radiobiological changes in a selected range of flora and fauna, but the specimens had long since bloomed into grotesque parodies of themselves and been destroyed.

Sometimes in the evenings, when a sepulchral light lay over the concrete bunkers and causeways, and the basins seemed like ornamental lakes in a city of deserted mausoleums, abandoned even by the dead, he would see the specters of his wife and son standing on the opposite bank. Their solitary figures appeared to have been watching him for hours. Although they never moved, Traven was sure they were beckoning to him. Roused from his reverie, he would stumble across the dark sand to the edge of the lake and wade through the water, shouting at the two figures as they moved away hand in hand among the lakes and disappeared across the distant causeways.

Shivering with cold, Traven would return to the bunker and lie on the bed of old magazines, waiting for their return. The image of their faces, the pale lantern of his wife's cheeks, floated on the river of his memory.

The Blocks (II)

It was not until he discovered the blocks that Traven realized he would never leave the island.

At this stage, some two months after his arrival, Traven had exhausted the small cache of food, and the symptoms of beriberi had become more acute. The numbness in his hands and feet, and the gradual loss of strength, continued. Only by an immense effort, and the knowledge that the inner sanctum of the island still lay unexplored, did he manage to leave the palliasse of magazines and make his way from the bunker.

As he sat in the drift of sand by the doorway that evening, he noticed a light shining through the palms far into the distance around the atoll. Confusing this with the image of his wife and son, and visualizing them waiting for him at some warm hearth among the dunes, Traven set off toward the light. Within fifty yards he lost his sense of direction. He blundered about for several hours on the edges of the landing strip, and succeeded only in cutting his foot on a broken Coca-Cola bottle in the sand.

After postponing his search for the night, he set out again in earnest the next morning. As he moved past the towers and blockhouses the heat lay over the island in an unbroken mantle. He had entered a zone devoid of time. Only the narrowing perimeters of the bunkers warned him that he was crossing the inner field of the fire-table.

He climbed the ridge which marked the furthest point in his previous exploration of the island. The plain beyond was covered with target aisles and explosion breaks. On the gray walls of the recording towers, which rose into the air like obelisks, were the faint outlines of human forms in stylized postures, the flash-shadows of the target community burned into the cement. Here and there, where the concrete apron had cracked, a line of palms hung precariously in the motionless air. The target lakes were smaller, filled with the broken bodies of plastic dummies. Most of them still lay in the inoffensive domestic postures into which they had been placed before the tests.

Beyond the furthest line of dunes, where the camera towers began to run and face him, were the tops of what seemed to be a herd of square-backed elephants. They were drawn up in precise ranks in a hollow that formed a shallow corral.

Traven advanced toward them, limping on his cut foot. On either side of him the loosening sand had excavated the dunes, and several of the blockhouses tilted on their sides. This plain of bunkers stretched for some quarter of a mile. To one side the half-submerged hulks of a group of concrete shelters, bombed out onto the surface in some earlier test, lay like the husks of the abandoned wombs that had given birth to this herd of megaliths.

The Blocks (III)

To grasp something of the vast number and oppressive size of the blocks, and their impact upon Traven, one must try to visualize sitting in the shade of one of these concrete monsters, or walking about in the center of this enormous labyrinth, which extended across the central table of the island. There were some two thousand of them, each a perfect cube fifteen feet in height, regularly spaced at ten-yard intervals. They were arranged in a series of tracts, each composed of two hundred blocks, inclined to one another and to the direction of the blast. They had weathered only slightly in the years since they were first built, and their gaunt profiles were like the cutting faces of an enormous die-plate, designed to stamp out huge rectilinear volumes of air. Three of the sides were smooth and unbroken, but the fourth, facing away from the direction of the blast, contained a narrow inspection door.

It was this feature of the blocks that Traven found particularly disturbing. Despite the considerable number of doors, by some freak of perspective only those in a single aisle were visible at any point within the maze, the rest obscured by the intervening blocks. As he walked from the perimeter into the center of the massif, line upon line of the small metal doors appeared and receded, a world of closed exits concealed behind endless corners.

Approximately twenty of the blocks, those immediately below ground zero, were solid, the walls of the remainder of varying thicknesses. From the outside they appeared to be of uniform solidity.

As he entered the first of the long aisles, Traven felt his step lighten; the sense of fatigue that had dogged him for so many months begin to lift. With their geometric regularity and finish, the blocks seemed to occupy more than their own volume of space, imposing on him a mood of absolute calm and order. He walked on into the center of the maze, eager to shut out the rest of the island. After a few random turns to left and right, he found himself alone, the vistas to the sea, lagoon, and island closed.

Here he sat down with his back against one of the blocks, the quest for his wife and son forgotten. For the first time since his arrival at the island the sense of dissociation prompted by its fragmenting landscape began to recede.

One development he did not expect. With dusk, and the need to leave the blocks and find food, he realized that he had lost himself. However he retraced his steps, struck out left or right at an oblique course, oriented himself around the sun and pressed on resolutely north or south, he found himself back at his starting point. Despite his best efforts, he was unable to make his way out of the maze. That he was aware of his motives gave him little help. Only when hunger overcame the need to remain did he manage to escape.

Abandoning his former home near the aircraft dump, Traven collected together what canned food he could find in the waist turret and cockpit lockers of the Superfortresses and pulled them across the island on a crude sledge. Fifty yards from the perimeter of the blocks he took over a tilting bunker, and pinned the fading photograph of the blond-haired child to the wall beside the door. The page was falling to pieces, like his fragmenting image of himself. Each evening when he woke he would eat uneagerly and then go out into the blocks. Sometimes he took a canteen of water with him and remained there for two or three days.

Traven: In Parenthesis

Elements in a quantal world:
    The terminal beach.
    The terminal bunker.
    The blocks.
  The landscape is coded.
  Entry points into the future=levels in a spinal landscape=zones of significant time.

The Submarine Pens

This precarious existence continued for the following weeks. As he walked out to the blocks one evening, he again saw his wife and son, standing among the dunes below a solitary tower, their faces watching him calmly. He realized that they had followed him across the island from their former haunt among the dried-up lakes. Once again he saw the beckoning light, and he decided to continue his exploration of the island.

Half a mile further along the atoll he found a group of four submarine pens, built over an inlet, now drained, which wound through the dunes from the sea. The pens still contained several feet of water, filled with strange luminescent fish and plants. A warning light winked at intervals from a metal tower. The remains of the substantial camp, only recently vacated, stood on the concrete pier outside. Greedily Traven heaped his sledge with the provisions stacked inside one of the metal shacks. With this change of diet the beriberi receded, and during the next days he returned to the camp. It appeared to be the site of a biological expedition. In a field office he came across a series of large charts of mutated chromosomes. He rolled them up and took them back to his bunker. The abstract patterns were meaningless, but during his recovery he amused himself by devising suitable titles for them. (Later, passing the aircraft dump on one of his forays, he found the half-buried jukebox, and tore the list of records from the selection panel, realizing that these were the most appropriate captions for the charts. Thus embroidered, they took on many layers of cryptic associations.)

Traven Lost Among the Blocks

August 5. Found the man Traven. A sad derelict figure, hiding in a bunker in the deserted interior of the island. He is suffering from severe exposure and malnutrition, but is unaware of this, or, for that matter, of any other events in the world around him. . . .

He maintains that he came to the island to carry out some scientific project—unstated—but I suspect that he understands his real motives and the unique role of the island . . . In some way its landscape seems to be involved with certain unconscious notions of time, and in particular with those that may be a repressed premonition of our own deaths. The attractions and dangers of such an architecture, as the past has shown, need no stressing.

August 6. He has the eyes of the possessed. I would guess that he is neither the first, not the last, to visit the island.

—Dr. C. Osborne: *Eniwetok Diary*

* * *

With the exhaustion of his supplies, Traven remained within the perimeter of the blocks almost continuously, conserving what strength remained to him to walk slowly down their empty corridors. The infection in his right foot made it difficult for him to replenish his supplies from the stores left by the biologists, and as his strength ebbed he found progressively less incentive to make his way out of the blocks. The system of megaliths now provided a complete substitute for those functions of his mind which gave to it its sense of the sustained rational order of time and space, his awareness kindled from levels above those of his present nervous system (if the autonomic system is dominated by the past, the cerebrospinal reaches toward the future). Without the blocks his sense of reality shrank to little more than the few square inches of sand beneath his feet.

On one of his last ventures into the maze, he spent all night and much of the following morning in a futile attempt to escape. Dragging himself from one rectangle of shadow to another, his leg as heavy as a club and apparently inflamed to the knee, he realized that he must soon find an equivalent for the blocks or he would end his life within them, trapped within this self-constructed mausoleum as surely as the retinue of Pharaoh.

He was sitting exhausted somewhere within the center of the system, the faceless lines of the tomb booths receding from him, when the sky was slowly divided by the drone of a light aircraft. This passed overhead, and then, five minutes later, returned. Seizing his opportunity, Traven struggled to his feet and made his exit from the blocks, his head raised to follow the glistening exhaust trail.

As he lay down in the bunker he dimly heard the aircraft return and carry out an inspection of the site.

A Belated Rescue

"Who are you?" A small sandy-haired man was peering down at him with a severe expression, then put away a syringe in his valise. "Do you realize you're on your last legs?"

"Traven . . . I've had some sort of accident. I'm glad you flew over."

"I'm sure you are. Why didn't you use our emergency radio? Anyway, we'll call the Navy and have you picked up."

"No . . ." Traven sat up on one elbow and felt weakly in his hip pocket. "I have a pass somewhere. I'm carrying out research."

"Into what?" The question assumed a complete understanding of Traven's motives. Traven lay in the shade beside the bunker, and drank weakly from a canteen as Dr. Osborne dressed his foot.

"You've also been stealing our stores."

Traven shook his head. Fifty yards away the blue and white Cessna stood on the concrete apron like a large dragonfly. "I didn't realize you were coming back."

"You must be in a trance."

The young woman at the controls of the aircraft climbed from the cockpit and walked over to them, glancing at the gray bunkers and blocks. She seemed unaware of or uninterested in the decrepit figure of Traven. Osborne spoke to her over his shoulder, and after a downward glance at Traven she went back to the aircraft. As she turned Traven rose involuntarily, recognizing the child in the photograph he had pinned to the wall. Then he remembered that the magazine could not have been more than four or five years old.

The engine of the aircraft started. It turned onto one of the roadways and took off into the wind.

The Terminal Beach

* * *

The young woman drove over by jeep that afternoon with a small camp bed and a canvas awning. During the intervening hours Traven had slept, and woke refreshed when Osborne returned from his scrutiny of the surrounding dunes.

"What are you doing here?" the young woman asked as she secured one of the guy ropes to the bunker.

"I'm searching for my wife and son," Traven said.

"They're on this island?" Surprised, but taking the reply at face value, she looked around her. "Here?"

"In a manner of speaking."

After inspecting the bunker, Osborne joined them. "The child in the photograph. Is she your daughter?"

"No." Traven tried to explain. "She's adopted *me*."

Unable to make sense of his replies, but accepting his assurances that he would leave the island, Osborne and the young woman returned to their camp. Each day Osborne returned to change the dressing, driven by the young woman, who seemed to grasp the role cast for her by Traven in his private mythology. Osborne, when he learned of Traven's previous career as a military pilot, assumed that he was a latter-day martyr left high and dry by the moratorium on thermonuclear tests.

"A guilt complex isn't an indiscriminate supply of moral sanctions. I think you may be overstretching yours."

When he mentioned the name Eatherly, Traven shook his head.

Undeterred, Osborne pressed: "Are you sure you're not making similar use of the image of Eniwetok— waiting for your pentecostal wind?"

"Believe me, Doctor, no." Traven replied firmly. "For me the H-bomb is a symbol of absolute freedom. Unlike

Eatherly I feel it's given me the right—the obligation, even—to do anything I choose."

"That seems strange logic," Osborne commented. "At least we are responsible for our physical selves."

Traven shrugged. "Not now, I think. After all, aren't we in effect men raised from the dead?"

Often, however, he thought of Eatherly: the prototypal Pre-Third Man, dating the Pre-Third from August 6, 1945, carrying a full load of cosmic guilt.

Shortly after Traven was strong enough to walk again he had to be rescued from the blocks for a second time. Osborne became less conciliatory.

"Our work is almost complete," he warned Traven. "You'll die here. Traven, what are you looking for?"

To himself Traven said: the tomb of the unknown civilian, *Homo hydrogenensis*, Eniwetock Man. To Osborne he said; "Doctor, your laboratory is at the wrong end of this island."

"I'm aware of that, Traven. There are rarer fish swimming in your head than in any submarine pen."

On the day before they left, Traven and the young woman drove over to the lakes where he had first arrived. As a final present from Osborne, an ironic gesture unexpected from the elderly biologist, she had brought the correct list of legends for the chromosome charts. They stopped by the derelict jukebox and she pasted them on to the selection panel.

They wandered among the supine wrecks of the Superfortresses. Traven lost sight of her, and for the next ten minutes searched in and out of the dunes. He found her standing in a small amphitheater formed by the sloping mirrors of a solar energy device, built by one of the visiting expeditions. She smiled to him as he stepped through the scaffolding. A dozen fragmented images of herself were reflected in the broken panes. In some she was sans head, in others multiples of her raised arms circled her like those of a Hindu goddess. Exhausted, Traven turned away and walked back to the jeep.

As they drove away he described his glimpses of his wife and son. "Their faces are always calm. My son's particularly, although he was never really like that. The only time his face was grave was when he was being born—then he seemed millions of years old."

The young woman nodded. "I hope you find them." As an afterthought she added: "Dr. Osborne is going to tell the Navy you're here. Hide somewhere."

Traven thanked her. When she flew away from the island for the last time he waved to her from his seat beside the blocks.

The Naval Party

When the search party came for him Traven hid in the only logical place. Fortunately the search was perfunctory, and was called off after a few hours. The sailors had brought a supply of beer with them, and the search soon turned into a drunken ramble. On the walls of the recording towers Traven later found balloons of obscene dialogue chalked into the mouths of the shadow figures, giving their postures the priapic gaiety of the dancers in cave drawings.

The climax of the party was the ignition of a store of gasoline in an underground tank near the airstrip. As he listened, first to the megaphones shouting his name, the echoes receding among the dunes like the forlorn calls of dying birds, then to the boom of the explosion and the laughter as the landing craft left, Traven felt a premonition that these were the last sounds he would hear.

He had hidden in one of the target basins, lying down among the bodies of the plastic dummies. In the hot sunlight their deformed faces gaped at him sightlessly from the tangle of limbs, their blurred smiles like those of the soundlessly laughing dead. Their faces filled his mind as he climbed over the bodies and returned to the bunker.

As he walked toward the blocks he saw the figures of his wife and son standing in his path. They were less than ten yards from him, their white faces watching him with a look of almost overwhelming expectantcy. Never had Traven seen them so close to the blocks. His wife's pale features seemed illuminated from within, her lips parted as if in greeting, one hand raised to take his own. His son's grave face, with its curiously fixed expression, regarded him with the same enigmatic smile as the girl in the photograph.

"Judith! David!" Startled, Traven ran forward to them. Then, in a sudden movement of light, their clothes turned into shrouds, and he saw the wounds that disfigured their necks and chests. Appalled, he cried out to them. As they vanished he fled into the safety and sanity of the blocks.

The Catechism of Good-bye

This time he found himself, as Osborne had predicted, unable to leave the blocks.

Somewhere in the shifting center of the maze, he sat with his back against one of the concrete flanks, his eyes raised to the sun. Around him the lines of cubes formed the horizons of his world. At times they would appear to advance toward him, looming over him like cliffs, the intervals between them narrowing so that they were little more than an arm's length apart, a labyrinth of narrow corridors running between them. Then they would re-cede from him, separating from each other like points in an expanding universe, until the nearest line formed an intermittent palisade along the horizon.

Time had become quantal. For hours it would be noon, the shadows contained within the motionless bulk of the blocks, the heat reverberating off the concrete floor. Abruptly he would find it was early afternoon or evening, the shadows everywhere like pointing fingers.

"Good-bye, Eniwetok," he murmured.

Somewhere there was a flicker of light, as if one of the blocks, like a counter on an abacus, had been plucked away.

"Good-bye, Los Alamos." Again a block seemed to vanish. The corridors around him remained intact, but somewhere, Traven was convinced, in the matrix super-imposed on his mind, a small interval of neutral space had been punched.

Good-bye, Hiroshima.

Good-bye, Alamogordo.

Good-bye, Moscow, London, Paris, New York . . .

Shuttles flickered, a ripple of integers. Traven stopped, accepting the futility of this megathlon farewell. Such a leave-taking required him to affix his signature on every one of the particles in the universe.

Total Noon: Eniwetok

The blocks now occupied positions on an endlessly re-volving circus wheel. They carried him upward, to heights from which he could see the whole island and the sea, and then down again through the opaque disk of the floor. From here he looked up at the undersurface of the concrete cap, an inverted landscape of rectilinear hollows, the dome-shaped mounds of the lake system, the thousands of empty cubic pits of the blocks.

"Good-bye, Traven"

To his disappointment he found that this ultimate act of rejection gained him nothing.

In an interval of lucidity, he looked down at his emaciated arms and legs propped loosely in front of him, the brittle wrists and hands covered with a lacework of ulcers. To his right was a trail of disturbed dust, the marks of slack heels.

In front of him lay a long corridor between the blocks, joining an oblique series a hundred yards away. Among these, where a narrow interval revealed the open space beyond, was a crescent-shaped shadow, poised in the air.

During the next half hour it moved slowly, turning as the sun swung.

The outline of a dune.

Seizing on this cipher, which hung before him like a symbol on a shield, Traven pushed himself through the dust. He climbed precariously to his feet, and covered his eyes from all sight of the blocks.

Ten minutes later he emerged from the western perimeter. The dune whose shadow had guided him lay fifty yards away. Beyond it, bearing the shadow like a screen, was a ridge of limestone, which ran away among the hillocks of a wasteland. The remains of old bulldozers, bales of barbed wire, and fifty-gallon drums lay half-buried in the sand.

Traven approached the dune, reluctant to leave this anonymous swell of sand. He shuffled around its edges, and then sat down in the shade by a narrow crevice in the ridge.

Ten minutes later he noticed that someone was watching him.

The Marooned Japanese

This corpse, whose eyes stared up at Traven, lay to his left at the bottom of the crevice. That of a man of middle age and powerful build, it lay on its side with its head on a pillow of stone, as if surveying the window of the sky. The fabric of the clothes had rotted to a gray tattered vestment, but in the absence of any small animal predators on the island the skin and musculature had been preserved. Here and there, at the angle of knee or wrist, a bony point shone through the leathery integument of the yellow skin, but the facial mask was still intact, and revealed a male Japanese of the professional classes. Looking down at the strong nose, high forehead, and broad mouth, Traven guessed that the Japanese had been a doctor or lawyer.

Puzzled as to how the corpse had found itself here, Traven slid a few feet down the slope. There were no radiation burns on the skin, which indicated that the Japanese had been there for less than five years. Nor did he appear to be wearing a uniform, so had not been a member of a military or scientific mission.

To the left of the corpse, within reach of his hand, was a frayed leather case, the remains of a map wallet. To the right was the bleached husk of a haversack, open to reveal a canteen of water and a small can.

Greedily, the reflex of starvation making him for the moment ignore this discovery that the Japanese had deliberately chosen to die in the crevice, Traven slid down the slope until his feet touched the splitting soles of the corpse's shoes. He reached forward and seized the canteen. A cupful of flat water swilled around the rusting bottom. Traven gulped down the water, the dissolved metal salts cloaking his lips and tongue with a bitter film. He pried the lid off the can, which was empty but for a tacky coating of condensed syrup. He scraped at this with the lid and chewed at the tarry flakes. They filled his mouth with an almost intoxicating sweetness. After a few moments he felt light-headed and sat back beside the corpse. Its sightless eyes regarded him with unmoving compassion.

The Fly

(A small fly, which Traven presumes has followed him into the crevice, now buzzes about the corpse's face. Traven leans forward to kill it, then reflects that perhaps this minuscule sentry had been the corpse's faithful companion, in return fed on the rich liqueurs and distillations of its pores. Carefully, to avoid injuring the fly, he encourages it to alight on his wrist.)

DR. YASUDA: Thank you, Traven. *(The voice is rough, as if unused to conversation.)* In my position, you understand.

TRAVEN: Of course, Doctor. I'm sorry I tried to kill it. These ingrained habits, you know, they're not easy to shrug off. Your sister's children in Osaka in Fortyfour, the exigencies of war, I hate to plead them, most known motives are so despicable one searches the unknown in the hope that . . .

YASUDA: Please, Traven, do not be embarrassed. The fly is lucky to retain its identity for so long. That son you mourn, not to mention my own two nieces and nephew, did they not die each day? Every parent in the world mourns the lost sons and daughters of their past childhoods.

TRAVEN: You're very tolerant, Doctor. I wouldn't dare—

YASUDA: Not at all, Traven. I make no apologies for you. After all, each one of us is little more than the meager residue of the infinite unrealized possibilities of our lives. But your son and my nieces are fixed in our minds forever, their identities as certain as the stars.

TRAVEN *(not entirely convinced):* That may be so, Doctor, but it leads to a dangerous conclusion in the case of this island. For instance, the blocks . . .

YASUDA: They are precisely to what I refer. Here among the blocks, Traven, you at last find the image of yourself free of time and space. This island is an ontological Garden of Eden; why try to expel yourself into a quantal world?

TRAVEN: Excuse me. *(The fly has flown back to the corpse's face and sits in one of the orbits, giving the good doctor an expression of quizzical beadiness. Reaching forward, Traven entices it onto his palm.)* Well, yes, these bunkers may be ontological objects, but whether this is the ontological fly seems doubtful. It's true that on this island it's the only fly, which is the next best thing.

YASUDA: You can't accept the plurality of the universe, Traven. Ask yourself, why? Why should this obsess you? It seems to me that you are hunting for the white leviathan, zero. The beach is a dangerous zone; avoid it. Have a proper humility; pursue a philosophy of acceptance.

TRAVEN: Then may I ask why you came here, Doctor?

YASUDA: To feed this fly. "What greater love—?"

TRAVEN *(still puzzling):* It doesn't really solve my problem. The blocks, you see . . .

YASUDA: Very well, if you must have it that way . . .

TRAVEN: But, Doctor—

YASUDA *(peremptorily):* Kill that fly!

TRAVEN: That's not an end, or a beginning. *(Hopelessly he kills the fly. Exhausted, he falls asleep beside the corpse.)*

The Terminal Beach

Searching for a piece of rope in the refuse dump behind the dunes, Traven found a bale of rusty wire. He unwound it, then secured a harness around the corpse's chest and dragged it from the crevice. The lid of a wooden crate served as a sledge. Traven fastened the corpse into a sitting position, and set off along the perimeter of the blocks. Around him the island was silent. The lines of palms hung in the sunlight, only his own motion varying the shifting ciphers of their crisscrossing trunks. The square turrets of the camera towers jutted from the dunes like forgotten obelisks.

An hour later, when Traven reached his bunker, he untied the wire cord he had fastened around his waist. He took the chair left for him by Dr. Osborne and carried it to a point midway between the bunker and the blocks.

Then he tied the body of the Japanese to the chair, arranging the hands so that they rested on the wooden arms, giving the moribund figure a posture of calm repose.

This done to his satisfaction, Traven returned to the bunker and squatted under the awning.

As the next days passed into weeks, the dignified figure of the Japanese sat in his chair fifty yards from him, guarding Traven from the blocks. Their magic still filled Traven's reveries, but he now had sufficient strength to rouse himself and forage for food. In the hot sunlight the skin of the Japanese became more and more bleached, and sometimes Traven would wake at night to find the white sepulchral figure sitting there, arms resting at its sides, in the shadows that crossed the concrete floor. At these moments he would often see his wife and son watching him from the dunes. As time passed they came closer, and he would sometimes turn to find them only a few yards behind him.

Patiently Traven waited for them to speak to him, thinking of the great blocks whose entrance was guarded by the seated figure of the dead archangel, as the waves broke on the distant shore and the burning bombers fell through his dreams.

Attack of the Jazz Giants*

Gregory Frost

1. Precipitating Events

In the grain mill outside Mound City, Doc Lewis and the boys had themselves four scared black men to burn. Doc, the officiating Grand Cyclops of the Klan hereabouts, sat way back on a cracked cane chair, two legs off the ground and daring the other two to snap. The dare had weight to it because, like his daddy before him, Doc had the heft of a hogshead keg. He'd lost all but a few strands of hair in the past few years as well, and the baldness bothered him much more than his increasing girth. In his youth, he'd gloried in his golden hair. In any case, the niggers couldn't see his features because Doc wore a

*The title is excerpted from ''A Short Poem'' by Leonard Gontarek, and is used with kind permission.

246

flour bag over his head. His boy, Bubba, had charge of the actual branding. It was one of very few events in which the squat, pug-faced boy showed anything at all like industry.

Before he reached for the hot iron, Bubba took a tin scoop, filled it from a sack of buckwheat flour, and then slapped it over his victim. An explosion as from a colossal powder puff, and the tremulous naked man became a blinking ghost, a nonentity, and was thereby reduced further from any kinship with his tormentors. The flour was Bubba's little joke.

Curly and Ed Rose, holding the victim by his upper arms, got powdered, too. But, half-drunk on 'shine, Doc's two assistant Night Hawks only laughed themselves silly and staggered a bit—two demented and pointy-headed art thieves trying to make off with a copy of Michaelangelo's *David*. They did not appreciate as did Doc the gravity of their efforts here. It was sport to them, that's all.

It was four men set to branding eight. They'd brought guns but didn't have to brandish them. Fear, solid as the chains round their victims' legs, kept the disguised foursome in power. They could do anything they liked, with impunity. Their victims prayed to survive or else die swiftly.

Bubba drew the iron out of the bread-oven coals, turned slowly, then drove the brand home. The flour puffed up, the black skin hissed. The man kicked and screamed and wrestled but Curly and Ed Rose had braced for that. Flour melted in a stream down a powdered thigh. By the time Bubba pulled the iron away, his victim had passed out. A fresh pink eye within a triangle adorned his left pectoral—a symbol of the magical forces he now lived under.

Bubba was a third-generation nigger-brander. He ought to have had some sense of the history behind his actions.

His grandaddy, the Captain, had maintained this tradition well after slaves had ceased to be property. At a time when carpetbaggers crawled over the body of the South like worms and the Black Codes kept shifting in their proscriptions, the identifying mark was for the black man's own good. First, the branding reminded him how easily the world could turn over on him. Second, it ensured that he knew he had a home, a place where he belonged. Back in the days of Reconstruction, Grandaddy had been a Grand Dragon.

Since then, the family had branded maybe five hundred. There were men and women in Chicago, New York, St. Louis and Kansas City who bore the cicatrice of the Lewis family plantation. No matter where they went, if things turned around, Doc would send out his Night Hawks to round them up. Many of those branded hadn't even been his workers. They'd been drifters, the homeless and directionless, passing through Mound City on their way to perdition. In other towns all across the south, they hanged those niggers. But his brand was known widely, so in a sense he was protecting them. He had worked this out long ago. Daddy was a man of vision, of foresight. Even those he'd branded couldn't have foretold otherwise.

2. The Homestead

How Doc got his name was a mystery that went to the grave with his father. Daddy Lewis had been a young captain in the Confederacy and so naturally they'd all called him Captain out of respect. Doc wasn't a medical practitioner, nor a vet, nor even a snake-oil salesman.

Somewhere before he turned ten, he got called Doc by the Captain and the name stuck. Maybe Daddy Lewis had had the percipience to know that his successor would need a nom de guerre to set him above the rest. Mystical power in names—a fact to which Doc could well attest.

He would happily have conjured something similar for Bubba, but that childish label had already malformed the boy's behavior well past the threshold of manhood. In fact, in moments of reflection Doc wondered if Bubba had ever really crossed that threshold. His desire to take pride in his son's actions had been endlessly frustrated, mostly by his wife, Sally.

Doc and she had two daughters as well: Debra and Psalmody. This latter name was the least likely thing Doc had ever heard, but the indomitable Sally had thought it a "beautiful, delicate, liquid word" and would not bend. Like the Captain, perhaps, she'd sensed something metaphysical about her child. At the same time, she couldn't tell you where she'd heard or what exactly was meant by the word, although it obviously referred to the Psalms. The solid biblical link carried the day. Sally could work Doc like a pump handle back then. Even now she could get under his skin with three or four well-placed words. She ought to—she was his cousin, had known him since childhood. This might also have accounted for a good deal regarding Bubba. His given name was Ezekiel. Biblically, he resembled the wheel, maybe a small ark or the fish that ate Jonah. Nobody was looking for anything metaphysical from him.

Psalmody had revealed her uniqueness early. At five, she'd asked her daddy what radiography was. Dutifully, Doc had looked the word up in a book and still didn't know to this day what it had told him. At six, Psalmody had wanted to know about positive rays, and at seven it had been genetics, but Doc had stopped researching by then. He didn't know what a father was supposed to do who couldn't offer his child the answers she sought. And, besides, he'd had a plantation to run.

It was 1925 now and Doc employed near eighty "workers." Curly and Ed Rose watched over the work force, same as they did everything else for him. He couldn't have imagined how he'd have gotten along without them.

Doc sensed that Curly had become enamored of Debra, his quieter daughter, his pale and delicate angel. Curly was a respectful young man, maybe a bit too fond of his sour mash but not so's it interfered with his work. Doc hoped they would marry and take over the farm. As for Psalmody, it was Bubba who seemed to have designs on her. Just looking at her, he could break out in a lustful sweat. The boy was troubling in his unceasing obtuseness. How could the two girls be such smart and lovely pastries and Bubba such a lump of dough? Surely never before in the family's long and proud history had there been so utterly beef-witted a child.

3. Intimations of Doom

The morning after the branding, Doc heaved himself out of bed, and went shuffling down the hall, scratching at his butt, toward the back stairs and the door leading to the outhouse. But, halfway down, he found his way blocked.

Sticking up from the first floor stood the enormous lower joint from an impossibly larger clarinet. It looked like some sort of black sarcophagus and it jammed the entire stairwell. The banister below had popped off a couple of its balusters where the clarinet piece exceeded the stairs' width. Doc glanced instinctively up at the ceiling but found no corresponding hole to explain the presence of the thing. The chrome pads and finger plates reflected him in his utter dismay, each one as big as his head. Who in his employ would have carted the infernal thing along the hall and down the stairs? In the middle of the night no less, and without waking him? Who would do it? An' what kind of a joke was it supposed to be? He didn't immediately recognize its musical disposition. All he cared was that, as incommodious as a kidney stone, it blocked his route to pee. The urgency of that need cut through his confusion, and he climbed quickly, apelike, back upstairs to the bedroom. One of the young maids, named Lizzie, had already arrived and was making up the bed. Somehow she'd known he was up—probably heard him clomping across the floor.

Doc hadn't the time to be shy. He snatched the chamber pot from under the bed, stuck his swollen member into it and glared defiantly at the girl while the echo of his release pinged off the pot. She openly observed his tool as she might have done a passing cockroach, too disinterested to reach over and squash it. With the pressure off, Doc's tool receded and he furiously tucked it back into his skivvies, blotching the flannel with the last remaining drops.

"Lizzie, what's that goddam thing on the back stairs?" he demanded. Doc never cursed in the house, so he knew that she knew how mad he was.

"Thing?" she asked. Never heard of it.

"Well, never you mind, girl, you go get me Carpy, right now. Don't say anything but that I want to see him pronto."

She nodded dimly and escaped, the bed half-made. Doc put down the brass pot. While he waited for the household retainer, he sat back on the bed. The matter on the back stairs was too perplexing to dwell upon, and his thoughts drifted.

Outside, the field workers were singing a "holler" about not goin' down to the well no more. Doc smiled vaguely at their singing, which brought back memories of other times on the bed: Sally on their wedding night, drunk and catty; Carpy's mother, laid back on it, willing to let him fuck her. The halcyon days of youth—it had all been ahead of him then.

4. The Homestead-II

Carpy was six years older than Bubba. Not nearly so dark as his mother, he neither much resembled his squat father. Muscular, yes, but long-muscled and trim. The only obvious trait of Doc's he'd acquired was the tendency toward baldness. Carpy's mother died shortly after his birth. His true parentage was kept from him, from the workers, and from Sally (who found out anyway and promptly stopped sleeping with her husband). She mistreated Carpy wickedly, never with any explanation or any apparent cause.

The most Doc dared for his eldest son was to teach him to read so that he could be promoted to the highest household position, that of overseer. It paid a tiny wage, but Doc had secretly hidden funds in a bank account for Carpy. He had rationalized this to himself over the years so as not to have to face the obvious conflict with his duties as a Cyclops. Unlike his old man, Carpy treated those dozens beneath his command with utmost kindness and compassion—a gentle foreman, fond of Lizzie, but secretly, hopelessly, in love with Psalmody. She was built like a goddess. Her breasts alone stuffed his brain full of immoderate thoughts, and thank God for that or he might have zeroed in on the rest of her.

Psalmody liked to run, decades before jogging would come of age. She refused to ride in the family Ford, preferring to race it along the dirt roads, barefoot, in loose-fitting boy's clothing. The sweat on her upper lip did things to Carpy that he couldn't explain. Certainly he had seen enough sweat in his life. Even Bubba registered her exudence of sexuality, but his elder half-brother was way ahead of him. Rarely, after all, were women excited by the vision of a loved one picking his nose. Carpy, a man of position and responsibility, never would do such a thing publicly; whereas Bubba's excavated mucous adorned chair arms, walls and the undersides of tables throughout the house. The thought of his hands on her would have made Psalmody faint. She was looking for someone of intelligence, of original thought, and pretty soon, too, or she would go crazy in this prison-farm. Everything that mattered to her existed somewhere else other than Mound City and its predatory environs. Although she didn't realize it, Carpy's gentle nature had already played upon the strings of her heart. History has a way of swinging around for another looksee.

5. Prelude to War

Carpy had no idea what the monstrosity confronting him might be, nor how it might have arrived. "It's like a big arrow was shot through the roof. Impossible stuff," he called it. "Mr. Doc, nobody in this house can be responsible. Fact, I don' know anybody who could. My word on that."

Of course Doc ought to have guessed that no servant had hauled the thing in here. His mind tried to put together an explanation: Too large to have been dragged and lacking a corresponding hole in the ceiling for Carpy's "arrow," the odd cylinder must have been assembled in place, brought in through the back door. The cause for this blasphemy remained an enigma, but the method at least he could resolve to his own satisfaction. He ordered that the thing be removed. "Break it into little bitty bits if you have to."

Carpy pushed hard against a polished fingerplate, which raised one of the connected pads a little ways. Deep below them, the earth seemed to belch out a flat, sonorous note. Carpy backed up against the wall. He and Doc traded worried looks. "Gonna take all the hands," he said, "everybody from the fields just to nudge this thing."

"Then, we gonna deal with it later," replied Doc. "Not messing about the workday over this little damn problem."

"Yes, sir, that seems best." Carpy withdrew past him, back up the steps. He peered down into the sarcophagal blackness of the instrument. Was that the top of a pale head way down inside there? The thing was some kind of sign, like chicken blood or a hanged man. This was a blight upon the family.

Halfway up the stairs, Doc found himself confronted by his wife. Sally had a way of looking at him that reduced his stature. That he was standing on a lower step of the stairs didn't help, either. He tried to take control of the situation quickly. "Damndest thing I ever seed," he said as he leaned back over the rail. Sally gave the thing a quick look. "Clarinet," she said sagely, "but you'd have to stand on the roof to play it."

"What the hell kind of clarinet is that?"

Sally replied, "A big clarinet." She moved to let him up.

Muttering, Doc stepped around her and headed for his room at full tilt. There, Lizzie had already removed the chamberpot and finished making the bed. The child did look after him well. He thought again of Carpy's mother, but dismissed the memory as both provocative and immaterial. Sally trod solemnly along the hall. He sensed her lingering in the doorway, and he turned around. He walked over and started to close the door. "I have to git dressed if you don't mind."

"You've dripped on yourself," she indicated, staring at his crotch.

Doc shut the door. He listened to her move off. "Sally," he said softly, "you are workin' my last nerve."

Once he had finished dressing, Doc went down to breakfast. He had barely scooped up his first forkful when a cry from outside stopped him. His name upon the air brought Doc running out to the porch. Sausage in his mouth and a checkered napkin bibbing his neck, he towered over Ed Rose, who stood in a panic on the ground. Ed blurted, "You gotta come quick, Doc. You gotta see this thing."

Doc told him to calm down. He threw off the napkin and followed his foreman into the fields. The steamy Mississippi morning pumped the sweat out of him as he waded through waist-high cotton plants. Branded workers had stopped their business to watch as the man himself strode past them. Ahead, a cluster of them surrounded "the thing."

It had crushed rows of plants but no one had been hurt. It was a thin gold tube, far longer than the thing inside the house, and it had spread a blue stain in a band over some of the cotton. The tube stretched out twenty yards before curving back—a piece from something much larger and more grotesque. In the flattened cotton the shape of the whole instrument could be discerned, as if

255

it had slept there overnight and then moved on at daybreak, leaving the sloughed hand slide behind. Doc walked in its rut while trying to formulate an identity for the thing. He had trouble.

"Hell," he said, "looks like . . . looks like . . ."

One of the fieldhands spoke up. "Like God's trombone."

Doc whirled around angrily but as quickly realized that was exactly what it looked like. "That's right. A big trombone." And the thing in the house—it, too, was some sort of instrument. What had passed across his land during the night? "This don't make no kind of sense." While he wore a consternated smile, he marked the worker who had spoken—a young man. A smart, clever, and un-branded young man. Wouldn't do to have a smart satchel-mouthed nigger roaming in their midst. Liable to foment all sorts of trouble. He would have to sublease Spangler's Mill again. Soon. As for the mystery trombone, it was so great a mystery that he saw no point in trying to wrestle it to earth. "Drag this curlicue outten here now, and you all get back to work," he told them. "And don't be worrying yourselves over what it portends. It don't portend shit."

They continued staring at the trombone shape for a while before moving off; all save the satchel-mouthed boy. He caught Doc in his stare, and it penetrated and drew fear like a venom from the white man's heart.

Doc retreated from the field. Back on the lawn beside his house, he grabbed Ed Rose by the arm and asked him, "Who is that boy?"

"A-which?" Ed answered.

Doc turned him around and pointed. The workers had all returned to their labors. He knew them, knew their shapes, but he could not pick out the one who had stared at him. "Where the hell'd he get to?" The cotton grew waist-high. Doc convinced himself that the boy was crouched down, hiding, afraid. He wanted very much for that particular bastard to be afraid. Ed interrupted his search. "By the way, Doc, you seen Curly this morning? He ain't around. Nobody's seen him since last night, when he went out after our little business. Said he couldn't sleep, had some kinda tune in his head."

"Too much booze in his head, you mean. He gets back, you send him to see me. I'm not in a tolerating mood this morning." Curly did not reappear all day. Doc's mood developed a razor edge.

That night, alone in his bed, he heard distant thunder, rhythmic and incessant. Jungle drumming derived from a jungle band whose members existed solely in the aether; travelers in the air, ghosts as surely as a skeleton scuffling on his grave.

The image jolted him awake. The sound of jungle thumping diminished. It rounded into words or something like words, briefly: "Juba, juba, juba," a droned spell, which pressed the consciousness out of him. He lacked the means to fight its power, but prayed to keep the evil music far out in the bush. "Don' ever let 'em in," he muttered, then faded away himself like a lost radio signal.

6. First Blood

Screaming woke Doc. Unmistakably Sally's voice, it sawed through the ceiling below. He wrestled his pants over his long johns, snapping up his suspenders while he ran along the hall. As he pivoted around the newel post, the screaming subsided into blubbering hysteria, and he followed it to the first floor. Such a sprawling God-damned house, this antebellum layer cake of his.

He stormed along the hall, cursing "God damn you, Sally, shut up," but his anger couldn't hold in the face of the new anomaly. It overwhelmed him—as big and broad as a church steeple. This time he knew what he looked at: He had forged the musical link. It was the bell of a trumpet, and for absolute sure it had dropped from out of the sky, because it had pinned somebody beneath it. One arm protruded, nearly severed by the swept gold rim. One arm, a white arm. A familiar white arm. Bubba's arm. His cold hand gripped tightly an equally cold branding iron. The dead idiot, what was he doing parading through the house with the fucking eye of God on a stick? Somebody would see, and some of them had surely been on the wrong end of it. A crawdad could have figured it out and put a name to it: Grand Cyclops and Son.

Doc got down on his knees to pry back the fingers. He drew the iron out of his son's hand. Sally continued her bubbly whining. He would've liked to have smacked her with the iron. Instead, he struck the trumpet bell. It clanged loudly. He thought, "Music destroyed my son." More than that, the trumpet like the clarinet was hollow.

Tossing down the bent brand, he tried to move the bell. He shoved it, grabbed onto the top and tried to tilt it up, he pushed it, climbed up the side and tried to pull it over. His bare feet squealed as they slid down the curved surface. He hung from the lip, his head back. He mewled to God, noticing abstractly that the ceiling remained intact. Yet the thing had passed right through it, must have done—the whole floor had buckled when it hit. He wiped the spittle off his lips and backed up into the counter. Lizzie stood there, struck stupid in her horror. She didn't even notice him.

What plague had been visited upon him? For what? He went to church like clockwork, prayed to and paid the Lord. He knew about original sin, the flood of Noah and the plague of locusts, about coveting your neighbor's wife, about the exodus. How could a man who comprehended those things be thus cursed?

He noticed his wife on her knees behind the bell. She had torn out some of her hair, and saliva foamed on her lips. Her anguish came in great heaves. Doc rushed over to her and tugged her hands down to her sides. "Calm," he said, "Calm now, honey. Easy does it." As if subduing a horse, he spoke. It worked for him but not for her. The strain of all she'd kept inside had broken Sally at last.

Eventually her daughters arrived at the scene. Debra reenacted her mother's squall, but Psalmody looked on with strange contentment, like Casandra watching as the wooden horse birthed inside her walls. Debra's screams galvanized Lizzie, and she snapped her skirts at and shooed both girls from the room, at which moment Carpy pushed his way in. He tripped over the bent iron and stopped still. Behind him came Ed Rose and a dozen field hands, but Carpy hardly noticed them. Ed ran over to Doc. The party had been on its way to move the thing in back, but trumpet or clarinet, it made little difference. Now they circled the bell. Silently, together, they bent down. They had no trouble grabbing hold of the rim; and, uttering a sharp "holler" as they often did in the fields, they lifted it all at once. Doc elbowed between them on his hands and knees to see if his son was all right. Probably the boy would have survived had it not been for the mute stuffed into the bell. It had acted as a hydraulic press, splitting the floor. Most of Bubba had been integrated with the boards.

The dark men set the bell down across the kitchen. They gathered around the depressed circle that contained Bubba's stain and Doc. They were silent. Their faces betrayed nothing. Doc found himself trapped like a sacrifice within them. One by one, they raised their fingers to their sweaty shirts as if to pledge allegiance, and each set of fingers carefully traced the hidden shapes of heterotopic eyes.

7. The Homestead-III

After the funeral, nothing was the same. The workers began to migrate, drifting away on the dry winds of August, but not before a group of them finally hefted the clarinet on the stairs and solved the mystery of Curly. Curiously, he had mummified inside the cramped space. The enormous black joint had hardly touched him. Why he had died at all became the new mystery. Ed Rose read the signs plainly enough and deserted before the sun came up on another day. The Cyclops should have mustered some terror then, but he had no Night Hawks left and his iron had disappeared. He needed guidance from a higher authority. Curly and the others had betrayed him, he felt.

Sally was locked away over in Vicksburg and not likely to be returning any time soon. Debra had taken the household helm. She intended to redecorate the whole place, telling her father, "I want to strip away the old life, Daddy. It's surely gone." Already, in the parlor she had installed one of those nice big Victrola humpbacks with the crank handle on the side.

Some weeks later, Doc awakened one sweltering night to the recurring thump of the jungle band. He got dressed and sneaked out the back door, careful of the crushed landing lest history repeat itself. The sound had grown in heat and intensity. It throbbed like the blood in his overworked arteries. Music. The battle hymn of a guerrilla war that had already claimed his former lieutenants.

"Oh, jass," cried a voice. "Jass, jass, I *love* it." The music slid around a wailing cornet. He knew already what that sound was—the workhouse radio, a device Carpy had brought in, arguably to keep the rest of the workers content enough to remain. But what was this hopped-up shit they were playing? "Juba," came a reply to chill his blood.

He peered around the edge of the open door. The whole of his depleted workforce sat grouped around the big wooden box. Some of them swayed in the rhythm. Their lidded eyes rolled loosely in their sockets. He might as well have been a ghost: they had no sense of him. A frenzied announcer broke in, babbling mythopoeic names—Chippie, Bix, Kid Ory, the Duke and the King. Names of power, and maybe capable of standing up to Ghouls and Dragons? And Cyclopes?

He wanted to go in there and rip apart that radio but was frightened by the energy pulsing through the room; scared rigid by the presence of Debra, like a ghost herself, cozy in their midst. He swallowed and drew back. This must be a nightmare from which he would shortly awaken. Even the crickets chirred with the beat.

Doc withdrew around the side of his house. Awhile on the steps, he breathed in the muggy night air. Jasmine mist hung thickly about him. There was enough pressure inside his skull to blow out a suture. He stared over toward the field where the trombone had lain but could see nothing. Finally, he climbed for the security of his own house.

Inside, someone had put on the parlor Victrola. The tune sounded like a washboard and banjo accompanied by a kazoo in a tub—just more of the insane noise that was pouring out of the workhouse. Drawn fearfully by it, Doc crept into the parlor, to find Carpy and Psalmody naked on the floor between the sofa and center table. He stared, brain on hold. He couldn't remember how to run away. The impassioned lovers didn't notice him but the eye in Carpy's shoulder rolled open and viewed him harshly. Doc stumbled back into the hall, his teeth clamped on the edge of his hand.

Slowly, an irrational anger took hold of him. Outmoded desire resurged in him against the invisible, the preternatural, which dwarfed him in its freedom. By God he wouldn't just stand here quivering. He'd whip this thing. Doc charged along the hall and down into the cellar. His secret identity hung hidden there—the white linen shroud and flour-sack hood of office. And there, across a keg of nails, lay a new branding iron. Its mark was new to him: a cross with extra arms. He didn't understand it exactly but the iron had a real heft that he liked.

Once in his guise of Cyclops, he took up his sceptre and rebounded up the stairs. At the top stood Lizzie in her nightdress. She seemed drunk or entranced. "Mr. Doc," she said gently, with acute sadness, but he would not be undone by so obvious a ploy. He struck her with the iron and, when she withstood the blow, struck her again. Hadn't he cared for her, hadn't he treated her justly?

The music seemed to race; someone had cranked up the Victrola. Its noise drowned out the thunder of his passing. He would descend upon the workers, scare them into their graves, and only then punish Carpy. Oh, that thankless task would be hardest of all. He had given that boy more than anyone could ask.

Doc stumbled, half-blind within his hood, down the porch steps, music the scent he followed through the night. He'd smash the radio first. "If thine eye offend thee," he recited triumphantly.

In the darkness, something struck him on the head. He paused. Another stinging tap—this one on the shoulder—

made him spin about. What was it? Chestnuts dropping out of season? Then another, harder blow caught him over one eye. Defiant, he raised the iron, and a dozen of the pesky things hammered into him. With a grunt, he collapsed onto one knee. He snatched at one of the objects as it tumbled in the grass. He thought he had hold of a chunk of hail for a moment but it was long and smooth and carefully finished. It was, dear God, a piano key. Alert to his folly, Doc tried to get up to retreat and found that a pile of the keys had amassed around him, the hem of his robe snagged beneath them. He whacked away as the wall grew up. He whipped the iron desperately, until exhaustion and a thousand blows made him reel.

The keys showered down, hard as buckshot. Black and white, they pummeled like fists, spreading dark stains across the shroud, until all that remained was the iron, stuck out like a lightning rod with a good-luck sign at the tip. The heaped keys glistened as bright moonlight reappeared, and the music tinkled artlessly away.

The Long-Awaited Appearance of the Real Black Box

Ratislav Durman

Edward Reindrop Horvat never had any illusions that he was an important person. His work as a restorer of Martian relics had no direct influence on the history of mankind; in fact, his influence was really quite negligible. The policy of Isolation had cut off all links between the Earth and Mars but, even without any further flow of artifacts from the Red Planet to Earth, there were still enough so that Edward had no fear that he would have to pass the years before retirement in another profession. The question was whether he would make it to retirement at all.

He was among the first conscripts yet the war did not interest him at all. At the obligatory political education classes during basic training they told him there were twenty reasons for war. The first two were so obviously ridiculous that he didn't bother to listen to the rest. He slept through them instead since the officer who gave the lectures obviously didn't care whether anyone listened to him or not.

By the time Edward arrived at the front the bitterness he had acquired in basic training had grown considerably. It bothered him that there was no one whom he could address with any conviction as "Sir" (the only man he knew was worthy of his "Good Morning, Sir" was killed in the first bombardment). It maddened him that instead of engaging in the highest sort of intellectual pursuits he was now forced to carry a rifle. It annoyed him that the only women he met were mindless automations of neurotic sexual compulsives who wanted to have one last orgasm before the end. These were the members of women's battalions with whom they were ordered to couple in the interests of "reducing psychic tension" among the troops.

But more than anything else it drove him into a rage that he was being forced to kill people who also had no interest in the war, who, if they were lucky, slept during political education lectures, just as he did. His dissatisfaction, however, did not last long. The physical exertions, the constant uncertainty and the everyday presence of death quickly extinguished every emotion. He became an automation which was fine since nothing more was expected of him.

Ten years went by, and death ignored him.

Anthony Sever would have been a soldier in any era and under any regime. Under Caeser, Joan of Arc or Rommel, he would certainly have risen no further than non-commissioned officer, a rank he certainly would have attained. However, his personal traits and the exigencies of the times in which he lived had made him general— and the head of the High Command at that.

He was always happiest at the front, in the thick of battle. Nevertheless his rank and position demanded that he put in an occasional appearance in the rear, whenever this was required by higher powers, or by the Great Leader. This time he had to go to the base "Q" in the delta.

Edward Reindrop Horvat had quickly, and despite his lack of ambition, risen to the rank of lieutenant. Soon after this, during attack, he had shown superhuman bravery. A cadet at any military academy in the world who had pronounced such an action feasible would have failed all his exams. It was no wonder that the commander of that sector of the front had rushed up to Edward and, tearing a medal from his own chest, had pinned it to him on the spot. Nor was it any wonder that Edward told the commander to shove the medal up his ass, to give him first aid instead since he was wounded. The commander believed that he was a reasonable man. He did not have Edward court-martialed, but he did strip him of all his rank and issued orders that he was never to be promoted again.

Though now only a private soldier, Edward often carried out missions which as a rule were only given to officers. Thus it came about that he was assigned to carry some documents to the base "Q" in the delta.

On his arrival in the delta General Anthony Sever had immediately ordered the execution of a guard for unmilitary bearing, demoted two officers to Private because he was dissatisfied with the cleanliness of the base, and sent a sergeant from communications center to the neuropsychiatric ward for stuttering. Colonel Liezovski, the commander of the base, hurried to meet the general before any really serious incident could take place.

"General, sir, I would like to inform you that the garrison of this base . . ."

"Fine, fine," said the general. "What's the problem, Colonel?"

"The new offensive weapons the enemy have been using lately calls for . . ."

"Keep it short," interrupted the general. "Keep it short."

"Yes, sir!"

"Good God," sighed the general, "you're incompetent, Captain Liezovski. If you keep on like this I'll kick you down to buck private, one rank at a time. And then I'll have you shot for sabotage. Is that clear?"

". . . the ultimate defensive weapon, the Defender EFI/1. More commonly known as the real black box. It's the invention of Colonel Doctor Levi from this base."

"Excellent," said the general. "That's what I like. You are a major now, so talk fast. I don't believe in your real black box. There's no such thing as a perfect defensive weapon."

"General, sir, the real black box creates a protective field around the soldier so that nothing can harm him."

"What about poison gases?"

"The protective field is selective, sir. It only lets in molecules of nitrogen and oxygen, in a ration of 3.5 to 1.5."

"And what about all those rays and waves? Lasers for example?"

"Absolute protection, General."

"It can't work," the general frowned. "I know that much physics. If this field doesn't let in waves—then how can the soldier see what's going on outside? Light consists of sort of waves doesn't it?"

"In the region of the eyes, sir, but . . ."

"Enough detail!" the general snarled. "I'm not interested in theory. Let's see how the damned thing works."

"General, permit me to introduce the inventor of the real black box, Colonel Levi."

Colonel Levi popped up from somewhere and marched

smartly up to the general and saluted him. At his side hung a small, inconspicuous black box.

"Good, let's see if it works!" said the general, drawing his pistol and emptying the whole clip at the colonel, who went down like an empty sack.

"And you call this the ultimate defensive weapon, Sergeant Liezovski?" raged the general.

"Sir, you didn't tell Colonel Levi to turn on the real black box."

"Why didn't he turn it on himself? You see what happens to incompetent soldiers."

"General, I am afraid that Colonel Levi was the only one who knew how to build the real black box, and as a precaution against possible espionage I forbade him to put anything down on paper."

"Nonsense," roared the general, "anything can be analyzed and duplicated once it's been built. But before we take it apart let's see whether this stupid gadget works."

"Yes, sir. We're going to fire artillery rounds at the person wearing the real black box. The test will take place on the firing range. We can watch from the communications center."

Edward Reindrop Horvat was on duty in the communications center when General Anthony Sever and Colonel Liezovski arrived, accompanied by an entourage of officers. He gave the general a snappy salute which was not returned: the general paid no attention to him. Instead, he went straight over to a television screen where the image of the sandy whiteness of the firing range could be seen. In a few moments a staff officer appeared on the range.

"It's no damned good," said the general. "Look at him glowing. He'll attract the enemy's attention."

"That's really immaterial, sir. What good does it do the enemy to see him if they can't harm him?"

"Well—they might be able to get him by closing him in somehow."

"No, sir. You could pour a ton of concrete on his head and still not capture him. The field can be used as . . ." The colonel searched for the proper word. ". . . as an icebreaker, if you see what I mean."

"If I didn't see what you mean, I wouldn't be a general," said Sever angrily. "Now let's get started."

"Begin!" ordered the colonel. "First we'll subject him to machine gun fire."

The field glowed even brighter in the place where it had been struck by bullets.

"You see, General?" the colonel said eagerly. "It's been repelling the bullets for a whole minute already!"

"Then why is he standing there like an old woman?" snapped the enraged general. "Why doesn't he act like a soldier? He ought to be running, crawling, fighting, taking cover. The damned box of yours is supposed to be for combat and I want to see how a real soldier behaves when he's wearing it."

The colonel reluctantly gave an order. The officer on the firing range started to walk about, but the general wasn't satisfied.

"Damn it! I said soldier, not a ballerina! Get that idiot out of there and give me a real soldier. Someone from the front lines!"

"General, you must realize that this is a base for scientific research," said the colonel, not without some pride. "The entire garrison is made up of scientists and technicians. Why, the unit in charge of guarding us has just come from basic training. I'm sorry, but we just don't have any cannon fodder."

"Colonel Liezovski—if you don't get a real soldier out on that firing range in two minutes I'll have you shot for high treason!"

Edward Reindrop Horvat realized, more instinctively than rationally, that his moment had come. He stepped forward and saluted again.

"General, sir, permit me to say something. I arrived yesterday from the front."

"You came here to take it easy, eh?" snarled the general.

"I came under orders, sir."

"I don't like shirkers, but at least you've had a taste of battle. You have one minute to get to the firing range. Move!"

"Yes, sir!"

They raked Edward Reindrop Horvat with mortar fire, then light recoilless cannon and howitzers before he finally realized that he was indeed invulnerable, that they could do nothing to harm him. He smiled and started to move off.

"Private Reindrop, you've moved too far to the left," he could hear the voice of Colonel Liezovski say through the loudspeaker. "You're out of view of cameras."

"You're incompetent, Captain Liezovski," said the general's voice. "Right, MARCH Soldier! Ten paces forward, MARCH!"

"Get lost, you idiot!" said Edward, still smiling.

For a time there was silence as they stopped firing anti-tank rockets at him.

"Drop an atom bomb on the goddamn deserter! A hydrogen bomb!" the general shrieked in Edward's headphones. It was so unpleasant that he took them off and threw them beyond the field of real black box. The temperature from the napalm was so high that they were instantly vaporized.

Several years passed before the front reached the river. The fighting thundered and exploded all around, but a lone civilian sat on the riverbank, glowing brightly. He fished calmly, showing no interest in the inferno which surrounded him.

By order number 15895-I, issued by General Anthony Sever in the interest of reassuring the populace, the man was declared an apparition.

Translated from the Serbo-Croatian by Dick Williams

Generation of Noah

William Tenn

That was the day Plunkett heard his wife screaming guardedly to their youngest boy.

He let the door of the laying house slam behind him, forgetful of the nervously feeding hens. She had, he realized, cupped her hands over her mouth so that only the boy would hear.

"Saul! You, *Saul*! Come back, come right back this instant. Do you want your father to catch you out there on the road? Saul!"

The last shriek was higher and clearer, as if she had despaired of attracting the boy's attention without at the same time warning the man.

Poor Ann!

Gently, rapidly, Plunkett *shh'd* his way through the bustling and hungry hens to the side door. He came out facing the brooder run and broke into a heavy, unathletic trot.

They have the responsibility after Ann and me, Plunkett told himself. Let them watch and learn again. He heard the other children clatter out of the feed house. Good!

"Saul!" his wife's voice shrilled unhappily. "Saul, your father's coming!"

Ann came out of the front door and paused. "Elliot," she called at his back as he leaped over the flush well-cover. "Please. I don't feel well."

A difficult pregnancy, of course, and in her sixth month. But that had nothing to do with Saul. Saul knew better.

At the last frozen furrow of the truck garden Plunkett gave himself a moment to gather the necessary air for his lungs. Years ago, when Von Rundstedt's Tigers roared through the Bulge, he would have been able to dig a foxhole after such a run. Now, he was just winded. Just showed you: such a short distance from the far end of the middle chicken house to the far end of the vegetable garden—merely crossing four acres—and he was winded. And consider the practice he'd had.

He could just about see the boy idly lifting a stick to throw for the dog's pleasure. Saul was in the further ditch, well past the white line his father had painted across the road.

"Elliot," his wife began again. "He's only six years old. He—"

Plunkett drew his jaws apart and let breath out in a bellyful of sound. "Saul! Saul Plunkett!" he bellowed. "Start running!"

He knew his voice had carried. He clicked the button on his stopwatch and threw his right arm up, pumping his clenched fist.

The boy *had* heard the yell. He turned, and, at the sight of the moving arm that meant the stopwatch had started, he dropped the stick. But, for the fearful moment, he was too startled to move.

Eight seconds. He lifted his lids slightly. Saul had begun to run. But he hadn't picked up speed, and Rusty skipping playfully between his legs threw him off his stride.

Ann had crossed the garden laboriously and stood at his side, alternately staring over his jutting elbow at the watch and smiling hesitantly sidewise at his face. She shouldn't have come out in her thin house-dress in November. But it was good for Ann. Plunkett kept his eyes stolidly on the unemotional second hand.

One minute forty.

He could hear the dog's joyful barks coming closer, but as yet there was no echo of sneakers slapping the highway. Two minutes. He wouldn't make it.

The old bitter thoughts came crowding back to Plunkett. A father timing his six-year-old son's speed with the best watch he could afford. This, then, was the scientific way to raise children in Earth's most enlightened era. Well, it was scientific . . . in keeping with the very latest discoveries. . . .

Two and a half minutes. Rusty's barks didn't sound so very far off. Plunkett could hear the desperate pad-pad-pad of the boy's feet. He might make it at that. If only he could!

"*Hurry*, Saul," his mother breathed. "You can make it."

Plunkett looked up in time to see his son pound past, his jeans already darkened with perspiration. "Why doesn't he breathe like I told him?" he muttered. "He'll be out of breath in no time."

Halfway to the house, a furrow caught at Saul's toes. As he sprawled, Ann gasped. "You can't count that, Elliot. He tripped."

"Of course he tripped. He should count on tripping."

"Get up, Saulie," Herbie, his older brother, screamed from the garage where he stood with Louise Dawkins, the pail of eggs still between them. "Get up and run! This corner here! You can make it!"

The boy weaved to his feet, and threw his body forward again. Plunkett could hear him sobbing. He reached the cellar steps—and literally plunged down.

Plunkett pressed the stopwatch and the second hand halted. Three minutes thirteen seconds.

He held the watch up for his wife to see. "Thirteen seconds, Ann."

Her face wrinkled.

He walked to the house. Saul crawled back up the steps, fragments of unrecovered breath rattling in his chest. He kept his eyes on his father.

"Come here, Saul. Come right here. Look at the watch. Now, what do you see?"

The boy stared intently at the watch. His lips began twisting; startled tears writhed down his stained face. "More—more than three m-minutes, poppa?"

"More than three minutes, Saul. Now, Saul—don't cry son; it isn't any use—Saul, what would have happened when you got to the steps?"

A small voice, pitifully trying to cover its cracks: "The big doors would be shut."

"The big doors would be shut. You would be locked outside. Then what would have happened to you? Stop crying. Answer me!"

"Then, when the bombs fell, I'd—I'd have no place to hide. I'd burn like the head of a match. An'—an' the only thing left of me would be a dark spot on the ground, shaped like my shadow. An'—an'—"

"And the radioactive dust," his father helped with the catechism.

"Elliot—" Ann sobbed behind him, "I don't—"

"*Please*, Ann! And the radioactive dust, son?"

"An' if it was ra-di-o-ac-tive dust 'stead of atom bombs, my skin would come right off my body, an' my lungs would burn up inside me—please, poppa, I won't do it again!"

"And your eyes? What would happen to your eyes?"

A chubby brown fist dug into one of the eyes. "An' my eyes would fall out, an' my teeth would fall out, and I'd feel such terrible terrible pain—"

"All over you and inside you. That's what would happen if you got to the cellar too late when the alarm went off, if you got locked out. At the end of three minutes, we pull the levers, and no matter who's outside—*no matter who*—all four corner doors swing shut and the cellar will be sealed. You understand that, Saul?"

The two Dawkins children were listening with white faces and dry lips. Their parents had brought them from the city and begged Elliot Plunkett as he remembered old friends to give their children the same protection as his. Well, they were getting it. This was the way to get it.

"Yes, I understand it, poppa. I won't ever do it again. Never again."

"I hope you won't. Now, start for the barn, Saul. Go ahead." Plunkett slid his heavy leather belt from its loops.

"Elliot! Don't you think he understands the horrible thing? A beating won't make it any clearer."

He paused behind the weeping boy trudging to the barn. "It won't make it any clearer, but it will teach him the lesson another way. All seven of us are going to be in that cellar three minutes after the alarm, if I have to wear this strap clear down to the buckle!"

When Plunkett later clumped into the kitchen with his heavy farm boots, he stopped and sighed.

Ann was feeding Dinah. With her eyes on the baby, she asked, "No supper for him, Elliot?"

"No supper." He sighed again. "It does take it out of a man."

"Especially you. Not many men would become a farmer at thirty-five. Not many men would sink every last penny into an underground fort and powerhouse, just for insurance. But you're right."

"I only wish," he said restlessly, "that I could work out some way of getting Nancy's heifer into the cellar. And if eggs stay high one more month I can build the tunnel to the generator. Then, there's the well. Only one well, even if it's enclosed—"

"And when we came out here seven years ago—" She rose to him at last and rubbed her lips gently against his thick blue shirt. "We only had a piece of ground. Now, we have three chicken houses, a thousand broilers, and I can't keep track of how many layers and breeders."

She stopped as his body tightened and he gripped her shoulders.

"Ann, *Ann*! If you think like that, you'll act like that! How can I expect the children to—Ann, what we have— all we have—is a five-room cellar, concrete-lined, which we can seal in a few seconds, an enclosed well from a fairly deep underground stream, a windmill generator for power and a sunken oil-burner-driven generator for emergencies. We have supplies to carry us through, geiger counters to detect radiation and lead-lined suits to move about in—afterwards. I've told you again and again that these things are our lifeboat, and the farm is just a sinking ship."

"Of course, darling." Plunkett's teeth ground together, then parted helplessly as his wife went back to feeding Dinah, the baby.

"You're perfectly right. Swallow now, Dinah. Why, that last bulletin from the Survivors Club would make *anybody* think."

He had been quoting from the October *Survivor*, and Ann had recognized it. Well? At least they were *doing* something—seeking out nooks and feverishly building crannies—pooling their various ingenuities in an attempt to haul themselves and their families through the military years of the Atomic Age.

The familiar green cover of the mimeographed magazine was very noticeable on the kitchen table. He flipped the sheets to the thumb-smudged article on page five and shook his head.

"Imagine!" he said loudly. "The poor fools agreeing with the government again on the safety factor. Six minutes! How can they—an organization like the Survivors Club making that their official opinion! Why freeze, *freeze* alone. . . ."

"They're ridiculous," Ann murmured, scraping the bottom of the bowl.

"All right, we have automatic detectors. But human beings still have to look at the radar scope, or we'd be diving underground every time there's a meteor shower."

He strode along a huge table, beating a fist rhythmically into one hand. "They won't be so sure, at first. Who wants to risk his rank by giving the nationwide signal that makes everyone in the country pull ground over his head, that makes our own projectile sites set to buzz? Finally, they are certain: they freeze for a moment. Meanwhile, the rockets are zooming down—how fast, we don't know. The men unfreeze, they trip each other up, they tangle frantically. *Then*, they press the button; *then*, the nationwide signal starts our radio alarms."

Plunkett turned to his wife, spread earnest, quivering arms. "And then, Ann, *we* freeze when we hear it! At last, we start for the cellar. Who knows, who can dare to say, how much has been cut off the margin of safety by that time? No, if they claim that six minutes is the safety factor, we'll give half of it to the alarm system. Three minutes for us."

"One more spoonful," Ann urged Dinah. "Just one more. *Down* it goes!"

Josephine Dawkins and Herbie were cleaning the feed trolley in the shed at the near end of the chicken house.

"All done, pop," the boy grinned at his father. "And the eggs taken care of. When does Mr. Whiting pick 'em up?"

"Nine o'clock. Did you finish feeding the hens in the last house?"

"I said all done, didn't I?" Herbie asked with adolescent impatience. "When I say a thing, I mean it."

"Good. You kids better get at your books. Hey, stop that! Education will be very important, afterwards. You never know what will be useful. And maybe only your mother and I to teach you."

"Gee," Herbie nodded at Josephine. "Think of that."

She pulled at her jumper where it was very tight over newly swelling breasts and patted her blonde braided hair. "What about *my* mother and father, Mr. Plunkett? Won't they be—be—"

"Naw!" Herbie laughed the loud, country laugh he'd been practicing lately. "They're dead-enders. They won't pull through. They live in the City, don't they? They'll just be some—"

"Herbie!"

"—some foam on a mushroom-shaped cloud," he finished, utterly entranced by the image. "Gosh, I'm sorry," he said, as he looked from his angry father to the quivering girl. He went on in a studiously reasonable voice. "But it's the truth, anyway. That's why they sent you and Lester here. I guess I'll marry you—afterwards. And you ought to get in the habit of calling *him* pop. Because that's the way it'll be."

Josephine squeezed her eyes shut, kicked the shed door open, and ran out. "I hate you, Herbie Plunkett," she wept. "You're a beast!"

Herbie grimaced at his father—*women, women, women!*—and ran after her. "Hey, Jo! Listen!"

The trouble was, Plunkett thought worriedly as he carried the emergency bulbs for the hydroponic garden into the cellar—the trouble was that Herbie had learned through constant reiteration the one thing: survival came before all else, and amenities were merely amenities.

Strength and self-sufficiency—Plunkett had worked out the virtues his children needed years ago, sitting in air-conditioned offices and totting corporation balances with one eye always on the calendar.

"Still," Plunkett muttered, "still—Herbie shouldn't—" He shook his head.

He inspected the incubators near the long steaming tables of the hydroponic garden. A tray about ready to hatch. They'd have to start assembling eggs to replace it in the morning. He paused in the third room, filled a gap in the bookshelves.

"Hope Josephine steadies the boy in his schoolwork. If he fails that next exam, they'll make me send him to town regularly. Now *there's* an aspect of survival I can hit Herbie with."

He realized he'd been talking to himself, a habit he'd been combating futilely for more than a month. Stuffy talk, too. He was becoming like those people who left tracts on trolley cars.

"Have to start watching myself," he commented. "Dammit, again!"

The telephone clattered upstairs. He heard Ann walk across to it, that serene, unhurried walk all pregnant women seem to have.

"Elliot! Nat Medarie."

"Tell him I'm coming, Ann." He swung the vault-like door carefully shut behind him, looked at it for a moment, and started up the high stone steps.

"Hello, Nat. What's new?"

"Hi, Plunk. Just got a postcard from Fitzgerald. Remember him? The abandoned silver mine in Montana? Yeah. He says we've got to go on the basis that lithium and hydrogen bombs will be used."

Plunkett leaned against the wall with his elbow. He cradled the receiver on his right shoulder so he could light a cigarette. "Fitzgerald can be wrong sometimes."

"Uhm. I don't know. But you know what a lithium bomb means, don't you?"

"It means," Plunkett said, staring through the wall of the house and into a boiling Earth, "that a chain reaction may be set off in the atmosphere if enough of them are used. Maybe if only one—"

"Oh, can it," Medarie interrupted. "That gets us nowhere. That way nobody gets through, and we might as well start shuttling from church to bar-room like my brother-in-law in Chicago is doing right now. Fred, I used to say to him— No, listen Plunk: it means I was right. You didn't dig deep enough."

"*Deep* enough! I'm as far down as I want to go. If I don't have enough layers of lead and concrete to shield me—well, if they can crack *my* shell, then you won't be able to walk on the surface before you die of thirst, Nat. No—I sunk my dough in power supply. Once that fails, you'll find yourself putting the used air back into your empty oxygen tanks by hand!''

The other man chuckled. ''All right. I *hope* I see you around.''

''And I hope *I* see . . .'' Plunkett twisted around to face the front window as an old station wagon bumped over the ruts in his driveway. ''Say, Nat, what do you know? Charlie Whiting just drove up. Isn't this Sunday?''

''Yeah. He hit my place early, too. Some sort of political meeting in town and he wants to make it. It's not enough that the striped-pants brigade are practically glaring into each other's eyebrows this time. A couple of local philosophers are impatient with the slow pace at which their extinction is approaching, and they're getting to see if they can't hurry it up some.''

''Don't be bitter,'' Plunkett smiled.

''Here's praying at you. Regards to Ann, Plunk.''

Plunkett cradled the receiver and ambled downstairs. Outside, he watched Charlie Whiting pull the door of the station wagon open on its one desperate hinge.

''Eggs stowed, Mr. Plunkett,'' Charlie said. ''Receipt signed. Here. You'll get a check Wednesday.''

''Thanks, Charlie. Hey, you kids get back to your books. Go on, Herbie. You're having an English quiz tonight. Eggs still going up, Charlie?''

''Up she goes.'' The old man slid onto the cracked leather seat and pulled the door shut deftly. He bent his arm on the open window. ''Heh. And every time she does I make a little more off you survivor fellas who are too scairt to carry 'em into town yourself.''

''Well, you're entitled to it,'' Plunkett said, uncomfortably. ''What about this meeting in town?''

''Bunch of folks goin' to discuss the conference. I say we pull out. I say we walk right out of the dern thing. This country never won a conference yet. A million conferences the last few years and everyone knows what's gonna happen sooner or later. Heh. They're just wastin' time. Hit 'em first, I say."

"Maybe we will. Maybe *they* will. Or—maybe, Charlie—a couple of different nations will get what looks like a good idea at the same time."

Charlie Whiting shoved his foot down and ground the starter. "You don't make sense. If we hit 'em first how can they do the same to us? Hit 'em first—hard enough—and they'll never recover in time to hit us back. That's what *I* say. But you survivor fellas—" he shook his white head angrily as the car shot away.

"Hey!" he yelled, turning onto the road. "Hey, look!"

Plunkett looked over his shoulder. Charlie Whiting was gesturing at him with his left hand, the forefinger pointing out and the thumb up straight.

"Look, Mr. Plunkett," the old man called. "Boom! Boom! Boom!" He cackled hysterically and writhed over the steering wheel.

Rusty scuttled around the side of the house, and after him, yipping frantically in ancient canine tradition.

Plunkett watched the receding car until it swept around the curve two miles away. He stared at the small dog returning proudly.

Poor Whiting. Poor everybody, for that matter, who had a normal distrust of crackpots.

How could you permit a greedy old codger like Whiting to buy your produce, just so you and your family wouldn't have to risk trips into town?

Well, it was a matter of having decided years ago that the world was too full of people who were convinced that they were faster on the draw than anyone else—and the other fellow was bluffing anyway. People who believed that two small boys could pile up snowballs across the street from each other and go home without having used them, people who discussed the merits of concrete fences as opposed to wire guard-rails while their automobiles skidded over the cliff. People who were righteous. People who were apathetic.

It was the last group, Plunkett remembered, who had made him stop buttonholing his fellows, at last. You got tired of standing around in a hair shirt and pointing ominously at the heavens. You got to the point where you wished the human race well, but you wanted to pull you and yours out of the way of its tantrums. Survival for the individual and his family, you thought—

Clang-ng-ng-ng-ng!

Plunkett pressed the stud on his stopwatch. Funny. There was no practice alarm scheduled for today. All the kids were out of the house, except for Saul—and he wouldn't dare to leave his room, let alone tamper with the alarm. Unless, perhaps, Ann—

He walked inside the kitchen. Ann was running toward the door, carrying Dinah. Her face was oddly unfamiliar. "Saulie!" she screamed. "Saulie! Hurry *up*, Saulie!"

"I'm coming, momma," the boy yelled as he clattered down the stairs. "I'm coming as fast as I can! I'll make it!"

Plunkett understood. He put a heavy hand on the wall, under the dinner-plate clock.

He watched his wife struggle down the steps into the cellar. Saul ran past him and out of the door, arms flailing. "I'll make it, poppa! I'll make it!"

Plunkett felt his stomach move. He swallowed with great care. "Don't hurry, son," he whispered. "It's only judgment day."

He straightened out and looked at his watch, noticing that his hand on the wall had left its moist outline behind. One minute, twelve seconds. Not bad. Not bad at all. He'd figured on three.

Clang-ng-ng-ng-ng!

He started to shake himself and began a shudder that he couldn't control. What was the matter? He knew what he had to do. He had to unpack the portable lathe that was still in the barn. . . .

"Elliot!" his wife called.

He found himself sliding down the steps on feet that somehow wouldn't lift when he wanted them to. He stumbled through the open cellar door. Frightened faces dotted the room in an unrecognizable jumble.

"We all here?" he croaked.

"All here, poppa," Saul said from his position near the aeration machinery. "Lester and Herbie are in the far room, by the other switch. Why is Josephine crying? Lester isn't crying. I'm not crying, either."

Plunkett nodded vaguely at the slim, sobbing girl and put his hand on the lever protruding from the concrete wall. He glanced at his watch again. Two minutes, ten seconds. Not bad.

"Mr. Plunkett!" Lester Dawkins sped in from the corridor. "Mr. Plunkett! Herbie ran out of the other door to get Rusty. I told him—"

Two minutes, twenty seconds, Plunkett realized as he leaped to the top of the steps. Herbie was running across the vegetable garden, snapping his fingers behind him to lure Rusty on. When he saw his father, his mouth stiffened with shock. He broke stride for a moment, and the dog charged joyously between his legs. Herbie fell.

Plunkett stepped forward. *Two minutes, forty seconds.* Herbie jerked himself to his feet, put his head down—and ran.

Was that dim thump a distant explosion? There—another one! Like a giant belching. Who had started it? And did it matter—now?

Three minutes. Rusty scampered down the cellar steps,

his head back, his tail flickering from side to side. Herbie panted up. Plunkett grabbed him by the collar and jumped.

And as he jumped he saw—far to the south—the umbrellas opening their agony upon the land. Rows upon swirling rows of them. . . .

He tossed the boy ahead when he landed. *Three minutes, five seconds.* He threw the switch, and, without waiting for the door to close and seal, darted into the corridor. That took care of two doors; the other switch controlled the remaining entrances. He reached it. He pulled it. He looked at his watch. *Three minutes, twenty seconds.* "The bombs," blubbered Josephine. "The bombs!"

Ann was scrabbling Herbie to her in the main room, feeling his arms, caressing his hair, pulling him in for a wild hug and crying out yet again. "Herbie! Herbie! Herbie!"

"I know you're gonna lick me, pop. I—I just want you to know that I think you ought to."

"I'm not going to lick you, son."

"You're not? But gee, I deserve a licking. I deserve the worst—"

"You may," Plunkett said, gasping at the wall of clicking geigers. *"You may deserve a beating,"* he yelled, so loudly that they all whirled to face him, "but I won't punish you, not only for now, but forever! And as I with you," he screamed, "so you with yours! Understand?"

"Yes," they replied in a weeping, ragged chorus. "We understand!"

"Swear! Swear that you and your children and your children's children will never punish another human being—*no matter what the provocation.*"

"We swear!" they bawled at him. "We swear!"

Then they all sat down.

To wait.

The Rocky Python Christmas Video Show

Frederik Pohl

On the screen of the television set the blank gray brightens to robin's-egg blue. We see the spires of a fairy-tale castle, with fluffy little clouds behind them. They are growing as we zoom in. The scene looks very much like the opening of a Disneyland special, and to make it even more so a zitzy stream of glittering comet dust darts in from the RIGHT. It turns into a Peter Pan figure who looks a lot like Jane Fonda. She hovers like a humming-bird, waving a wand at us. We zoom in for a closeup.

JANE:
    Hello. I'm not Peter Pan. I grew up. It was the world that didn't.

Now that we get a better look at Jane, she isn't nearly as much like Peter Pan as she is like Barbarella. She's wearing a Buck Rogers kind of spacesuit which leaves her head and face free.

JANE:

I'm what you'd call a forensic anthropologist now.

She zips away rapidly REAR and comes back escorting the skyline, which, as it approaches, changes from fairy tale to Everytown. The castles are actually church spires—Methodist, Baptist, Congregationalist, R.C. Jane reaches down with her wand and touches one of the spires, and the zitzy fairy dust becomes snow. We are looking at a New England town in winter. It could well be Thornton Wilder's Our Town.

JANE:

What I'm trying to do is show whose fault it was. I mean, I already know whose. It was yours, all of yours. You fuckers. But I want to nail it down so there's no argument.

Sound of caroling comes up: God Rest Ye Merry, Gentlemen. *The camera comes down and looks through open church doors on the congregation. Jane comes to rest on the steps of the church, looking inside for a moment before she turns back to us.*

JANE:

Take Christmas. I mean, take Christmas—*please*. Listen to this guy.

The caroling has stopped and the minister, who looks like Robert Morley, is offering a prayer.

MINISTER:

And at this time of rejoicing, Lord, we ask of Thee a special care for our sons and brothers who now battle in Thy service in far-off lands. Save them from harm.

Let their valiant sacrifice be rewarded with the destruction of those who set themselves against Thee and our sacred cause, we beseech Thee in Thy holy name.

Jane shakes her head.

JANE:
How do you like that guy? Oh, you know, some ways Christmas must have been a lot of fun in the old days, right? Giving presents and all? Celebrating the passing of the winter solstice and the lengthening of the days? Remembering the birthday of this Prince of Peace fellow, and everybody saying they were going to love everybody? I mean, love everybody except those *other* guys.

The congregation rises and begins to come out into the winter day. Two boys start a snowball fight. Their mothers, flustered but laughing, call to them to stop it, but the boys go on.

JANE:
So why'd you always have to go and screw it up? I mean, do you think we *like* having to wear these Goddamned suits?

One of the snowballs catches Jane behind the ear and knocks her sprawling. She looks up, resigned.

JANE:
It could've been worse. It could've been a hand grenade. You know, a lot of the time it was. Why, I remember a time, a war or two ago—

She stops to think, rubbing her ear. Then she shakes her head, wincing.

JANE:
No, that one wasn't a hand grenade. It was a soldier, and he got me with the butt of his gun. Tell you about it another time, but first I want you to meet some friends of mine.

She pushes away the backdrop that is the New England town scene, which has frozen into inaction, and reveals that the set of a TV game show is already in place behind it. On this set we see eight young men, all in uniform, though the uniforms aren't the same. Jane strips out of her spacesuit and is revealed in the tails and tights of a girl tapdancer. She puts on a top hat; her wand has become a circus ringmaster's whip. Music up; she flourishes the whip and speaks.

JANE:
Welcome to our version of "The Dating Game!"

She points to the man in the first position. He is wearing the uniform of a British soldier of the 1914 war; his head is bandaged, and his helmet is perched on top of the bandage.

JANE:
Bachelor Number One, will you tell us why you're here?

BACHELOR NUMBER ONE:
I ain't no bachelor, miss. Got a wife an' two kiddies back 'ome, least I fink I do, if the Zeppelins 'aven't got 'em yet.

JANE:
That isn't what I asked you, is it?

BACHELOR NUMBER ONE:
Oh, you mean *why*, like. Why I'm *here*, you mean. I s'pose it's the syme as all these other blokes, I expect. Coz we're dead?

JANE:
Because you had that real big *date*, right. That's the All New, Everybody Plays Dating Game, you see? And now, all you studs, please tell us where you met your date.

She gestures to them, and one by one they respond:

BACHELOR NUMBER ONE:
Wipers it was, miss.

BACHELOR NUMBER TWO:
(He wears a GI uniform from World War Two. He is missing an arm.)
They told us we were supposed to take this mountain. I think they said it was named Monte Cassino.

BACHELOR NUMBER THREE:
(He wears a Union infantry uniform from the Civil War. He is black and resembles Eddie Murphy.)
Near Petersburg, ma'am. Dey blowed up de mine an' we went in, an' den dey started shootin' down at us.

BACHELOR NUMBER FOUR:
(He wears a Red Army uniform, though it is in rags. He is skeletally thin.)

Lake Ladoga, the siege of Leningrad. I fell through the ice and froze.

BACHELOR NUMBER FIVE:
(He is Oriental, small, wearing what looks like black pajamas. They are completely burned away on one side, and his flesh is blistered.)
I was carrying rocket grenades down the Trail when the napalm came.

BACHELOR NUMBER SIX:
(He wears the fur-collared flying suit of a U.S. Navy pilot, vintage of 1954. He is also badly burned.)
I was shot down north of the Yalu. I landed all right, but the plane was burning and when I tried to get out they shot at me.

BACHELOR NUMBER SEVEN:
(He wears the uniform of one of Napoleon's hussars. He is seated with Bachelor Number Eight at a common desk.)
I too froze in Russia. It was on the way back from Moscow, very cold, and we had no food.

BACHELOR NUMBER EIGHT:
(In Wehrmacht uniform. He is blind.)
And I also froze, kind lady. It was more than one hundred thirty years later, but it was in almost the same spot as the Frenchie.

JANE:
Thanks, guys.
(To audience.)
We could've had lots more—hey, we could've had *millions*, all the way from Thermopylae to Grenada, only

you know what it is when you have to stay under budget. And, listen, not just *soldiers*. Women, children, old people—remember Hiroshima? Or the time they wiped out the Catharists in France? "Kill them all," the Catholic general told his troops, "God will know which are His own." And I'm not even talking about, like, say, the *Mongols*, or that all-time goldy oldy, the Second Punic War.

(She scratches her crotch reminiscently.)

Then there were all the other little things that went along with the war for the civilians. You know what I mean?

You have to use your imagination a little bit here, folks—remember I told you about the budget? So we couldn't bring you all the starved children and all like that, and I have to play all the civilian women myself. So there was this soldier; he came into the cellar where I was hiding and there I was. He got me right behind the ear with the butt of his rifle and he was already opening his pants. . . .

Jane turns away and walks toward the wings, lost in thought.

BACHELOR NUMBER EIGHT:
(Indignantly.)

That must have been an Ivan. We German soldiers do not rape.

BACHELOR NUMBER FOUR:
No, you just bayonet babies.

BACHELOR NUMBER EIGHT:
A damnable lie! I personally bayonetted no babies.

The youngest I killed had no less than fifteen years, absolutely, I am almost sure.

Jane isn't listening. She has begun strutting across the stage, top hat, tails and cane on her shoulder; she is doing aerobic exercises, and is paying no attention to the eight "bachelors."

BACHELOR NUMBER ONE:
   Miss? Beggin' yer pardon, miss? We've got a kind of an argle-bargle here.

JANE:
(She stops at the wing RIGHT, and looks at them, irritated.)
   Oh, shut up, okay? It doesn't matter which of you it was, does it? I mean, after he stuck me with *that* thing he stuck me with his *other* thing so I died anyway. Anyway, you probably all got off on it.

BACHELOR NUMBER TWO:
(Also indignant.)
   Hey, lady, that's a load of crap. We never done nothing like that.

JANE:
   What, never?

BACHELOR NUMBER TWO:
   You bet your pretty little bottom, never. General Mark Clark would've crucified us. Anyway, the Eye-tie broads was giving it away.

JANE:
   For a can of Spam, you mean?

(She looks at him thoughtfully, then grins and turns to the wings. She pulls an army cot out onto the stage and sits on the edge of it. She pats the cot.)

So what do you think, GI Joe? Remember, I don't want your Spam and I'm not interested in you. But you've got your gun. I couldn't stop you, could I?

BACHELOR NUMBER TWO:
(Dangerously.)
What're you trying to prove, lady?

JANE:
What do you think? A heroic fighting man has a right to a little R&R, hasn't he? If you mean to sin, why wait to begin? I can't stop you. Anyway, if you've killed my kids and blown up my house, what's a little gang-bang?

BACHELOR NUMBER TWO:
You're really asking for it!
(He starts toward her, grimly horny. Then he stops in consternation, feels his groin, shakes his head. He looks at her angrily.)
Hell, lady, you really take the starch out of a fellow.

JANE:
(Sympathetically.)
Testosterone running a little low? I guess you haven't killed anybody lately, that it?

All eight of the bachelors are muttering as Jane pushes the cot back into the wings.

BACHELOR NUMBER TWO:
You make us sound like a bunch of animals! We

were *soldiers.* I got a Silver Star. If I'd been an officer I bet it would've been the Medal of Honor!

BACHELOR NUMBER SEVEN:
 The Emperor himself shook my hand!

BACHELOR NUMBER FIVE:
 It was the shells we carried that made our comrades in the South able to throw off the imperialist yoke!

BACHELOR NUMBER FOUR:
 Even when we were starving, we fought!

BACHELOR NUMBER FIVE:
 We done what dey tole us to do, ma'am. We was supposed to break right through to Richmond, an' we dang near done it, too. We would've, iffen de generals hadda got some more troops into de Crater 'fore we was all kilt ourselfs.

JANE:
 Oh, gosh, nobody said you weren't all *brave.* I mean, not counting if you pooped your pants sometimes, right? But you went right on and did the job you were supposed to do. The thing is, what were you so brave *about*?

BACHELOR NUMBER ONE:
 It was the Huns, miss. They was doin' awful fings in Belgium.

BACHELOR NUMBER SEVEN:
 For the Emperor!

BACHELOR NUMBER THREE:

Dey whupped us, ma'am, when we was slaves. Freedom! An' we kilt dem back.

BACHELOR NUMBER EIGHT:
For the Aryan race!

BACHELOR NUMBER FOUR:
For the Soviet motherland!

JANE:
(As the bachelors are all speaking at once.)
Boys, boys! Let's kind of hold it down, okay?
(She looks at Bachelor Number Six.)
What about you, Ensign? Don't you have anything to say?

BACHELOR NUMBER SIX:
(Grinning.)
Seems to me you're doing all the talking, hon. Me, I'm just a fly-boy. Drop a couple five-hundred pounders, shoot up a column of trucks, back on the ship for a malted milk and the night movie—except for that damn MIG. I bet it was a Russky pilot that got me. No damn slopey could've flown like that.

I know what you're saying, though. I was always glad I was a carrier pilot. We didn't get into that real lousy stuff they did on the ground. So don't talk to me about rape and looting and all that—I wasn't anywhere near it. I was in the air, and we had a nice clean war.

JANE:
Do you suppose they felt the same way in the *Enola Gay*?

BACHELOR NUMBER SIX:

Now, wait a minute, honey! You've got the wrong guy here. I never dropped any atomic bombs!

JANE:

They didn't give you any atomic bombs to drop, did they?

BACHELOR NUMBER SIX:

Damn right they didn't, and you know why? Because the U. S. of A. *decided* not to use the Bomb then! We could've, easily enough! We had 'em! Plenty of them. Only we held them back for humanitarian reasons.

JANE:

And maybe also, a little, because they were scared that the Russians had them too?

(Bachelor Number Six shrugs and looks away, losing interest.)

And then *everybody* had them, remember? England and France, and India and China, and Brazil and South Africa and Israel and Pakistan—And people said that was really okay, because that was MAD, the Mutal Assured Deterrent, the thing that would keep anybody from ever using one, because everybody knew that nobody could possibly win a nuclear war?

They were wrong about one of those things, remember? But they were right enough about the other. Nobody won.

Here, take a look. Give me a hand, will you?

She goes behind the desks and pulls out a new backdrop, puffing with the effort. Bachelors Numbers Six and One help her, then go back to their places. All the others crane their necks to see.

We are now looking at the New England town again, only it has been nuked. All the church spires are broken and burned out. A few people are moving about in the dirty, ash-tainted snow. We see that some are children in rags, looking hungry, freezing in the cold weather. A few adults look obviously sick. One or two figures seem more energetic; they are shepherding the others to a waiting "ambulance"—it is someone's large sleigh, pulled by a swaybacked old horse.

Jane takes off her hat and gathers up the tails of her coat to tuck into the waistband of her tights.

JANE:

The trouble was, the deterrent didn't deter everybody.

She picks up a TV remote controller from the floor, aims it at the screen and flicks from scene to scene. We see New York, Tokyo, Moscow, Beijing, Chicago, Rio de Janeiro, Tel Aviv, San Francisco, Capetown, Paris, Rome, Copenhagen, Melbourne, Singapore, Mexico City, St. Louis, Cairo, Stockholm. They are all in ruins. Jane is talking while she changes channels.

JANE:

It only took one to start it, you know. Then everybody got together to finish it.

BACHELOR NUMBER TWO:
(He is bewildered and angry.)

Hey, it wasn't supposed to happen that way! They was supposed to make sure there wasn't any more wars!

BACHELOR NUMBER ONE:
    They said the sime about mine, too, miss.

JANE:
    Well, what the hell, one out of a million isn't bad,
is it? Because this time they were right.

BACHELOR NUMBER SEVEN:
    (He is incredulous, but dares to be hopeful.)
    Pardon, mamselle, is it that peace is here at last?

JANE:
    You bet, sweetie. Only it's a little late for you guys,
isn't it? I mean, being all dead and like that.
    *(She comes over to them and pats the nearest one on
the shoulder—insistently.)*
    So really, now, you better all just lie down again,
okay? Go ahead. That's the way. . . .

*Grumbling, all eight bachelors get up and tip their
desks down onto the floor. When they do so, we see that
each of the desks is actually a plain pine coffin. The eight
men reluctantly climb in, one after another, each one
putting the lid on for the one before him.*

*Jane, grunting, lifts the last lid in place to cover Bach-
elor Number Eight. Then she begins putting her suit back
on. Now we see that it isn't really a spacesuit. It's an
anti-radiation suit, and it is spotted and stained with
long use.*

JANE:
    (Bowing to audience.)
    Well, Merry Christmas to you all, and good will to
men, and peace on Earth. *Really.* I mean, this is the war
that finally meant it.

(She gazes at the screen, then flicks the remote controller and the screen goes blank. All is black. The only thing we see is Jane herself, alone and brightly lit on the empty stage. She puts on her helmet, but before she closes it she adds:)

There aren't enough of us left for anything else.

Afterword: The End of War

There was a time when science fiction writers seemed to be inventing all of the new ideas. Youthful SF readers in the thirties were inspired to become rocket engineers—then went on to build the rockets that up to then had existed only in fiction. Atomic power and, unhappily, atom bombs were science fiction commonplaces, along with television, personal radios, and many other devices and concepts too numerous to mention; many of which exist today. It is however the regrettable fact that in recent times SF invention has given way to a rather mindless repetition that produces uninspired copies of copies of Tolkien, rehashes of ancient plots strung out in mind-numbing volumes. Even more depressing are the military-minded writers, and even publishers, who consider war to be a Good Thing, almost a commonplace event. They tell us over and over again that violent conflict and destruction will be with us forever. The idea that there will always be war is an abomination and an insult to human intelligence. War is about fear and death—and nothing else. Those who write about the glories of future conflict are writing the pornography of war.

This volume is an attempt to correct that false assumption, to balance negative with positive. The most imaginative science fiction writer today is named Gorbachev. He invented a story plot called *Glasnost and Perestroika*—then made the story come true. No other SF writer ever managed to produce a story with such daring and novel concepts.

The authors of the stories in this anthology have risen to Gorbachev's challenge. All of them are aware of that very simple yet tremendously vital concept:

We are what we think we are.

External reality is created by internal opinion, attitude and prejudice.

The Cold War is now over—though many politicians still need to be convinced of that fact. It began as a state of mind, grew strong as it fed on fear and greed, until it became a monster that divided the world, fanned prejudices, bred war machines that impoverished us all. There never was a physical threat—no matter what the Cold Warriors told us with their fictional theories of Domino Effects, "lost" countries, Evil Empires.

Stalin's paranoid fear of the threat of invasion had a basis in reality. He was well aware that Napoleon had invaded Russia and had been turned back only with the greatest difficulty and loss of life. He was there when Russia was invaded by America, Britain and other western countries at the end of the First World War, when the Allies fought on the side of the Whites during the revolution. He rose to power fighting the invading Germans in the Second World War. He believed, and proved to his own satisfaction, that force was the answer to every problem. He murdered his enemies, and those he believed to be his enemies, filling the Gulags as well. When the Soviet forces drove the German invaders back to Berlin he saw to it that all of the Soviet occupied countries had communist governments—whether they wanted them or no—to act as a buffer against any future invasions from the west.

The right-wing politicians of the west responded to the "threat" with enthusiastic paranoia of their own. The Red Beast was coming and had to be restrained. Capitalists have always seen socialists as a threat to their very existence—completly ignoring the fact that Marx was wrong and there is no eternal war between the classes. Socialism and capitalism have blended quite happily in Scandinavia for decades. Despite the fact that the exhausted Soviet Union not only had no desire to invade Western Europe, but was physically incapable of doing so, the Cold War began. What a boon for the armament industries this was! America became a socialist country at last—although the benefactors were these big businesss that produced the weaponry, not the people. So it began.

And now it has ended. Yet nostalgia still exists for those bad old days. Stalin the murderer is a hero in Georgia. Lawrence Eagleburger believes that "For all its risks and uncertainties, the Cold War was characterized by a remarkably stable and predictable set of relations among the great powers." Oh, really. The fear that I and all of the world felt during the Cuban missile crisis—to take a single example—was imaginary?

This attitude is unacceptable. There is no time for nostalgia, no going back. We must accept the fact that the armistice has been signed; the Cold War is over. There were no winners—only losers. We must think deeply about what Georgi Arbatov—a longtime Soviet observer of American attitudes—said after all the Soviet cutbacks. "We deprive you of an enemy . . . This compels you to introduce many changes in traditional political thinking.''

That's it in a nutshell. We must analyze our attitudes and our prejudices and when they prove worthless or dangerous they must be rejected.

There is nothing new in this; dreadful examples litter history. The Irish potato famine was caused by a fungus infection. But the thousands of deaths were caused by social and political attitudes. To begin with, the English viewed the Irish as inferiors and foisted a slave economy upon them. Forcing them to exist on the monocrop of potatoes, a simple slave food that they could grow themselves. So when the blight came there were no other food supplies available. In Ireland. There was plenty of food in Britain, but that was not carried across the Irish Sea because of Victorian work-ethic values. You must work for what you receive. No work—no food. Starvation and death followed.

Nationalism is in reality mankind's biggest enemy; jingoism and the national state the continuing threat to world peace. How we love to hate each other! During the Second World War, when the Germans invaded Yugoslavia, the guerrilla bands fled to the mountains. Where they killed each other, not the Germans. Serbs slaughtered Croats, Moslems killed Christians. The same thing happened again when *glasnost* reached Azerbaijan. What did they do with their new-found freedom? Why they killed each other, of course. National and religious prejudices, long submerged by force, instantly emerged with deadly consequences.

Before we sneer at their simpleminded hatreds—let us think of our own. No less of an authority than George Kennan, former U.S. Ambassador to Moscow, firmly believes that the ''Soviet Threat'' never existed. In all his years of close observation of the USSR he has

". . . Never seen any desire, intention or incentive on the Soviet side . . ." to attack Western Europe or initiate a first nuclear strike. If what he says is true—then the entire Cold War had no basis in fact. We were playing out another set of prejudices. It is chilling and very frightening to realize that General Curtis LeMay, head of the Strategic Air Command, did not have the power to throw helpless women out of windows, as they recently did in Baku, but instead he bragged that he could have reduced the Soviet Union to ". . . a smoldering, radiating ruin in two hours."

Why does this happen? What makes normal human beings into apparently bloodthirsty monsters? Is mankind forever doomed, forever damned? No. Absolutely not. The explanation is there if we only take the trouble to see it. Intelligence is basically responsible. The one characteristic that raised us up now threatens to destroy us. Intelligence begets invention—and finally attitude.

Mankind differs in only one vital way from the other animals. We may be physically related to the other primates, but we differ in *kind*. In all other animals function follows gene form. A bower bird does not have to be taught how to build its complex nest; a terrier will quickly and efficiently kill the first rat it ever sees.

We don't work that way. We invented everything that we now do. We invented culture. That important fact must never be forgotten. Like our machines and our cultivated crops, obvious inventions, we invented culture as well. Many varied and different cultures. All of them work in a more or less satisfactory manner—or they would not exist. This was all well and good when populations were small, the distances between them great. This is no longer true. Populations grow without control, cultures and nations push against each other more and more.

Which would be all right if we respected each other's culture, if we saw all cultures as being equal.

But we don't. Once this culture, this artifact has been invented, it is hallowed with divinity. It is god-given, perfect, unchangeable. Change is the enemy; those who question their culture are rejected, often killed. Myth is defended against the heresy of fact. Each religion is correct; all of the thousands of others wrong. Each nation is best; all of the others enemies.

This is "received" intelligence and questioning it is heresy. The correct name for it is faith. Most of the time faith is believing in something because we have been told to believe in it. Faith is the continued acceptance of that belief in face of strong, real evidence to the contrary. Faith is strong because it had a very real function at one time. It made society possible and prevented anarchy. But now faith has become our enemy, science our only hope. So perhaps there is good reason for the word "science" in science fiction. Because science is the enemy of unreasoning faith. Science knows—it does not "believe"—it *knows* that all facts are challengeable, all theories subject to test. The bigots of religion twist and misunderstand this term. They say that since evolution is a "theory" their theories of origin must be entertained as well. No. They misuse the word. In this context "process" is to be preferred. The Process of Evolution has been proven time and time again. Details may change; the process exists.

I am not attacking religions. I am attacking all faith-structures that attack and threaten me. The complex, and incorrect, faith structure of soul-foetus-baby threatens world existence by overpopulation. Because one group would have us follow their belief that there is such a thing as a "soul" that enters a foetus 9 months before birth, therefore abortion is akin to murder—we are all under threat. Look at the reality; through science and medicine we have brought death-control into the world. Infant mortality is lower, diseases like smallpox no longer exist, people live longer. So we are breeding ourselves out of existence. To match death-control we must have birth-control. Family planning and zero population growth. Why don't we? Primarily because of faith in a complex and completely wrong theory. Fertilized egg—soul—baby. It states that there is a thing called a soul. This is supposed to enter a fertilized ovum. Then this developing mass of growing cells is called a "baby" and it is forbidden to interfere with its growth. No matter what the cost to its mother and society as a whole.

The faith structure of fundamentalist Muslims threatens Salman Rushdie's life. This same faith structure also chops off hands, stones women to death, kills thousands.

The faith structure of all-Reds-equal-and-bad caused the CIA to destroy the democratically elected government in Chile, to murder the president and thousands more. I do not attack Christianity. I don't have to—it attacks itself. Christian Catholics in North Ireland murder Christian Protestants. And vice versa.

This list, tragically, can be extended forever. There are still conflicts of greed, where stronger power structures seek the control of smaller ones just because they have the strength to do so. There is no such thing as abstract evil—another faith-structure—but there sure are plenty of evil men. They grab power, then quickly come to believe that they are different, ordained to rule. Another faith-structure. All war, all intolerance in the world today, is the product of belief, the product of faith-structures. If we keep this always before us we may perhaps begin to do something about war.

Perhaps we can end it once and for all. The mere fact of our saying out loud that the end of war is possible is the first step. We must have new ideas about war and how to live with each other, alongside each other.

Which, to come full circle, is the idea behind this book. You will not find the solution to the world's problems here. But you will certainly find plenty of ideas, food for thought, concepts to consider.

The idea comes first, then the action. We must produce new models for the postwar world. Perhaps some of them are on the pages you've just read. I do not know—but I am hopeful.

Science fiction writers are thinking writers who challenge, who hopefully challenge, outmoded and dangerous faith-structures. They not only know that change is possible and a continuing process; they know that you can *change* this change, make things happen to order. This is important. Change is not automatic or inevitable. If we see a negative change occurring—carbon dioxide in the atmosphere for instance—we have the intelligence and the ability to change that. If we have the will. That is the overpowering understanding that must never be forgotten. Beliefs must change if we are to survive. Dangerous faith-structures must be challenged. Intelligence must come before faith. Tolerance must take the place of intolerance. The true religion is one that believes in tolerance—not hatred. I'll let you live—if you let me live. Never forgetting that we all live on spaceship Earth. There are no national boundaries visible from space. Live and let live. Let us seek out and find a way to put this into effect.

> Let there be an end to war.
> Here is a beginning.

> —Harry Harrison